INTO THE WIND

Also by Annie Baret

Threads of Fate
Rhythms of Nature
Patterns of Life
Elemental Forces

INTO
the
WIND

A Free Rider Novel

ANNIE BARET

Ktenoura Books

USA

Published by Ktenoura Books, Alexandria, Virginia

ISBN 978-0-9860534-4-3

Second Edition 2016

Cover by BespokeBookCovers.com

Cover photographs by Anita Schroeder

At any given moment, life is completely senseless. But viewed over a period, it seems to reveal itself as an organism existing in time, having a purpose, trending in a certain direction.

Aldous Huxley

Chapter 1

The concrete floor was cold against Joe Crawford's buttocks. Behind his back, the wall of the padded cell was only slightly warmer.

The small cubicle was bare except for a drain in the center. He couldn't break any lights, flood the toilet, or impale himself on sharp edges. Not that he wanted to. But he had been antagonistic earlier and now he was being punished for it.

His hosts, ignoring Crawford's fuck-you attitude, had demonstrated exquisite hospitality, providing an orange jumpsuit and plastic sandals. They had also given him a blanket, but he had passed it on to a shivering crackhead named Gus. Now Crawford was feeling the chill of the December morning.

Before he could ask for another blanket, the officers had called him from the bullpen to the booking station. Perhaps it was the raw atmosphere or maybe he was just in a bad mood. He had refused to provide fingerprints or pose for a mug shot.

The officers hadn't argued. Instead they had escorted him to a padded cell and left him there – literally in the cooler – to ponder his uncertain future.

That future, like much of Crawford's past, was irrevocably tied to Simon Lang, a man who had haunted Crawford's life for many years. But Lang was supposed to be the one who ended up in prison.

Crawford might have committed a few illegal activities of his own, but as they had been done in a quest for retribution, he didn't consider them worthy of jail time.

Even as he shivered, Crawford decided that requesting a second blanket was a lost cause. A bootless errand his grandfather used to say when the odds for success were nil.

Crawford and his sister Claire had joked about bootless errands when they were children. Claire was now living in Texas with her fiancé, and Simon Lang appeared to have forgotten about her. But even if he hadn't, the O'Hancy family would protect her. Claire had told Crawford that after years of hiding from Simon Lang, she was happy to settle into a comfortable, uncomplicated existence.

That might be fine for Claire, but Crawford wasn't ready to let the past go. He was going to destroy Simon Lang.

Or at least he would if he got out of jail any time soon.

Chapter 2

One Day Earlier

Crawford stretched his legs and leaned back in the oversized leather armchair. With its domed back, deep seat, and rolled arms, it looked like something from 1930s Paris. It probably was. The brown upholstery would have been shiny and smooth at one time, but it had dried and cracked, forming a miscellaneous patchwork of lines and pentagonal shapes that resembled the Death Valley salt flats.

The furrows etched across the surface of the chair could pass for fractals – those detailed, seemingly endless mathematical patterns, often holistic and continuous, that were said to mimic nature. Crawford knew that even though a fractal appeared complicated, its origin was no more than the repeated iteration of a straightforward equation.

Infinite complexity from a simple algorithm. It could be a metaphor for his life.

From where he sat he could see both the pink Formica top of the rickety kitchen table and the sagging mattress on the bed. This small efficiency apartment bore little resemblance to his multimillion dollar condo, which had boasted elegant furnishings and a spectacular view. But after the FBI discovered where he lived, he had placed the condo on the market. For the time being, this anonymous apartment suited most of his needs. More importantly, the Feds didn't know where it was.

Crawford had a mixed relationship with federal law

enforcement officers. They were an aggravation he could do without, but they were investigating Simon Lang. The Feds knew Lang was a criminal. They were just too ham-handed to secure the information that would convict him.

Or perhaps their lack of success was because they were forced to adhere to a façade of legality in their pursuit of justice. Crawford seldom bothered with the law. At various times, he had used burglary, eavesdropping, fraud, embezzlement, arson, and property damage in his crusade against Simon Lang.

But Crawford, despite his nefarious and multifarious activities, had been no more adept than the Feds at taking out Lang.

When neither he nor the federal government had achieved their purpose, Crawford had reluctantly decided to join forces. He became a contact, a source of information, for the FBI. But he had done it on his own terms.

That was the point about the apartment. Crawford's past, not to mention his present life, wouldn't stand up to examination by law enforcement. He was the one who determined when and where he spoke to the FBI.

Crawford adjusted the headset and took another sip of lukewarm coffee, hoping the caffeine would galvanize his brain waves and stimulate his neurons. He was monitoring the telephone lines of LB Freight, a large West Coast trucking company run by Simon Lang.

So far he had overheard chats between secretaries,

orders for lunch, and complaints about the air conditioning system. But mostly he had listened as bets were placed on the weekend's football games. It was Las Vegas, after all. Betting was as much a part of the lifestyle as golf courses and swimming pools.

Crawford absent mindedly studied the coffee table in front of him. With its turned legs and fluted columns, the table had once been a stately piece. Now the top was stained with an assortment of water marks. The abstract blobs looked like a Mandelbrot set – which was nothing more than a kind of fractal – only less predictable.

He was engaged in a mathematical pursuit, calculating how many smaller circles would be required to cover the large round water stain at the end of the coffee table, when his mind jerked to attention.

"Fucking hell!" he muttered.

He listened to the end of the recorded segment. Then he played it back again. It was a conversation between Simon Lang and Graciela Martín, the chief financial officer of LB Freight.

"The O'Neill supply chain issue has resurfaced. I thought we destroyed everything." Simon Lang's voice resembled the testy, menacing growl of a wounded animal.

"We did," Graciela assured Simon. *"There's nothing left. No paper. No computer files."*

"It appears we overlooked something, Gracie. I want you to go through everything again. What about the employees who were involved?"

"They have all left LB Freight," she replied. *"Ernest O'Neill and Michael Colby are dead. The only ones still alive are George Chaplin, Darius Taylor, and Wesley Bernard."*

Crawford was hoping he had misheard, that perhaps his imagination had inserted those names, that none of this was real. But there was no mistake. He let out a long, slow hiss of breath. When he realized his hands had closed into fists, he carefully loosened his fingers one at a time. But he kept listening.

"We're going to have to get rid of them," Simon told her.

"I don't think they present a problem, Simon. Chaplin is a homeless drunk, Taylor is dying of cancer, and Bernard is living in Mexico."

"Somebody knows something," Lang replied. Then he gave a bark of harsh laughter. *"He called me Apollyon. What does that mean?"*

"Apollyon was the angel of the abyss," Graciela replied.

Crawford thought there was an edge to her voice, but he couldn't tell what it meant. Evidently Simon couldn't either.

"Well, it doesn't matter," Simon decided. *"I'm calling Alice. I want this resolved once and for all."*

"What brought this to your attention, Simon?" Graciela asked.

"Anonymous message."

"Blackmail?"

"Nothing I can't handle," Simon told her.

The next recording was of a conversation between Simon and his daughter, Alice, who had gone to Mexico to avoid a warrant for her arrest.

"Get rid of them," he told Alice. *"Start with Bernard. Then I want you to come home. When you get here you can take care of the other two."*

Crawford took off the headset and wearily rubbed his neck. His scheme to take down Simon Lang, simple in its original concept, had become a labyrinthine game with unknown parameters. Each day brought a new twist, another hurdle, or an added complication.

It was the fractals all over again. When you magnified a fractal, you plunged into its depths, finding irregularities that teased you with their familiarity and taunted you with their differences.

When you sought retribution, you never knew where it was going to take you.

Chapter 3

Graciela Martín listened as Simon Lang issued instructions to his daughter. He didn't realize that all she had to do was press a button to hear his calls.

Simon was so accustomed to her presence that he often didn't notice her. That was fine with Gracie. It made it easier to keep tabs on her temperamental boss.

"Apollyon," she thought. The word had come out of nowhere, almost as a warning. She had told Simon that Apollyon was the angel of the abyss. As she had expected, he didn't understand what she meant.

Apollyon was the destroyer.

Gracie stared at the pastel desert painting on the wall, the one the decorator had said would enhance the ambiance of the office, the one that didn't intrude on the subtle chrome and gray color scheme. But what she saw was a black angel, wings spread wide, rising from a fiery pit of orange flames.

She had known this time would come. She would set the wheels in motion.

Chapter 4

FBI Special Agent Chloe Mathews pushed the elevator button for the fourth floor of the LB Freight offices in Las Vegas. The FBI believed the company was involved in weapons smuggling, drugs, prostitution, and gambling, but they needed proof. Chloe was there to get it.

When the door closed and the elevator began to ascend, she checked her appearance in the mirror. Her newly highlighted hair, incorporating multiple strands of lilac and tangerine, was held in place by gel. She had inserted cheek plumpers to make her face round. And she was wearing a sleeveless dress with more than a hint of décolletage. The hemline stopped a few inches above her knees.

She didn't think anyone would mistake her for an undercover FBI agent. She thought she looked like the quintessential administrative assistant, and she had the credentials to prove it. Her résumé contained a carefully fabricated background with excellent references.

Chloe was also carrying a false driver's license and social security number in the name of Agnes Reynard. In medieval French allegories, Reynard was a fox. Clever and charismatic, the fox usually triumphed at the end of the story.

Chloe wanted to be that fox. She wanted to convict Simon Lang.

Undercover work wasn't new to Chloe. In her previous

assignment out of the Phoenix FBI office, she had infil-
trated the Bosqueros motorcycle gang at a gathering in
Boulder City, securing information that had resulted in
the arrests of a number of its officers.

She had also identified a rogue FBI agent, a man
named Steve Carson-Burleigh who had been taking
kickbacks from the Bosqueros. Caught up in his own
game of corruption, he had let himself be lured into a
trap and killed. He hadn't analyzed the situation, hadn't
fully understood what was going on around him.

It was all about knowing the game, Chloe reminded
herself. You had to be able to anticipate what was going
to happen, and how and why.

Before she left Buffalo, New York, to take the Phoenix job, her boss, Regina Bentley, had talked about it.

"You can know the rules and not know the game,
Chloe. Keep that in mind."

And Chloe had. She had known when she volunteered to take part in the investigation of Simon Lang
that it would be a dangerous operation, and she had
taken steps to make certain she had things under control. She had even asked her friend, Patty Moriarity, for
advice on becoming an administrative assistant.

"It's an ish job," Patty told her, "but as an undercover
op, you won't be in it very long."

"What's an ish job?" Chloe asked.

"Shit job," Patty explained. "It's a dead end."

Not a literal "dead end" if Chloe could help it.

"What will I have to do?" she asked.

"Answer the phone, do word processing, run errands. When I was an administrative assistant, I spent a lot of time reminding the boss about appointments."

"Doesn't sound too hard," Chloe concluded.

"Depends on the boss," Patty reminded her.

When the elevator reached the fourth floor, Chloe found herself in a vast open area. The thick carpet was a muted silver in color. The walls were painted a soft gray. The décor consisted primarily of glass and chrome.

A long, curved receptionist desk topped with frosted glass snaked its way toward the floor-to-ceiling window. Like the yellow brick road, it seemed to point the way to the Emerald City, or in this case, the Las Vegas Strip.

Behind the desk a young woman with sleek black hair pulled into a bun was speaking into a headset. She was as cool and contained as the office. She looked like she belonged in an upscale New York City boutique. The name plaque on the undulating desk read Alicia Armstrong.

Chloe thought of her own hair style. Perhaps she should not have gone in for the highlights. It had been a spur-of-the-moment decision, like many of her choices in life.

"You never think about the consequences. You always make up your mind before you consider what you're getting into," Grandma Mathews used to warn her, standing by the kitchen stove, hands on her hips, wearing an apron with bright orange flowers. "Your parents were the same, and look where it got them. Dead before they reached their thirties. You'll be lucky if the same thing doesn't happen to you." Then her grandmother would shake her head, wipe her hands on the hem of the apron, and go back to stirring whatever she was cooking.

Chloe was now thirty-one years old and still breathing. She credited her impressive longevity to instinct and quick reactions. She might make a few mistakes now and then, but she always managed to come out ahead.

And while the highlights might have been one of those assorted misjudgments, they weren't going to deter her. She straightened her back and approached the desk.

"Ms. Reynard?" the receptionist said as she looked up at Chloe. "Mr. Lang is expecting you. I'll see if he's free."

Chapter 5

Simon Lang, who was over six feet tall and weighed more than two hundred pounds, was an impressive figure. When he was younger, he had been a handsome man. Now he was considered distinguished. His black hair was liberally tinted with silver, and there were deep creases in his face.

Chloe caught a brief flicker of curiosity in Lang's eyes as she entered the office. Simon Lang was a successful businessman. Split-second assessments were probably second nature to him. He had already seen her résumé and references. Now he had seen her. She wondered what he was thinking.

Lang extended a large hand and introduced himself. Then he led her to a cluster of elegant chrome chairs in the corner of his office and invited her to take a seat. He sat down in another chair and turned to gaze at the vista of Las Vegas spread out in front of them.

"It's a city I never get tired of watching," he said. "It's got everything. The good, the bad, and the ugly. The high rollers and the dead beats. The layabouts and the movers and shakers. The scrupulous and the untrustworthy."

He turned his head suddenly to look at her. "Which are you, Ms. Reynard?"

Chloe knew better than to be caught off guard. She looked back at him steadily.

"I doubt if any of us can be classified in just one way,

Mr. Lang. I'm competent and hard-working. I'm also reliable. My past employers gave me excellent references."

Lang looked at her for a few seconds, but his eyes gave nothing away. "What would you like to know about LB Freight?" he asked.

A great deal, she thought. But Simon Lang wasn't going to provide the kind of information she was after.

"I understand the job involves working with your truck fleet," she replied. "How big is your operation?"

"We have five hundred trucks," he told her. "About three times that number of trailers. We do long haul, regional, specialty, and bulk shipments. We do some hazmat, but not a great deal. We've modernized the tractors, made them more aerodynamic. Electronic dashboards. Full size cabs. The trailers have been updated to be more efficient, as well. Our safety record is outstanding. A lot of our drivers have over a million miles without an accident."

Lang went on to describe the LB Freight trucking operation in fluent detail. She might have been listening to the chief executive officer of a legitimate company make a report to his board of directors.

"I'm impressed," she told him. It was the truth. "What are the areas in which you want to see improvements?"

"There are always problems," Lang admitted. "We've got a decent utilization rate, but I'd like to push it higher. We can't find as many drivers as we need, and once we train them, we can't always keep them. But we've upgraded our benefits package for drivers, so I think we'll start doing better in that area."

Chloe hadn't known if Lang would be a hands-on manager. A CEO who was running illegal operations might focus on that side of the business, leaving his staff to handle the legitimate activities. But Lang appeared up to date on every aspect of the fleet.

"I'd like to know more about the position you have available," she said.

"The job is in Robbie's office. He's my son. I'll let him fill you in," Lang said. He stood up, indicating that the session was over.

"It was a pleasure to meet you, Ms. Reynard. I'm sure you'll fit into our office nicely."

That must be the strangest interview in history, Chloe thought. *Lang hadn't asked about her background or experience. But it sounded as if she might get the job.*

Lang escorted her to the door and turned her over to his executive secretary. This wasn't the receptionist, but another woman whose name plaque read Ms. Lincoln.

"My name's Peggy," she told Chloe with a smile. "I'll take you to meet Robbie."

Peggy, who appeared to be in her late twenties, had a generous smile. Instead of favoring the boutique style of Alicia Armstrong in her dress, Peggy had on a comfortable, well-cut suit and sensible shoes.

"Have you worked here long?" Chloe asked as the

two women walked the short distance to the suite occupied by Robbie Lang.

"Several years," Peggy replied. "I didn't expect to stay this long, but here I am."

"Why was that?" Chloe asked.

"You mean why did I stay or why didn't I leave?"

Chloe laughed. "Both, I guess."

Peggy looked around to be sure no one else was in earshot. Then she whispered to Chloe. "This used to be an awful place to work when Lenny Lang was alive. He was the son of Mr. Lang. I wouldn't wish death on anyone, but all of the women here are glad he's not around anymore. I wasn't planning to stay, but once Lenny was out of the picture, there was no reason to leave. The salary is good and Mr. Lang is a fair-minded boss."

"Fair-minded in what way?" Chloe asked.

"He lets me set my own schedule," Peggy replied. "That's important because I'm taking classes at UNLV. That's the University of Nevada, Las Vegas," she added.

"What do you do as executive secretary?" Chloe asked.

"I'm really just a glorified administrative assistant," Peggy admitted, "but I liked the sound of executive secretary. When I asked Mr. Lang if I could rename my position, he said why not."

She and Chloe exchanged a grin before Peggy knocked on the door of Robbie Lang's office.

Chapter 6

Robbie Lang was in his mid-thirties, soft-spoken and somewhat absent-minded. Chloe discovered that he was in charge of hiring, training, and supervising LB Freight's drivers.

The job announcement for the administrative assistant position had listed a series of duties, including monitoring whether drivers were receiving the required training, were being routinely tested for drugs and alcohol, had up-to-date medical exams, and were keeping their log books accurately.

Patty might consider it an ish job, but Chloe knew that working closely with the drivers would provide the opportunity she needed to find out where they were going and what loads they were carrying.

"Are you also the fleet manager?" Chloe asked.

"No. My brother, Lenny, used to take care of that. But he died. Now my dad does it."

"I'm sorry to hear about your brother," Chloe commiserated. She knew that Lenny had been killed in a shoot-out. "Does Mr. Lang keep track of fuel receipts, or do you?"

"He's got the fuel receipts," Robbie told her. "We keep them electronically. All I have are the drivers' log books. But that's enough." He glanced at a side table where the books were piled haphazardly.

"I want you to take the position," he said to Chloe. "Can you start tomorrow?"

"Of course," Chloe replied, already planning how she would organize the log books. They would provide a lot of information, but her task would be more complicated than she had expected. The records didn't appear to be kept in an orderly manner. Some were probably missing, and the ones that were available wouldn't necessarily be accurate.

The fuel receipts kept by Simon Lang could provide some of the data she needed. They would reveal where the drivers had purchased fuel and how much. Maybe she could find a way to get a look at those, too.

Chloe brought her attention back to Robbie. Evidently feeling that the official interview was over, he had begun to talk about life in Las Vegas. He was describing a local nightclub called Les Trois Épices. Something about music. He seemed to be waiting for her response.

"What's your favorite kind of music?" Chloe asked. She had lost track of the conversation, but it was a safe enough question.

"Gypsy jazz," he told her. "We're Roma, you know."

That was odd, she thought. Robbie was the second person who had told her he was Roma. The first was Joe Crawford.

She wondered if Crawford knew the Langs had a Romany heritage. She would have to ask him.

Chapter 7

Joe Crawford handed Chloe a thumb drive containing the software he had developed.

"All you have to do is plug it into your PC at LB Freight when you start work tomorrow," he told her. "The application will install itself. Then remove it and get out of there."

He didn't tell her he had been using similar software for some time to keep track of Simon Lang and his family. He hadn't told the FBI, either.

"This will enable the FBI to tap into LB Freight computer records and emails, right?" she asked as she examined the small device. "And I'm not going to get out of there. I'm going to help Robbie with the driver training materials tomorrow."

"Hanging around LB Freight is dangerous," Crawford warned her. "Simon Lang doesn't hesitate to murder people who get in his way."

"I'm a professional," she told him. "I know what I'm doing."

Crawford wanted to argue with her, but she changed the subject.

"Before I hack into the LB Freight computer system, I'd like to see the court order," she said.

Crawford had known she would insist on following the rules, and had come prepared. He pulled the document from his back pocket and handed it to her.

Crawford watched as Chloe eagerly unfolded the piece of paper. In his association with the FBI, he hadn't intended to do more than provide background information on Simon Lang's criminal activities. Then his FBI contact had blackmailed him into working with Chloe. It was supposed to have been a one-time arrangement when he escorted her to the Bosqueros gathering in Boulder City. Now he was helping her carry out another undercover assignment. This one involved LB Freight.

He had learned in their previous assignment that Chloe liked following the rules. In fact, her devotion to prescribed behavior sometimes had a tinge of religious fervor.

Crawford understood that. He was equally committed. Only his religion was revenge. Rules formed the structure of Chloe's life; redressing a wrong was the hallmark of his.

But while Crawford couldn't shake his allegiance to vengeance, Chloe occasionally broke free of the rules, running after an impromptu idea like the mad hatter searching for the answer to a riddle.

Crawford hadn't figured out the pattern, but whatever motivated Chloe, it was clear she enjoyed challenges. He thought he might be one of those challenges.

She knew he operated outside the law, that he didn't accept the status quo. Nevertheless, he and his straightforward, follow-the-rules FBI agent had become a team.

But it was more than that. They were sleeping together. That didn't fit into any rule book that he knew of.

"This looks OK," Chloe noted, carefully scrutinizing the wording, the dates, and the signatures on the court order. Everything, in fact.

It should look OK, Crawford thought. He had taken the original court order and added enough details to keep her happy.

"Tell me how the software works," she said.

"It directs LB Freight data packets to the FBI router," he explained. "Each packet will be split between the intended server and the covert FBI server. The FBI will get a copy of everything LB Freight sends or receives."

"What else?"

Crawford smoothed the knuckles of one hand under her chin and studied the face of his woman. The one who was having an affair with an outlaw. The one who was pretending to be an administrative assistant.

Dark eyebrows arched above wide, clear blue eyes that could sparkle with enjoyment or blaze with anger. Her nose was small and straight, and her chin was determinedly firm. Normally she had smooth brown hair. Just now, it was somewhat spiky and oddly streaked with color.

Chloe had told him that in preparation for her undercover assignment, she wanted to cultivate the persona of the job she was to fill. "If I act like an administrative assistant even when I'm away from work," she had said, "I'll be less likely to do something out of character."

She must have decided to become a sassy administrative assistant. She was wearing a short, tight dress that skimmed her hips. She was also radiating enthusiasm. But that was typical Chloe. That didn't have anything to do with her new job at LB Freight.

Crawford didn't want to talk about software. For once, he didn't even want to talk about LB Freight and Simon Lang. He wanted to put Chloe on his motorcycle, take her to his cabin in the mountains, and engage in a round of steamy sex. Afterward, they would sit in the hot spring and look at the stars.

Just now she wasn't interested in sex. "The software," she reminded him. "Won't the IT staff discover it's there?"

"They won't know they're being intercepted," he assured her.

"And they can't trace it to me?" she asked.

"No."

"How do you know?"

"The software will plant malicious code on the server motherboard and erase itself from the PC. But even though it is on the server, the techs still won't find it. The infected server will appear to be functioning as usual and the code will be invisible to LB Freight's security programs."

"What if they replace the motherboard?"

"The code will regenerate itself."

"What else haven't you told me?"

Crawford didn't answer. He was operating on the principle that it was best if she didn't know too much about his activities.

Chloe was smart. Sooner or later, Ms. Follow-the-Rules would realize what he was doing, and she wouldn't approve of his tactics. Then he would lose her.

But right now, they were together. He would go with that.

Chapter 8

Chloe placed the thumb drive in the zipper compartment of her purse. She slid the court order between the cardboard and the inner packaging of a cereal box. She didn't expect Simon Lang to search her apartment. The only address he had for her was false. But Chloe didn't want to take chances.

She was alone this evening. Crawford had been distracted and in a hurry, and she hadn't invited him to stay. They had agreed to meet the following afternoon to compare notes.

Chloe changed into a pair of stretch leggings and a matching T-shirt. She always felt better when the various items of clothing she was wearing paired well. Especially the lingerie. She hadn't brought much with her from Buffalo, but she did have a drawer full of beautifully coordinated panties and camisoles.

She picked up a bottle of water and made her way to the exercise room. Walking through the house, a mid-century modern in the Scotch Eighties section of Las Vegas, made her feel like she was in a time warp.

The roof of the single story dwelling was low, flat, and irregular. One wall was made entirely of glass. The high windows struggled valiantly to reduce the light and heat of the desert. The main living room had wooden beams and a stone fireplace for the chilly months of the year. Throughout most of the residence, the decorator had used atomic-age chrome furniture and eye-popping pastel colors.

According to Patty, the house had been custom-built for a casino boss with organized crime connections. When the original owner turned up dead in a car bombing, the house was placed on sale and the Moriarity family purchased it.

Patty had grown up in the house. Now she and her boyfriend, Graham, lived there. Chloe was subleasing the portion that had once served as the maid's quarters.

As she went through her exercise routine, Chloe considered what she would wear for her first day of work at LB Freight. A dark-colored dress, she decided, remembering Alicia Armstrong's sleek appearance and Peggy Lincoln's neat, professional attire. She would add a sweater for warmth. And red lingerie. Matching, of course. That would give her courage.

Having resolved the wardrobe issue, Chloe's thoughts turned to her relationship with the enigmatic Crawford. They were a mismatched pair if there ever was one, but neither of them wanted to end the relationship.

She had been the one to bring up the matter the last time they visited his cabin in the mountains of Esmeralda County. Crawford wasn't going to initiate a conversation about a difficult subject. The man saved his words like a miser holding on to his money.

"Where are we going with this?" she had asked him. They had been basking in the warmth of the hot spring, sitting on the stone bench he had placed there, and gazing at the stars.

"With stargazing?"

"No. Our relationship."

"Where do you want it to go?" he had asked as he stared at the sky.

"I asked you first," she replied. She placed her hands on the sides of his face and turned his head so that he was looking directly at her. She could see the glimmers of fire in his dark green eyes. They reminded her of flecks of iron oxide in green bloodstone, protection against the evil eye.

"What I want isn't going to matter in the end, Sweet Cheeks."

"I told you not to call me that."

"I like calling you that," he said. "When you get mad, your eyes spark."

He was baiting her, trying to get himself out of an awkward conversation, but she persisted.

"Crawford, I asked you a question. Answer it, please."

"It won't work," he told her. "We can't have a relationship. You're an FBI agent. Everything I do is illegal."

Having said that, he settled back on the bench. In his mind, he had finished the conversation. But she wouldn't let him go.

"In case you hadn't noticed, we're already having a relationship."

She brought her face to within a few inches of his, until they were almost nose to nose, staring at each other. In the starlight, his eyes were ghost-like, shadowed and haunted.

For a few long moments, it was as if the earth had

stopped revolving. Nothing moved in the desert around them. The small desert rodents ceased rustling among the dry branches. Even the coyotes on their nightly rounds were silent.

"Oh, hell," Crawford muttered.

He pulled her onto his lap, wrapped his arms around her and captured her mouth with his.

They hadn't finished the conversation, and Chloe hadn't brought up the matter again. Neither of them had the answer. Talking about it wasn't going to change things.

Chapter 9

Crawford sank into the leather armchair, placed his computer on the coffee table, and pulled out his cell phone. He had fulfilled his promise to provide Chloe and the FBI with software to tap into LB Freight Internet communications. With that out of the way, he could concentrate on other tasks. He wanted to discover what it was about the O'Neill supply chain issue that worried Simon Lang. And he wanted to locate and warn the three men Simon Lang intended to kill.

The conversation between Simon Lang and Gracie Martin had occurred that morning, and Simon would already have contacted his daughter. Alice Lang was a contract killer. She would be looking for the three men. But there might be a way to save them.

It was time for the Squad to go into action.

Fifteen years earlier, Simon Lang had forcibly taken over the company known as Lang Brothers Metal Works, and renamed it LB Freight. In his zeal to remake the company into a major regional enterprise, Lang had abandoned long-standing personnel policies and safety procedures. Working conditions had immediately deteriorated. Employees who opposed the changes or tried to bring in union representatives were either let go or given dangerous, unhealthy assignments. Lang had gone so far as to arrange for the most recalcitrant of his employees to be exposed to toxic metal-working chemicals. The workers who had come into contact with the airborne particles containing nitrite and untreated mineral oils contracted cancer. Many of them had died. Most of the remaining few were terminally ill.

Crawford and his associates, who called themselves the Squad, were determined to correct the injustice. Stopping Simon Lang was the first goal. The second was to sink LB Freight into bankruptcy. Then the Squad planned to turn the company into an employee-owned corporation.

The O'Neill supply chain issue – whatever it was – might provide sufficient evidence to prosecute Simon Lang. But there was a snag.

Darius Taylor was a member of the Squad. While working at LB Freight, he had been exposed to toxic chemicals. Now he had cancer. The doctors had told him he might have six months to live.

Darius had several items on his bucket list and the time had come to take care of them. He and his wife had always wanted to visit Hawaii. They were there now.

Crawford wanted information, but he didn't want to call Darius and interrupt what might be the Taylors' last vacation.

He called Diego Gutierrez, another member of the Squad, and asked him to find the location in Mexico of Wesley Bernard, and warn Bernard that Simon Lang had placed a hit on him. Maybe Bernard could get out of town before Alice Lang tracked him down.

Crawford also tasked Diego with locating the homeless George Chaplin. But that matter wasn't as urgent. Before Alice could shoot Chaplin, she had to return to the United States. Then she had to track down a homeless man. That would take a few days.

Crawford also wanted to review the LB Freight personnel files for Ernest O'Neill, Darius Taylor, and the other men.

Chloe would start work at LB Freight in the morning, but if he asked her to get the files, she would demand a search warrant. He didn't have time to wait for a warrant. Besides, he didn't want to alert the FBI to anything that might involve Darius Taylor.

He considered breaking into the LB Freight office. He had done it before. But there were security cameras everywhere. Both the LB Freight security staff and the FBI were monitoring the footage. If Crawford disguised himself, none of them would recognize him. But it was possible Chloe would see the tapes. She would spot him immediately, even in a disguise.

Crawford called Sid Allenby, who was de facto co-leader of the Squad.

"Send Diego and Harrison," Sid recommended. Harrison Knight was another member of the Squad. "No one at the FBI knows them. They can pose as workmen."

"After-hours workmen?"

"Sure. I'll prepare a requisition." Sid had once been a production machinist with LB Freight. He was familiar with the inner workings of the company.

"I've asked Diego to look for a man named Wesley Bernard. Simon Lang wants Alice to get rid of him," Crawford said.

"Gaining access to LB Freight will take only a few hours," Sid replied. "Then Diego can get back to looking for Bernard."

Crawford had agreed, and Sid had set up the operation.

That was the reason Diego Gutierrez and Harrison Knight had entered the LB Freight premises.

Now Simon Lang was holding them both captive.

Chapter 10

"What happened?" Crawford asked Sid.

"One of the guards picked up Diego and Harrison, held them while he asked Lang for instructions, and took them to an unknown location," Sid reported. "Diego bribed the guard to let him make a phone call. That's how I learned about it."

"It's a setup," Crawford decided. "Simon Lang wouldn't keep an employee who accepted a bribe."

"Yeah," Sid replied. "I agree. Diego couldn't provide much information. The only thing he could tell me was that it didn't take more than an hour to get to wherever they are. And before you ask, I couldn't trace the call."

"If it took only an hour, they aren't far from Vegas."

"Right," Sid agreed. "Got any ideas?"

Crawford had a lot of ideas about where the men might be – too many to investigate. But he could narrow down the search. "I'll take it from here," he told Sid.

Uncle Joey Lancaster, the new president of the Bosqueros motorcycle gang, always knew what was going on around town. He also handled weapons purchases and sales for the bikers.

Uncle Joey had sold Crawford a P556 pistol a few weeks ago, and Crawford had converted it to a short barreled rifle. The conversion had been simple, involving only the exchange of a few parts. Counterfeiting the tax stamp had taken more time.

Crawford had both the weapon and the stamp. All the new owner had to do to demonstrate that his firearm was registered was engrave his name, city, and state on the frame. Crawford would throw in the fraudulent paperwork free of charge.

The Bosqueros prized SBRs with ten-inch barrels – rather than the usual sixteen-inch ones – for their portability, versatility, and maneuverability. Uncle Joey would be eager to get his hands on the weapon, especially one that could be made to look legal.

Crawford had originally had another use in mind for the SBR, intending to trade it for a shipment of C4 explosives, but the C4 could wait. The important thing was to remove Diego and Harrison from Simon Lang's control. As Crawford had warned Chloe, Lang made a practice of murdering anyone who got in his way.

Just as Crawford expected, Uncle Joey agreed to the trade – the SBR in exchange for information on where Lang was holding the two men. As usual, Uncle Joey refused to deal on credit. He would provide the information when he had the SBR.

Before leaving to meet Uncle Joey, Crawford received another call from Sid.

"Arthur Blackcotton was seen in Vegas," Sid warned.

"Who the hell is that?"

"You know him by the name One-Eye," Sid had replied. "Be careful. The rumors are that he's after the man the Bosqueros call Ghost. He wants the girlfriend, too."

Chapter 11

Now Crawford was being held in the McCullough Detention Center, and he had only himself to blame. He should have listened to Sid's cautionary advice about One-Eye. The fractals had been a warning. He hadn't paid enough attention to those damn inherent complications.

One-Eye had gone to prison for the murder of a boy who refused to get out of his way. Then he had lost an eye in a prison fight. Later he had raped a teen-aged would-be biker chick before turning her over to his pals. The police had found her body several weeks later, but there had not been enough evidence to charge One-Eye or anyone else with her murder.

While Chloe and Crawford were attending the Bosqueros get-together in Boulder City, One-Eye had tried to kidnap Chloe. Unfortunately for One-Eye, he hadn't expected to encounter a trained professional. Instead of letting herself be captured, Chloe had fought back, kneeing One-Eye in the groin and throwing him to the ground.

As a result of the altercation, the Bosqueros had evicted One-Eye and his cronies from the club. Evidently One-Eye hadn't forgotten or forgiven.

This morning when Crawford had set out to meet Uncle Joey, he had been riding his BMW 1600, keeping his speed under control and listening to the engine. He had removed the touring screen and the wind was blasting his face.

Chloe had sent for her Fatboy and wanted to ride

with him. But he liked it when she was behind him on the same bike, her arms wrapped around him, her face against his shoulder.

He was thinking of Chloe. That was why he hadn't noticed One-Eye until it was too late.

One-Eye had forced Crawford's motorcycle off the road, sending him catapulting into the ditch. Crawford felt as Phaethon must have when Zeus knocked him from the sky with a thunderbolt. But Phaethon's flaming body had fallen into a river. Crawford hit the dirt.

It wasn't Crawford's first fall and he was wearing a full face helmet, protective vest, and knee guards. They hadn't been his idea, but using them was easier than arguing with Chloe.

He had somersaulted through the air before doing a tuck and roll, ending on his back, with the bike taking the brunt of the impact. A stunned Crawford had shaken his head to clear it. Through the din in his ears, he heard One-Eye shout, "You're a dead man, Ghost."

One-Eye, like all the Bosqueros, addressed Crawford as Ghost. It was Crawford's biker name. One-Eye didn't know it, but Crawford really was a dead man.

Since his return from the Army, Crawford had been enough of an annoyance that Simon Lang had placed a bounty on his head – a hundred grand, dead or alive. Having his worth measured at a measly hundred thou had rankled, but Crawford had taken Lang up on his offer. He had faked his own death and collected the money, paltry though it was.

One-Eye had called him a dead man, Crawford

mused as he sat on the floor and listened to the sounds that filtered through the small barred window of his cell. Perhaps One-Eye was smarter than he looked. It wouldn't be hard. The infamous Arthur Blackcotton bore a number of prison tattoos. His one remaining eye was bloodshot, his mouth was small and pinched, and his cauliflower ears stuck out from his misshapen head like a kid's drawing of a space monster.

Nah, Crawford thought. There wasn't anything smart about One-Eye. Dangerous, maybe. But smart? Not a chance in hell.

After issuing his prophecy, One-Eye had disappeared, the tires of his truck spinning gravel that struck the asphalt like sparks from a fiery chariot.

With only a few cuts and scratches, Crawford had been examining his bike, standing among the discarded fast food wrappers, empty soda and beer cans, abandoned tires, and what looked like a perfectly good copy of Pilgrim's Progress, when the highway patrol arrived. It was an officer Crawford had met before.

Trooper Reinhart regularly appeared in Crawford's life, much like a *chovihano,* a Gypsy shaman, out to rescue a lost soul. That wouldn't have been a problem, but Trooper Reinhart thought Crawford's name was Donlevsky.

This time Crawford wasn't carrying identification as Donlevsky. He wasn't carrying any identification. And then there was the matter of the short barreled rifle in the bike's panniers. All in all, it would have been difficult to explain. Crawford hadn't tried.

Chapter 12

Crawford lolled against the wall of his cell. He was getting a crick in his neck. So much for the padding, or maybe it was a result of the bike accident. He was woozy and his head ached.

He was allowed to make one phone call.

He could notify FBI Special Agent Tom Jefferson of his incarceration. It was, after all, Jefferson who had recruited him to work with Chloe Mathews.

But even though Jefferson knew Crawford ignored any laws he found inconvenient, he wouldn't be happy to learn about the SBR. At the least, Crawford would get a lengthy harangue; at the most, Jefferson would just leave him in jail.

Alternatively, Crawford could call Sid, but the cops would record the conversation. He didn't want them to know about Sid or the other members of the Squad.

He had to make a decision. He chose Sid.

He went to the window of his cell and shouted at the corrections officer, "I want to make a phone call."

Crawford would use the Squad's code name for Sid, and identify himself as "Ghost." After taking the call, Sid would have to get rid of his cell phone. He wouldn't be pleased. It would be the third replacement this month.

From across the bullpen, Gus raised his head. "That's the way to tell 'em," he encouraged Crawford. "We might be in the slough of despond, but we have our rights."

Crawford hadn't thought of Pilgrim's Progress since high school. Now he was being stalked by it.

The officer in charge of the detention center was Sergeant Akers, an earnest young man fresh out of the Marines. He kept his eyes on the television set for a few moments before he stood up. He was watching a reporter discuss the purported crimes of the Bosqueros.

"I'm here at Virgil's Roadhouse," the reporter stated, "where the Bosqueros leaders allegedly met to discuss their operations. As you can see, the business, often frequented by bikers, is now closed for repairs."

The one-story, wood frame roadhouse was getting a new kitchen, as well as assorted upgrades, including a fresh coat of paint. Crawford wondered if Virgil was going to redecorate the interior. He hoped not. He liked the bar stools with their cracked vinyl seats, the pool table with its scuffed green felt, and the juke box that only worked when you kicked it.

On Tuesdays, Virgil operated a tattoo parlor in the back room. Crawford, an amateur artist, had provided a few designs, including one of the roadhouse with its American flag over the front door.

Virgil sponsored live honkytonk piano music on the weekends, but only to a small self-selected audience. He couldn't be bothered to advertise.

Virgil's Roadhouse was the Bosqueros' distribution point for drugs. Virgil was also a gun runner, bringing weapons in from Mexico. Being an equal opportunity provider, he sold illegal arms to both the Bosqueros and Simon Lang.

Guns and drugs were the primary sources of Virgil's income. The roadhouse, while profitable, was a cover for his other business interests.

Given the variety of clientele that passed through the roadhouse, it might as well have been Grand Central Station. The graffiti in the hallway to the bathrooms was equally wide-ranging, with everything from the scatological, to the sexually crude, to the erotic, to the highbrow.

"What is the numerical value of a potato?" someone had written.

"Meeny," another had answered.

"No, you dickheads," a third had scrawled. "It's Mississippi."

"I never understood that piece of graffiti," Uncle Joey had complained to Crawford when they chanced to encounter one another in the roadhouse hallway one day. Uncle Joey had been buying guns. Crawford and Virgil had been discussing the latest shipment of C4.

"Don't worry," Crawford had told him. "Even Einstein couldn't figure it out."

If Virgil was redecorating, the layers of felt pen and spray paint graffiti might be only memories now. Future customers would be free to set forth their own forms of creative expression, but something irretrievable would have been lost.

The next time he passed by Virgil's, Crawford would make it a point to check out the graffiti. If the one about the potato had been painted over, he could always redo it.

But first he had to get out of jail.

"The FBI is searching for the owner of the road-house, Virgil Bascom," the reporter continued, "but so far they haven't been able to locate him."

"That's because he's in Mexico," Sergeant Akers muttered. "The FBI can't chase its own tail."

Having stated his opinion of the FBI, Akers appeared ready to strike a deal with the prisoner. He turned to Crawford. "Sir, you can make a phone call after we have your fingerprints and photo." His voice and manner were professional.

"Fuck that," Crawford responded. He didn't want to be professional.

Gus let out a bark of laughter and Crawford gave him a half smile.

"I could tell you a few things," Gus shouted. He had wrapped the blanket around himself like a cocoon. He didn't seem to be shivering as much as before.

"Same here," Crawford replied. But they weren't close enough for a collegial conversation, and he didn't want to get Gus into trouble by yelling at him across the central booking area. He turned around and stared at the walls.

He and Gus might tell each other a few things, but there was a lot he hadn't told Chloe.

The software he had turned over to her bypassed LB Freight security protocols and gave Crawford administrative control. He could infiltrate the entire LB Freight network.

The court order, even after his amendments, didn't cover that part.

Once he got out of jail, he planned to use the software to obtain diagrams of LB Freight's security structure, including their video surveillance. She didn't know that, either.

And there was something else he hadn't mentioned. He was routing everything through his own server, where he was filtering the information. The FBI would get only what he released.

And if references to Darius Taylor and the O'Neill supply chain appeared in the LB Freight emails, the FBI would never see them.

Chapter 13

Simon Lang was a *rom baro*, a big man politically and physically. He had a massive body and an ego to match.

Lang had taken over the family business, wresting control of his father's scrap metal company from his brothers, Aaron and Jacob, and forcing them into retirement. Then he had brought in his own sons and daughter and placed them in charge of various divisions.

He had expanded operations, setting up offices in Los Angeles and San Diego, and investing in trucks to haul the loads. LB Freight had become a major West Coast transport company, hauling everything from appliances to illegal weapons and drugs.

The Lang family had other interests only marginally associated with LB Freight. Simon ran an illegal sports betting operation and several high-end escort services that dealt in cocaine and prostitutes. The Langs also provided murder for hire services to a few select clients. Lenny, Simon's son, had once been the designated hit man, but Lenny had been killed in a somewhat murky incident in Prague. Alice, Simon's daughter, had taken over the contract kills after Lenny's demise.

Now Lang needed her skills. He knew that bringing her back was a risk. She was wanted for the murder of an FBI agent named Steve Carson-Burleigh. But it was a chance he had to take.

Alice could make San Diego her base of operations, and stay out of Vegas. The FBI wouldn't think to look for her in California.

Lang's other son, Robbie, was a good-hearted boy of mediocre intelligence and no talent for business. Robbie was of limited use in the company, but Simon was fond of his son. He had placed Robbie in charge of the drivers.

Without Lenny and Alice, Lang was running the business almost singlehandedly. He had assumed control of the freight and equipment side of things, formerly managed by Lenny. He was also temporarily in charge of the scrap metal business, normally Alice's responsibility. It was taking a lot of his time.

Then something else had come up.

Enrique Castellanos was the LB Freight contact in the crime syndicate known as the Bosqueros. There was also a motorcycle gang of the same name, a subsidiary of the syndicate. Simon Lang and his family had little to do with the motorcycle gang, but they often acted in conjunction with the syndicate. The two enterprises frequently exchanged information of interest to both parties.

Simon had learned through Enrique Castellanos that an FBI agent in Las Vegas named Tom Jefferson was leading an investigation of LB Freight.

Screw Thomas motherfucking Jefferson, Lang had thought.

He had considered bribing Jefferson and adding him to the LB Freight payroll. The Langs often recruited law enforcement personnel and paid them off regularly.

But Lang dropped the idea when he found that Jefferson had a reputation for being squeaky clean.

Had Alice been available, Lang would have placed a hit on Jefferson. But the news about the FBI investigation had arrived almost simultaneously with the warrant for Alice's arrest.

The only alternative left to Lang was to undertake his own investigation of Jefferson.

It wasn't hard to discover that Jefferson often went to a restaurant on the outskirts of Las Vegas known as Bruno's Pizza, and that he generally ate at the same table. Lang had his men install a listening device under the table.

Not long after that, his men had brought him a recording of Jefferson discussing the investigation of LB Freight with Joe Crawford and an FBI agent named Chloe Mathews. Lang learned that Mathews planned to take a position with LB Freight, and that Crawford was going to help her with technical surveillance.

At the time, Lang didn't know what Chloe Mathews looked like, but he had since obtained a photo. When Agnes Reynard showed up yesterday for an interview, Lang had recognized her. She had changed her appearance, but Lang had been in the business a long time. It wasn't easy to fool a *rom baro*.

Now Ms. Reynard-Mathews was working in Robbie's office, which was just down the hall. It was a convenient way to keep an eye on both of them. Lang had decided to play a game with Ms. Reynard-Mathews, planting useless information for her to ferret out.

He would also start a few rumors about her. And not just rumors. He would provide solid evidence against her, and he would make sure the FBI discovered it.

That might take care of the Reynard-Mathews woman, but there were other obstacles in Simon Lang's path. The FBI had obtained a warrant to monitor LB Freight Internet usage. Lang blamed Crawford for that turn of events.

Lang had told the LB Freight information technology staff to keep an eye on Ms. Reynard. He had used the excuse of industrial espionage, saying that Reynard hadn't yet been fully vetted. The staff were also running hourly and random checks for any kind of intrusion or interference.

The IT staff had reported to him a few minutes ago that the server was functioning as usual. Either the FBI and Reynard-Mathews hadn't yet tried to crack his system, or they had tried and been unsuccessful.

The last few years had been difficult ones for LB Freight. There had been a series of unexplained burglaries and fires. Purchase orders had mysteriously been altered, leading to expensive modifications on the deliveries. Files and records had disappeared.

Lang believed those setbacks had been caused by Joe Crawford. He knew Crawford was trying to destroy him, and that Crawford was involved in the death of Lenny, the banishment of Alice, and the presence of Ms. Reynard-Mathews in the LB Freight office.

Simon and Lenny had tried to get rid of the madman, the *divia-mus*, but Crawford kept changing his name and reappearing like a ghost from the past. After Alice had taken care of the men involved in the O'Neill supply chain issue, she would deal with Crawford. This time the troublemaking *pikie* would stay dead.

Setting aside his plans for Crawford, Simon Lang focused on the two men who had entered the building last night. Harrison Knight was a former employee of LB Freight. A would-be union organizer, he hadn't lasted long in the company. The other intruder was a man named Diego Gutierrez. Gutierrez had never worked for LB Freight, but his father had. Aurelio Alejandro Gutierrez had died of cancer a few years ago.

Why had two men with former connections to LB Freight tried to gain access to the files? What did they want? Lang thought of the anonymous message he had received. Perhaps Knight and Gutierrez were connected in some way to O'Neill.

It was Gazsi Yanko who had notified Lang of the unauthorized entry of Gutierrez and Knight. Yanko was getting on in years, but his loyalty to LB Freight went back to the days of old Isaiah Lang, Simon's father.

The two men had said they were going to the file room when Yanko stopped them.

"They told me they were supposed to move old file boxes to the warehouse," Yanko reported. "But the work order didn't have Ms. Lincoln's signature on it. I know she handles that stuff now. When I called her she said it wasn't legit. She's having the staff put all the personnel files on the computer. When they're finished with the paper documents, they destroy them."

"At first I thought the men were thieves," Yanko

went on. "But they didn't try to get to the cashier's cage or any of the safes, and we don't keep expensive equipment in the office. They didn't have materials to start fires or blow up the building. There's something strange about this. I got a feeling."

Lang had learned to trust Yanko's "feelings."

"Hold the men in the south warehouse," he instructed Yanko. "Make friends with them and learn what you can. If they want to make a call, let them. We'll trace the call. But don't let them get hold of a phone with GPS."

"I got an old phone without GPS," Yanko had replied. "I think it still works."

Yanko had locked up the men, but had willingly provided food and drink. After that, he had hung around and chatted with them. When Dlego Gutierrez asked to make a phone call and offered money, Yanko accepted. Then he told Simon what had occurred.

The conversation between Gutierrez and a man he called Charon hadn't yielded any usable information. When Lang's staff tried to trace the number Gutierrez had called, they learned it belonged to a burner phone that was no longer functioning.

The two men could stay where they were for the moment, Lang decided. Tomorrow he would move them to a more remote location. Then he would interrogate them. If he hadn't learned anything by the time Alice arrived, he would turn Gutierrez and Knight over to her. Alice knew how to take care of unwanted visitors.

Chapter 14

"Get your butt off the floor," Jefferson said to Crawford as the guard opened the door. "I explained to Sergeant Akers about the sting operation and why you were carrying the SBR."

Jefferson's voice echoed loudly in the small cell, making Crawford's ears ring.

His deal with Uncle Joey hadn't been a sting operation and Jefferson had known nothing about it. Now Jefferson was angry. His round, boyish face was tense, his lips narrowed. His lowered brows almost covered his eyes. If he hadn't looked so much like Beaver Cleaver, he would have resembled a wolf preparing to attack.

"I was just about to call you," Crawford informed him.

"You're a fucking liar. Let's get out of here."

Jefferson didn't speak again until they were in the parking lot.

"Explain. Everything. Now." Jefferson didn't sound like the Beaver. His voice had the rapid-fire intensity of James Cagney.

"How did you find me?" Crawford replied. The officers had returned his biking outfit. He zipped the jacket over his protective vest. The weather was unusually cold for Vegas.

"What the hell were you doing?" Jefferson growled.

"We're finally getting somewhere in the investigation of LB Freight. This latest stunt of yours could destroy everything."

"It was your friend Trooper Reinhart, wasn't it?" Crawford replied. "He pops up in the most inopportune places. Did you ask him to follow me?"

While Jefferson ground his teeth, Crawford took the opportunity to look around. He didn't see his bike. It might still be at the scene of the accident. He would send someone to pick it up.

He pulled out his cell phone, glanced at it, and returned it to his pocket. The phone had been in the custody of the detention center for several hours. They – or Jefferson, for that matter – might be tracking it. He would get a new one before he made any calls.

Jefferson hadn't answered, so Crawford continued. "What happened to the SBR?"

"The sergeant only half believed what I told him. He confiscated it. What the fuck were you planning?"

"You don't want to know."

Chapter 15

A few hours later, Crawford pulled up to the Lazy Lake Casino in west Las Vegas. It was some distance from the Strip and frequented mostly by locals and deadbeats.

There were several antiquated surveillance cameras, but he didn't think they would be a problem. The exterior cameras were caked with pigeon droppings. The ones inside the casino had never been plugged into a monitoring bank. They might be rolling, but they weren't recording.

The McCullough Detention Center had, with some arm-twisting on Jefferson's part, agreed to delete all record of the man with no name. Jefferson had told them the outcome of a long-running FBI investigation was at stake.

Sergeant Akers hadn't been overly impressed – his contempt for the FBI was only slightly less than obvious – but he had gone along with the request.

Crawford didn't think Akers had been acting in a spirit of cooperation among law enforcement agencies. Gus, who was still in the bullpen, was in the midst of a diatribe on the injustices he was suffering. It was more likely that Akers wanted FBI Special Agent Jefferson out of the detention center before Gus said something to embarrass them.

As Crawford and Jefferson were leaving, Gus ended his denunciation and gave Crawford a wry grimace. "The wicket gate," Gus called after him. "Don't forget."

Crawford had other things to worry about than the wicket gate, whatever that was. Even with Akers' assurance that he would delete the information on his brief incarceration, Crawford would have to take precautions. Both Simon Lang and One-Eye wanted him dead.

The Langs had law-enforcement contacts throughout the tri-state area. They wouldn't need an official record. An informal telephone conversation could be just as revealing. And just as lethal.

Crawford didn't think One-Eye had any cooperative police contacts, but he still wasn't taking chances. One-Eye had found him this morning. Crawford had to make sure it didn't happen again.

Crawford had a new phone – one of the throwaways he and Sid kept on hand. Sid had picked up the motorcycle and was checking it for damage. Crawford was driving an old Ford pickup. It was a 1971 F100 with a four-barrel intake, fresh paint, and a radio. It belonged to Sid's brother, Carter, who had just finished reworking the engine.

Crawford's driver's license bore the name James Whistler. He now sported a mustache and blonde wig, and was wearing an oversized trench coat, courtesy of Sid, with khaki slacks and a faded T-shirt.

He looked like a sexual deviate. He ought to fit right in.

He found Chloe in the nonsmoking section of the casino sitting at a row of slot machines. She was playing a penny slot machine called Jaguar Princess. He sat down beside her and put a hundred-dollar bill into a Woolly Mammoth machine.

"Are you sure you're OK? You don't look good." Chloe examined him as carefully as she would a search warrant.

"I'm fine," he said. "I was wearing the protective gear you suggested."

Actually she had insisted, but he wasn't going to squabble about it. The clothing might have saved his life. At the least, it had prevented much more serious injuries. "The nurse at the detention center treated my cuts," he added.

"Yes. Jefferson told me you had been arrested. What's going on?"

"I wasn't arrested and Jefferson should mind his own business," Crawford replied as he jabbed a few buttons on the slot machine. He promptly lost twenty dollars.

Chloe shrugged and changed her approach.

"I started work at LB Freight this morning," she reminded Crawford.

"Were you able to install the software?" he asked.

"The IT techs were all over my machine. They said something about setting it up for a first-time employee. But after Robbie left, I went into his office to pick up some materials. I plugged the device into his PC."

"Did you remember . . .?"

"To remove the thumb drive?" she asked with a grin. "Here it is." She handed it to him and he shoved it in his pocket. Then he returned to his study of the player control buttons on the slot machine.

"I've got more information on LB Freight," she said. "I overheard a conversation today between Graciela Martín and Simon Lang."

That got Crawford's immediate attention. He stopped playing slots and turned to look at her. He was down fifty dollars anyway.

"What were they talking about?" he asked.

"Something about old personnel files, but it wasn't what they said, it was how they said it. I think they're having an affair."

"Huh." He turned back to the machine and lost another fifteen dollars.

"Do you know anything about the personnel files?" Chloe asked.

He didn't answer.

"Crawford," Chloe warned. "Talk to me."

He lost the last of his money.

A woolly mammoth stared at him from the plexiglass panel of the slot machine. The colorful drawing was designed to attract customers, but it wasn't exactly friendly. There was a mean, cynical look in the eyes of the beast. Crawford stared at the gigantic curving horns. In the dim light of the casino, the horns appeared to be moving. Something that might be a volcano was erupting behind the beast, sending dark clouds of smoke into the atmosphere.

Danger.

"We've got to slow down the investigation," he told Chloe.

"Why?" she demanded.

"Did I ever tell you about *baxt?*"

"No. Tell me now." She turned in the swivel chair to look at him, her knees touching his. "Is that a new disguise? You look like a flasher."

"Would you arrest me if I flashed you?"

"Yes," she told him. "Keep talking."

"*Baxt* is the Romany word for luck. It can be good or bad. Mostly it's just tricky."

"Like you."

He ignored the digression. "We thought we had a plan. Now we're gonna have to improvise."

"You mean we're not going after Simon Lang?"

"Not yet. Lang is holding two of my men."

"How did that happen?" Chloe asked.

He might as well tell her. She would get it out of him sooner or later. "They entered LB Freight last night."

He didn't go into the telephone call between Lang and Graciela on the O'Neill supply chain matter. Nor did he mention the names of Diego and Harrison. Chloe was an FBI agent. He and the Squad were breaking the law.

She studied his face for a long time, her eyes never leaving his. "You don't make things easy, do you?" she said. "What do you want me to do?"

Chapter 16

"You realize you're asking me to lie to Agent Jefferson?" Chloe said for the fourth or fifth time. He had lost count.

"Those men helped you convict the Bosqueros," Crawford reminded her. Diego, Harrison, and several other members of the Squad had been involved in Chloe's previous undercover case.

"You think good and bad are interchangeable, don't you?" she said.

"Some actions can be both at the same time. My men were trying to help a friend."

"They should be arrested for breaking into LB Freight."

"They didn't exactly break in. They went in through the door."

She didn't bother to reply.

"If we don't rescue them, Simon Lang will kill them. Do you want to take that chance?"

"No, of course not, but I want to do things right. You're asking me to operate outside the law."

"Yeah, Sweet Cheeks, I know. You like to follow the rules. But things are workin' against us this time."

"That's what you meant about *baxt*, isn't it?"

"Yeah. Finish your game and let's go."

"I'll cash in the rest of my money," she said.

"How much did you start with?"

"Five dollars."

"Bet it all," he told her. He reached down and hit the cash out button on the Jaguar Princess before she could stop him.

The resulting noise was deafening. A cacophony of bells, sirens, music, and trumpet blasts sounded above the usual din. Multicolored lights flashed and whirled. Patrons at other slots turned to look.

Chloe stared at the machine. "You won," she said, somewhat bemused.

"No, you won. Big time," Crawford told her. The tally on the machine was $4,000. "Get your voucher and we'll cash it in."

Before she could pick up the coupon, the face of the woolly mammoth splintered with a sharp crack. The animal had looked dangerous before. Now it appeared to be charging out of the front of the slot machine with a bullet hole in its head.

"That was a gunshot. Get down," Crawford said as he pushed Chloe to the floor. He pulled out his gun.

"I know a gunshot when I hear it," she snapped. "And what are you doing with a gun?"

She reached for her weapon, but she had been working at LB Freight that morning, and wasn't armed.

"Give me your gun," she whispered. "You shouldn't have it in here anyway."

"No," he said. As he glanced toward the rear of the building, he saw One-Eye vanish down a hallway that led to the restrooms.

Crawford considered following him, but his first priority was to protect Chloe. Besides, she wouldn't approve if he shot One-Eye.

"I'm a better shot than you," Chloe reminded him. She was still fussing about the gun.

"We're not gonna shoot anything," he murmured. "We're gonna get outta here." He pointed toward a side door. "Let's move."

He managed to maneuver their way through an assortment of patrons. Some had ducked below the machines and were plastered to the floor. Others were sitting in the chairs and screaming. Chloe continued to argue with him. There were no more shots and he put the gun back in his pocket.

Outside everything was chaos. A few people were crying and shouting; others were running toward their vehicles. Casino personnel were trying to calm everyone and bring about order.

"The police are on their way," a man told Chloe and Crawford. "You can wait over there."

Crawford paid no attention. He led a protesting Chloe to the pickup and pushed her in. He climbed into the driver's seat, pulled out of the parking lot, and headed for the highway.

"Did you see who fired the shot?" Chloe asked.

"Yeah. It was your old friend, One-Eye. He was the one who rammed my bike earlier today."

"He's after you, isn't he?"

"He's after both of us."

Chloe leaned back in the passenger seat. "I guess he hasn't forgotten what happened in Boulder City. You should have let me kick him."

"It wasn't necessary. You had already thrown him to the ground. And that wasn't all that happened in Boulder City. I started a rumor about him," Crawford admitted.

"The one about One-Eye consorting with the Feds?"

"Consorting?"

"Yeah, you know what that means. Did anyone believe you?" she asked. "One-Eye isn't exactly the consorting type."

She was right. Crawford had started the rumor as camouflage, a form of self-protection, trying to place the blame for some of the weekend's events on One-Eye. But the Bosqueros probably hadn't believed it. They knew Chloe had obtained evidence against them. And they knew the man they called Ghost had brought her to the gathering.

Baxt was unpredictable. He couldn't afford to forget that.

"We forgot the voucher," Chloe said, breaking into his thoughts.

"*Baxt,*" he said, more to himself than her. "You can't win 'em all."

Chapter 17

Sylvia Blackshear watched as Crawford and Mathews pulled out of the parking lot. Then she made a call.

"I'm at the Lazy Lake Casino. One-Eye just shot at your persons of interest," she reported, "but no one got hurt."

"Where is One-Eye now?"

"I saw him leave in a GMC Sierra. Black. He was alone." She provided the license number.

"What about Crawford and Mathews?"

"I've lost them for the moment. But she left her vehicle in the parking lot. I'll get back on her tail when she returns to collect it."

After ending the call, Sylvia slipped past the police into the casino and returned to the row of slot machines. The Jaguar Princess hadn't been damaged in the shooting.

She picked up the voucher for $4,000 and tucked it in her pocket.

Chapter 18

"Where are we going?" Chloe asked. "My car's at the casino. And I want to report to Jefferson. Now that we have installed the software, the FBI can start monitoring LB Freight's emails."

"I'll send someone after your car," Crawford said. Normally he would ask Diego, but Diego was being held by Simon Lang.

Crawford's head was still ringing. He tried to concentrate, but the neurons in his brain were bogged down in mental quicksand.

Thoughts of One-Eye, Simon Lang, and the SBR were intermingled with other worries. How had that highway patrol trooper – he couldn't remember his name – found him? Where were Diego and Harrison being held? Would the Squad be able to save Wesley Bernard? What about the homeless George Chaplin? It was too late for McNeill and Colby.

Events from the past crept in to Crawford's thoughts. He remembered getting rid of the bodies of the McCauley brothers. They had worked for Simon Lang. Then Crawford had gone to Prague, and Lenny Lang had followed him. Now Lenny was dead.

How many more deaths?

"Are you feeling all right?" Chloe asked. "You can go now. The light is green."

He looked at her in confusion.

"You're ill," she said. "Pull over and let me drive."

"No, I was just . . ."

"Pull over," she said fiercely. "You may have more injuries from the accident than you realize. Did you get a full examination from the detention center medical personnel? Something more than a Band-Aid? This isn't like you."

"I'm OK."

"No. You're not OK. You just signaled left and turned right."

"I know what I'm doing." But he couldn't remember what they were talking about.

"Crawford!"

"Sweet Cheeks!"

"Pull over before I arrest you," Chloe said through clenched teeth.

"You wouldn't."

"Watch me."

"OK," he mumbled, as he stopped the truck on the shoulder of the highway. "I need to think."

She traded places with him, but didn't put the truck in gear. "I want to call Jefferson before we go any further," she said, reaching for her phone.

"No. Not yet. We have to rescue Diego and Harrison. Then there's Darius."

"I thought only two men had been captured," she said. "Are there three?"

The sound in Crawford's head was deafening. He couldn't think how to explain everything. "Just drive, will you?"

For once she didn't argue. "Where do you want to go?" she asked. When he didn't reply, she provided her own answer.

"To the hospital. I think you've got a concussion."

"No," Crawford said. "No hospitals. We'll go to Sid's place."

Chapter 19

"Good thing you were wearing that helmet Chloe made you buy," Sid told Crawford. "It saved your life."

"Don't let her know. I'll never hear the end of it."

"I already know," Chloe told them from the doorway. "And the first thing we're going to do is buy you a new one. The helmets are only good for one crash. How's your head?"

"Fine."

"I think you should see a doctor."

"No."

"Stubborn cuss, isn't he?" Sid remarked. "But his pupils look normal and he's speaking clearly."

"I'm fine," Crawford complained. "You let me sleep for six hours. I thought you were going to wake me."

"He's acting like Cranky Kong," Sid muttered to Chloe. Then Sid's voice became a southernized mimicry of the Donkey Kong character. "*What in tarnation do you want? Fetch me my paper. There's too many baddies around here.*"

Sid was a tall, burly African American, friendly, relaxed, and outgoing. He and Crawford had formed a partnership of opposites. Sid was sociable and persuasive. Crawford was brusque and often rude. As improbable as it seemed, the two were good friends.

"I still think he has a concussion," Chloe told Sid.

"We've got work to do," Crawford growled, "and

you can stop talking about me."

"There's carryout in the living room," Chloe said as she left the two men together in the hallway. "We have a plan."

Crawford looked at Sid. "You found Diego and Harrison?"

"No, but Chloe has an idea. She spent all afternoon working it out."

"What?"

"You won't hear it until you eat something," Chloe called from the living room.

"You heard the lady," Sid advised him. "Food first."

"Did you take care of that other thing?" Crawford murmured to Sid, being careful not to let Chloe hear.

"Yeah. Everything is set for in the morning. Two a.m. But first we find Diego and Harrison."

"The first thing that happens is you tell me what the fuckin' plan is," Crawford complained.

"*Food first,*" Sid repeated in Cranky Kong's squeaky voice.

Crawford glared at him, went on down the hall, and as he entered the living room heard Sid behind him still quoting Cranky Kong.

"*Give me the banana, and take that good-for-nothing Donkey with you. Don't forget to shut the gate on your way out.*"

Crawford didn't have a gate, so he shut the door in Sid's face, leaving him standing in the hall.

Chapter 20

"I'll drive," Chloe said as she took the key to the Ford pickup. Crawford had dutifully eaten his share of the Chinese carryout, but she still hadn't told him what she planned to do.

She didn't want to involve him. She wanted him to wait for her at Sid's.

"You need to rest," Chloe said. "Head injuries are dangerous."

"I'll rest when this is over, damn it."

Sid had been on Chloe's side. "Try to stay calm," Sid cautioned. "Agitation and emotional turmoil are bad for a head injury."

"What do you fucking know about head injuries, Mr. Donkey Kong?"

"Whoa, Dude, I always preferred Funky Kong myself," Sid replied. "*Buckle up and blast off! You're outta here!*"

"Don't start," Crawford warned him.

"I looked up head injuries on the Internet this afternoon while I was listening to you snore," Sid told him, reverting to his normal voice. "Don't overdo it. The Squad needs you."

In the midst of his irritation, Crawford knew Sid was right. The Squad was the important thing.

"Asshole," he muttered to Sid as he followed Chloe out the door. Sid just grinned.

"Where are we going?" Crawford asked Chloe as he got into the truck.

"To my place."

"Where's your car? Did you pick it up?" Crawford asked.

"Yes. But there's a problem. Someone followed me from the casino."

It wouldn't be hard to follow Chloe in her red Audi R8, Crawford thought. But she hadn't sought his advice when it came to rental cars.

When Chloe had seen the Audi, speckled with dust and bird droppings, parked behind the office of Trevor's Rental Car, she had made Crawford stop. Then she had approached the dealer, a flashy young man wearing custom-made alligator cowboy boots. "I want to rent that car," she had said.

"The Audi belongs to a friend of mine," Trevor told her with a wide smile. "I'm just keeping it for him. I've got a nice Mazda I can show you."

It had taken Chloe only two minutes to talk Trevor into letting her test drive the Audi. After that, it was a done deal.

"You sure know how to drive," an awe-struck Trevor had said as he climbed out of the passenger seat. "I think I can talk Fergus into renting it to you."

"I can talk to him," Chloe volunteered.

"He's at the correctional center in Carson City," Trevor said. "They have visiting hours tomorrow. I'll just drive up to see him."

"What's he in for?" Crawford had asked.

"Aggravated identity theft," Trevor said. "But don't worry. The car's clean. I can get the paperwork for you by Tuesday."

"Are you sure this is a good idea?" Crawford had asked as he and Chloe left the rental car lot.

"The best way to work undercover is to become the person you're pretending to be," Chloe said.

"You're going to pretend to be a sports car driver?"

"I won't be pretending," Chloe had told him with a grin. "I'll just put down sports cars as a hobby on my job application." And that's what she had done.

When Chloe and Crawford returned to pick up the car, they found Trevor had washed and polished it and vacuumed the interior. Chloe drove the car to her apartment, where Crawford searched it carefully, but Trevor had been correct. There was nothing illegal hidden in the Audi.

Now someone had tailed Chloe in her bright red sports car.

"Who was following you?" he asked as Chloe pulled into the lane of traffic and headed for Patty's house. He and Sid had already scanned the surrounding streets and houses on the lookout for One-Eye. Crawford checked again, this time more carefully.

"I couldn't see the driver. I went into a shopping center, circled around, and when I came out, the car was still behind me."

"What color and make? Did you get the license?" he asked.

"It was a metallic gray Ford Focus," she told him, "Nevada plates. I called in the license number and asked for identification."

"Called it in to the FBI?"

"Yes. Where did you think I would call it in?"

Crawford, like Sergeant Akers, didn't think the FBI could chase its own tail. He wouldn't have bothered to ask the Feds. He would have called it in to Diego, who had more law enforcement contacts than the subdivisions of a fractal. An infinite number probably. But Diego was currently unavailable.

The person following Chloe could have been One-Eye. Or it could have been someone hired by Simon Lang, who might make a practice of tailing his employees. But it might also have been one of the Bosqueros, intent on revenge for the recent arrests of the group's leaders.

There was nothing he could do about it at the moment except keep her close and try to protect her. But maybe he could persuade her to find another rental car. "What did you do after you called it in?" he asked, keeping his voice level in an effort to avoid agitation and emotional turmoil.

"For a while, I kept up the evasive maneuvers, but I still couldn't lose the Focus. I decided someone must have put a GPS tracker on the Audi. I went to one of the large casino parking lots, left the car, and called Freddy's Auto Service."

"You called Freddy?" Crawford stammered. He was experiencing emotional turmoil, but he couldn't help it. There was good reason. Freddy ran a chop shop in North Las Vegas. Crawford had stopped there once with Chloe, but he had hoped she had forgotten about it.

"Look at it this way," she said. "I was being followed by an unknown person or persons. I was in an unfamiliar city. Freddy may run a shady operation on the fringes of the law, but at least he's a known quantity."

"Yeah, OK," Crawford admitted. He and Freddy had an understanding. Neither of them interfered with the other. "What happened?"

"Freddy's mechanic – his name is Eugene – found a tracker sending out ten-second updates. He disabled it, but he wanted to do a more thorough check. He took the car back to the service station."

Crawford thought about the ramifications. Eugene was an expert at avoiding notice. He wouldn't have allowed anyone to follow him back to the shop, even if he *was* driving a red Audi. But Chloe had probably taken a taxi from the casino to Sid's house. If someone had followed her, Sid could be in danger.

"Did anyone follow you to Sid's?" Crawford could hear the urgency in his own voice.

"No, of course not." Her tone was frosty. "I know how to avoid surveillance. But I didn't have to worry. Freddy drove me."

"Freddy drove you?" It wasn't agitation that made Crawford's voice squeak. It was utter stupefaction.

Freddy ran a multimillion dollar chop shop. He didn't offer impromptu chauffeur services to casual customers.

"Yes," Chloe said with a smile. "He taught me some new tricks on how to lose a tail."

"Does he know you're an FBI agent?"

"We didn't discuss my occupation. I couldn't remember if you had introduced me before, so I gave him the name I was using at the time, Dee Atkins. We talked about Pilgrim's Progress."

"Huh," Crawford replied. That was too many coincidences. Maybe he really did have a concussion.

"Yeah, Freddy said he was going to play the part of Good-Will in the church play. You know, the character who said if you knock, the gate will open for you."

Freddy? In a church play?

"No. I'd forgotten that," Crawford muttered. He wondered if the gate was a wicket gate. Gus had told him not to forget the wicket gate.

"Oh, and Freddy had a message for you."

"Yeah?"

"You owe him one," Chloe said.

More than one, Crawford thought.

"I told him I'd pay him and pick up the car tomorrow," Chloe added.

"I'll pick it up for you." Crawford wanted to find out what his debt to Freddy was going to entail. But he also wanted to learn what kind of device had been placed in Chloe's vehicle. He hoped Freddy had kept the tracker.

Chapter 21

"This is Patty and her friend Graham," Chloe said. The couple had evidently been waiting for them. "They're going to help us."

"Patty and I worked together in Phoenix," Chloe explained, "and she knows who I am. Graham is a musician. He's got a gig in Vegas now."

Crawford was still waiting to hear how Chloe planned to rescue Diego and Harrison. She hadn't told him she was involving two strangers. He nodded at Patty and Graham. He never shook hands with people he didn't like. He hadn't decided about these two.

Graham was wearing black leather trousers and a torn black T-shirt. Muscles bulged over the leather bands on his arms. A choker studded with spikes hugged his football-player sized neck.

Graham held out his hand and was waiting. Crawford didn't move. When he looked up, Chloe was frowning at him. Patty, who was no more than half the size of Graham, appeared ready to fight for her musician boyfriend. Crawford looked at the circle of faces, gave up, and shook Graham's hand.

"The name's Dojcsak," Graham said. At least it was a name Crawford had heard before. Pronounced somewhere between doy-jack and chock, the name indicated a Hungarian heritage. Crawford's ancestors had also been Hungarian.

"Crawford," he growled in return.

"I'm Patty Moriarty," the woman said. She had on Alice in Wonderland leggings, combat boots, and a sequined top. Her hair style resembled Chloe's.

Crawford began to understand what was happening. Patty had provided the inspiration for Chloe's disguise.

He had known that Chloe was subleasing the apartment, but this was the first time he had met Patty. As an undercover operative, Chloe wouldn't have wanted to lease an apartment in her own name. With Patty she didn't have to.

Crawford shook Patty's hand and waited for Chloe to explain what they were doing. He thought he was showing admirable patience. Chloe evidently approved. She smiled at him.

But he wasn't ready to relax. He still didn't know the plan.

Chloe disappeared into the bedroom, leaving him standing in the living room with Patty and Graham.

Crawford edged toward the outside door. He was ill at ease. He had been more comfortable in jail with the crackhead, and wondered how Gus was doing. Once Diego and Harrison were removed from Lang's temporary prison, Crawford would ask Diego to check on Gus.

Patty glanced at her two companions. "Well," she said briskly. "I'm going to leave you two to get acquainted." With that she followed Chloe.

Patty closed the door behind her, but Crawford could hear her voice coming from the bedroom. "So that's mojo man, huh?" She didn't sound overly impressed.

Chloe's reply was muffled and Crawford was too far away from the bedroom door to make it out.

Graham didn't seem inclined to talk and Crawford had no use for social conversation. He went to the window and checked again to be sure they hadn't been followed.

Graham opened a black molded plastic case that was sitting on the floor and took out a saxophone. "We're going to be late," he explained. "I hope you don't mind if I warm up here. I won't have time when we get there."

"Huh," Crawford replied. He didn't know where they were going, but evidently Graham did.

Graham was a skilled musician. He could discern minute differences in intonation, and fuse disparate melodies and variations into a harmonious composition. He was accustomed to interpreting indistinct and nuanced sounds and gestures. Taking Crawford's mumble as concurrence, he smiled, took off the choker, and began to play – scales, assorted notes, basic patterns, and progressions.

To Crawford the miscellaneous sounds were mellow and unobtrusive. He only half listened. He was assembling a list of things to do and questions to answer. One-Eye. Darius. Diego and Harrison. Freddy.

This all went back to Simon Lang. Crawford remembered meeting Simon when he was a child. "Watch out for that man," his father had said. "He's the worst of the brothers."

It was an old memory, one that Crawford hadn't thought of for many years. He wondered why it had come back to him now. The music from Graham's saxophone swirled through the air. The tune was vaguely familiar. Crawford glanced up to find that Graham was watching him.

"I thought you might recognize it," Graham said. "You're Hungarian, aren't you?"

"My ancestors were," Crawford replied.

"It's a jazz tune from the thirties," Graham told him. "I always find it soothing. It calms me down before a performance."

"What is it?" Crawford asked. He could remember his grandmother singing it.

"*Te Vagy a Fény*," Graham said. "You Are the Light." He lifted the saxophone to his lips and continued to play.

When Chloe and Patty returned, the men had settled into a comfortable silence. Graham was polishing his saxophone. Crawford was thinking about Pilgrim's Progress. He would go back and find that book. Gus might like to have it.

Patty hadn't changed clothes, but Chloe was wearing a black dress that skimmed one shoulder and fit tightly at the waist.

Her skirt swirled as if in time to Graham's music. The notes still hovered in Crawford's mind, clearer now, as if the melody had swept away the debris, allowing light to enter.

Chloe had a fluffy black scarf in one hand. In the other she carried a small evening bag.

It was just large enough to hold her gun.

Chapter 22

"It won't work," Crawford insisted. Actually he thought the plan was fucking stupid, but he managed to keep that observation to himself. Graham's music must have calmed him down.

Chloe was driving again. Patty and Graham had taken another vehicle and were going to meet them.

"Yes, it will," Chloe insisted. "We want to find out where Simon Lang took Harrison and Diego. Robbie isn't included in Lang's inner circle, but he knows more than his father realizes. I called Robbie while you were sleeping. He's going to meet us at Les Trois Épices. That's where Graham is playing."

"You can't go out in public," Crawford insisted. "One-Eye is trying to kill you."

But that wasn't the only concern Crawford had. Robbie Lang wasn't known for his astuteness. Simon Lang would want to keep his only surviving son out of trouble. Lang likely had bodyguards following the congenial and inattentive Robbie. They would report back to Simon on Robbie's activities.

"One-Eye is trying to kill both of us, but you're not staying out of sight," Chloe rejoined.

"I'm in disguise," Crawford argued.

"You were wearing the same disguise at the Lazy Lake, but that didn't keep One-Eye from shooting at you. And don't tell me he was shooting at me. His shot hit your machine, not mine."

"Maybe he's a bad shot," Crawford suggested.

"Yeah, sure."

He could tell she was trying not to argue with him. Ms. Do-Right would want to avoid agitating anyone with a suspected concussion.

"You can back me up, but stay out of sight. Have you been to Les Trois Épices?" she asked.

Crawford had not only been there, he had once owned the place. Now Les Trois Épices, a top rated restaurant and bar, was included in the real estate holdings of the Squad. Crawford would stay out of sight, but he and Maurice Vipond, the manager, would keep an eye on Chloe.

"I know the place."

"Good. Patty and I have reservations. When we learn anything, I'll call you."

He gave her his new phone number. But she wouldn't need to call to get his attention. He wasn't going to be far away.

Chapter 23

Robbie Lang, slim and blond, bore little resemblance to the other members of his family, all of whom had dark hair and eyes. If Crawford didn't know better, he might think Simon's wife, Venetia, had taken a lover. But Venetia wasn't the type to cheat on Simon. Neither did Crawford think that Robbie was a throwback to a grandparent or great-grandparent. Through several generations, the Langs had run true to type. Crawford decided Robbie had to be the result of a spontaneous mutation.

"Robbie likes to model himself on Albert Campion," Chloe had told Crawford, explaining that Campion was a fictional character who was seemingly affable and unintelligent, but who always managed to solve the mystery by the end of the book. "Campion is smarter than he appears," Chloe added.

But that was the end of the similarity between Robbie and Albert Campion. Like One-Eye, Robbie wasn't any smarter than he looked. But that didn't stop him from wearing horn-rimmed glasses just as Albert Campion had. Robbie also kept a parrot named Autolycus.

"The parrot can say "Help! Fire!" Chloe told Crawford.

That was probably more than Robbie could do in an emergency, Crawford thought. But that was another observation he kept to himself.

"How do you know?" he had asked instead.

"I stopped by Robbie's condo today to drop off

training materials for the new drivers," Chloe replied. "That's when I met his parrot. Robbie's condo is in the same building as your old one."

"He never did show good taste," Crawford muttered.

"You two have that in common, do you?" Chloe had asked. But she hadn't waited for an answer.

Through the one-way window, Crawford watched Chloe and Patty as they laughed and chatted with Robbie Lang. Robbie was evidently hosting the event. He bought drinks and danced with the women. Patty left her boots under the table and danced in her stockings. Chloe was wearing high-heeled sandals that glittered when she moved.

Robbie and Chloe had both ordered Scotch, but Chloe seldom touched her drink. When Robbie left the table, Chloe poured most of hers into his glass.

When Robbie came back, Chloe smiled at him and asked him a question. He picked up his drink – not seeming to notice that the glass had been refilled – and began to talk.

"I'd like to know what he's saying," Crawford said to Maurice. "Can we hook up a listening device?"

"If you had let me know ahead of time," Maurice said, "I could have set up something. But it would be hard to get to the table now. Lang's escorts are sitting over there," he nodded toward the corner of the bar where two tough-looking men moodily watched the gathering. "And the noise level is pretty high. Not sure we could get much anyway."

"Any chance of hearing what the bodyguards are saying?"

Maurice thought about it for a few seconds. "Maybe," he said. "They're next to the wall. I might be able to rig something."

While Maurice was gone, Crawford watched the events at Chloe's table. Robbie was facing the one-way window. Chloe's face was partially angled toward Crawford. Patty rarely sat still.

During the break, Patty excused herself to join Graham, leaving Chloe and Robbie together. Maurice returned. "We're listening to the escorts," he reported, "but all they're doing is complaining about the food. They didn't like the watermelon and cucumber salad."

Crawford wasn't concerned about the salad. "We need a lip reader," he said.

"You've got one," Maurice laughed. "You just saw her. She was sitting at the table with your mark."

"Patty?"

"Yeah. Graham's girlfriend. She said she learned because her parents made her wear headphones to rock concerts. That was the only way she knew what people were saying."

Chapter 24

Ten minutes later Patty was sitting with Crawford in the small stuffy room behind the one-way window.

"Cool beans," she said. "I always wanted to be part of an op. What do you want me to do?"

"Tell me what Robbie is saying."

"Chloe will tell you later," Patty reminded him. "You two are pretty close, aren't you?"

Crawford ignored her question. He wasn't going to discuss his private life with Patty. "We're running out of time. We need the information now."

"Mojo man takes over," Patty murmured.

What the hell did that mean?

"Chloe just has to get him to talk," Crawford muttered.

"She will," Patty said comfortably. "She can get anyone to talk."

"Can you tell what they're saying?" Crawford reminded her.

"Chloe heard there was an attempted break-in at LB Freight last night. Everyone was whispering about it, but she was out of the office most of the afternoon and didn't hear what actually happened. Chloe has her dead face on. She sometimes does that so people don't know what she's thinking." Patty paused to take a drink of soda. "This is way YOLO."

"Huh?" Crawford murmured. He watched as Robbie

leaned over to pat Chloe's hand.

"You only live once," Patty replied. "You like her a lot, don't you? I know she likes you. That's why she stayed in Nevada instead of going back to New York."

That was a surprise. Crawford thought Chloe had stayed because she wanted to convict the Langs without breaking the law. It was a moral challenge, a way to show him that you could triumph over evil and still stay within the rules.

Chloe rarely spoke of her feelings. Crawford never did. The one time Chloe had brought up the matter of their relationship – the one that mimicked a fractal in its complexity – Crawford had muttered something about how it would never work. That wasn't what he had wanted to say. The trouble was, he didn't know what he wanted to say.

But Chloe had evidently talked to Patty. Now Patty knew more than he did about Chloe's feelings. Crawford stared out the one-way window. Chloe smiled at Robbie as she removed her hand from underneath his. Crawford felt better now that Chloe and Robbie weren't holding hands. He brought his mind back to their purpose.

"What are they talking about?" he asked Patty.

"Robbie said the break-in wasn't a big deal. Did you know about the break-in? Is that what this is about?"

"Huh," Crawford responded.

"I keep telling her to listen to her intuition," Patty said. "About how she feels about you."

Intuition? Crawford asked Patty what else Robbie

was saying.

"Two men tried to get into the building with a fake work order, but Yanko stopped them. Did you know about the fake work order?" she asked, turning her head to look at Crawford.

"Just keep lip reading." His voice sounded curt, even to himself.

"You should chill," Patty told him. "And don't bark at me." She continued to stare at him.

"Please," he added.

Patty smiled slightly and obligingly turned back to the window. "Chloe must have asked him who Yanko was. He's saying Yanko has worked at LB Freight since it was Lang Brothers Metal Works. I remember my parents talking about the metal works. A lot of people didn't like the takeover."

Crawford growled, making a sound deep in his throat, but he didn't say anything. He was trying not to bark at her.

"OK. OK. I'll tell you what he's saying. Yanko is a night watchman. He used to work for the old man. Who's the old man?"

"Isaiah Lang," Crawford said. "Go on."

"Chloe asked him what happened to the two men. Were they turned over to the police? But you would know if that happened, wouldn't you?"

Crawford motioned for her to continue.

"The police and everything!" Patty sounded as if she were congratulating herself. "Honkenbonkers!"

"No police," Crawford told her. "Keep watching."

"I'm on it," she replied, turning back to the window. "He's saying his dad is holding the men temporarily."

"Where?" Crawford demanded. He was half out of his chair.

"That's what Chloe is asking. She's worried that the burglars might be locked in the office where they could endanger the employees. And they would. But you don't think so, do you?"

"No. I don't think so," Crawford admitted. Chloe wasn't the only one who could get people to talk. "What is Robbie saying now?"

"The men aren't in the office. They're at the warehouse on Route 15."

"North or south?" Crawford demanded.

"South. That's what you were after, isn't it?"

But Crawford wasn't there to answer her question. He had stepped out of the small room and was making a phone call.

Chapter 25

"Are you in or out of this one?" Crawford asked Chloe as they pulled into the parking lot of the South Route 15 Warehouse.

They were going in without a search warrant. He wasn't sure she would want to accompany them.

Sid had been waiting outside the one-story building. He had brought two other Squad members. One of them was Carter, his brother, who had driven trucks for LB Freight until he was fired on trumped up charges. The other was Barney Watson, whose brother had died of cancer after leaving LB Freight.

Chloe was already out of the truck.

"Exigent circumstances," she replied as she checked her gun. The one she had been carrying in her evening bag. "We have probable cause that a crime has been committed."

Well, damn. She was in.

"Besides, you need me," Chloe added. "I'm a better shot than you. I'm also an expert driver in case we have to get away quickly."

There was never anything halfway about Chloe.

Chapter 26

Crawford gathered his posse into a huddle. "Did you take care of the cameras?"

"Got 'em," Sid assured him.

"We have to move quickly. We don't have much time," Crawford reminded the group.

"You think Robbie will tell Simon what we discussed, don't you?" Chloe asked.

"Robbie may not realize the importance of what he said to you. But Simon will. They may already know we're here. Let's move."

"How are we going to get in?" Chloe asked.

"I'll break in through the delivery area. Wait at the front door and I'll open it for you. Once we're inside I want you to take the offices and meeting rooms. Sid and Carter will cover the open floor storage. Barney will check the dispatch area. I'll handle the stockrooms."

"You've been here before," she murmured. But it wasn't really a question and Crawford didn't answer. "It would be faster if we all came with you," she added.

"I'm going to blast a hole in the wall. You don't want to be a part of that."

"There is a reasonable basis to believe the safety of the prisoners is threatened," she replied. "Let's go."

As it turned out he didn't need to use any of his dwindling supply of C4. He could save it for the next time he wanted to blow a hole in something.

Chloe was right. He had been there before.

A year ago Crawford and Sid had broken into the warehouse, at which time they had turned on the overhead sprinklers and flooded the dry storage area. It was part of their ongoing attempt to bankrupt LB Freight. Their entry had been through a high window in the men's restroom. They found the same window had never been secured.

Once inside, Crawford cut the connection to the cameras, and the group quickly dispersed. After a few minutes they reported back, meeting at the small canteen.

No one had found any sign of Diego and Harrison. The search was taking too long. There should have been night watchmen at the warehouse, but they hadn't encountered any guards.

"There must be other areas we haven't seen," Sid whispered.

"If I wanted to lock someone up, I might put them in a security cage with the high value items," Chloe murmured, her voice no louder than the hum of the cold drink machine.

Crawford glanced at Sid. "Secure storage is sometimes in the open floor area," Sid told them. "But we didn't see any blocked off aisles. If there's a cage with high value items, Carter and I missed it."

"It could be walled up," Crawford said. "All you would see is a locked door."

"Back wall," said Carter. "That's where the flammable liquids and acids are stored, along with the oversized items. The shelves don't go all the way to the outside wall."

"That's where we'll look," Crawford decided. "Sid and Carter will go along the right side. I want Chloe and Barney to keep to the center. I'll take the left wall. Keep your eyes open for guards."

In the dim lighting, the rows of metal shelves holding office and vehicle supplies cast elongated shadows across the bare concrete floor. Large shipping containers filled with items that LB Freight was transporting for customers were stacked in an open area. Forklifts were parked along the wall.

Crawford silently cursed as he hit his ankle on the front guard of a stock chaser. He bent over to rub his shin and found himself looking at a stack of T-shirts bearing the LB Freight logo.

You never knew when an official T-shirt would come in handy. He stuffed one inside his jacket.

He was passing a pile of used pallets when he saw the guard. The old man had entered through the back door and was taking off his coat. He was looking toward the wall, but something, perhaps a movement of air, caused him to turn around and see Crawford.

The two men stared at each other for a few seconds. Crawford with the gun in his hand, and the man with a surprised look on his face.

"You're Mike Colby's son," Yanko said. "I remember you from when you were a kid. What are you doing here?"

Chapter 27

Crawford was wearing the same wig and mustache he had donned to keep his date with Chloe at the Lazy Lake. He should have done more to disguise himself. But even then, Yanko might have recognized him. The old man had a long memory and he had always been credited with a kind of sixth sense.

"I'm looking for some friends of mine," Crawford said.

"So you sent them. I wondered."

"Where are they?" Crawford asked. He hoped they were all right. He didn't want to waste time talking to Yanko.

"Don't worry. We haven't hurt them."

Crawford remembered that Yanko had a way of answering questions that hadn't been asked. That peculiarity reminded him of his prospective brother-in-law, a man he still didn't like.

"I was sorry to hear about your dad," Yanko remarked. "He died very young."

"He died because Simon Lang poisoned him and the others."

"No. Mr. Lang wouldn't do that, even if he didn't like what your dad was doing."

"What was that?" Crawford asked.

"Going around asking questions. Gathering data, he called it."

"What about?"

"Working conditions and the like. He wouldn't listen to me. I told him to let it go."

"He died of cancer," Crawford said, "not from asking questions."

"He fretted too much."

They were losing time. Crawford went back to his primary concern.

"Where are the men?"

"You mean Jimmy and Harry?"

"Yeah." *So Yanko and Simon Lang knew their names. That spelled even more danger for the Squad.*

"I won't tell you."

"I'll find them," Crawford replied.

"You'll have to kill me first."

"No. I'm not going to kill you."

"Then why are you carrying that gun if you're not going to kill someone?"

"I like to scare people," Crawford said dryly.

"You don't scare me."

Crawford believed him. Yanko wasn't scared. It wasn't just bravado. The old man was enjoying their encounter.

Yanko had always been loyal to his employers. First to Isaiah Lang. Now to Simon. Crawford wanted to warn him about Simon.

"The Lang family wouldn't hesitate to double cross

you," he told Yanko. "They're all crooks and murderers. You should get away from them."

"That's funny coming from you," Yanko said.

Just then Chloe arrived. "We have what we came for and we're ready to go," she told Crawford. She glanced curiously at Yanko.

"So you've got a gun moll with you," Yanko said.

"I'm not a gun moll," Chloe retorted. She turned to Crawford. "If he's the guard, we should arrest him. I've got a pair of handcuffs."

"You won't put any handcuffs on me," Yanko scoffed. "I know what women like to do when they handcuff men."

"Just what is that?" she asked. Crawford caught a hint of mischief in her eyes, but otherwise, her face revealed nothing of what she was thinking. *Her dead face*, Patty had called it

"Don't try to use your femmy fatal wiles on me," Yanko warned.

"I'm not a femme fatale," she said. "And I'm not a gun moll."

"You look like a gun moll, dressed up in your fancy clothes and shiny shoes," Yanko told her. "But I'm not sure about your hair."

Crawford, who wasn't sure about her hair, either, listened as the two sparred.

"There's nothing wrong with my hair," she replied.

"Too many purple and orange splotches," Yanko advised her. "And it's too short."

"Do you know this man?" Chloe asked Crawford.

"We met when he was a boy," Yanko said. "You wouldn't believe it now, but he used to be a skinny lad with a shaved head and a ring in his nose." He turned back to Crawford. "You know I'm going to have to tell Mr. Lang I saw you, Colby."

"You do what you need to do, Yanko," Crawford said. "We're going now."

"You aren't going to arrest me?" Yanko sounded almost disappointed.

"Not this time," Crawford confirmed.

He kept his gun visible as Chloe turned to go. Then he had one last thought. "Do you know anything about the O'Neill supply chain issue?" he asked Yanko.

"No, and I wouldn't tell you if I did."

Crawford found a pen and wrote an email address on a piece of paper. "If you learn anything, send me a message," he said.

"Not likely," Yanko muttered.

"Wasn't that dangerous?" Chloe asked Crawford as they got into the pickup. Sid, along with Barney and Carter, had already left in the van with Diego and Harrison.

"You mean leaving Yanko? He didn't deserve to be arrested."

"I meant giving him your email address."

"It's an untraceable email account, anonymous and encrypted."

He didn't tell her he had designed it himself. Then he had sold the setup to his future brother-in-law for a lot of money.

Much more than it was worth.

Chapter 28

"What is the O'Neill supply chain issue?" Chloe asked.

He should have known she would remember every-thing.

"I haven't figured it out yet," Crawford told her.

"Is that why Diego and Harrison went to LB Freight? To look for information?"

"Yeah."

"Will Yanko tell Simon Lang we were there?"

"Yeah. Simon will know."

"Are Diego and Harrison in danger?"

"Simon Lang knows who they are," Crawford told her. "We have a safe house for Diego and his wife. Harrison is going to L.A. to visit his sister."

It was the first time he had taken Chloe to his apartment. Now the FBI would know where it was. But it didn't matter, Crawford consoled himself. The Squad had others. They maintained several safe houses in and around Vegas.

It would have been nicer – and much safer – if they had been able to go to his condo, but he had emptied it out. He wouldn't want to live in the same building as Robbie, anyway. He didn't want to share a lack of good taste with the parrot master.

When Chloe had insisted that Crawford rest, he had persuaded her to sit next to him on the sofa. He claimed that having her beside him would reduce any residual agitation and emotional turmoil he might be feeling after their evening's activities.

She had taken off her shoes and was leaning comfortably against his shoulder, her purple and orange hair just under his chin. He had propped his feet on the coffee table, and was explaining to her that a Mandelbrot set was a group of complex numbers that, when graphed, produced a fractal that looked something like a squashed ladybug.

"Why would you want to squash a ladybug?" she asked lazily.

"That's not the point."

"Then what is the point?"

"Chaos and infinity," he replied. "Or maybe it's just art."

Chloe sat up to look at him. "I knew you were an artist, but I didn't know you were a mathematician."

"I'm not really."

"Then how do you know about fractals?"

"I taught myself a little about mathematics."

"When you were learning how to hack into computers?"

"Yeah."

"What else did you teach yourself?"

"Mechanics, plumbing, electricity."

"I'll remember that if I need a handyman." She settled back beside him. He put his arm around her.

He was trying not to lie to her, but he wasn't telling

her the whole truth either. He hadn't mentioned that he could tap telephones and disable security systems. Then there was fraud, arson, counterfeiting, forgery, and burglary. Manipulating locks. Altering court orders. Converting firearms. Detonating C4. Disposing of dead bodies. Coming back from the dead. The list was seemingly endless.

"Will you draw me a fractal?" she asked.

"Can't," he replied. "But I could make one for you on the computer."

"Maybe tomorrow," she said softly. "Yanko knew you from before, didn't he?"

She was changing the subject. Maybe this was how she conducted interrogations, engaging the alleged perpetrator in an irrelevant conversation and then slipping in a pertinent question. He considered how much he could tell her.

"I met him when I was about sixteen years old."

"How many years ago was that?"

"Probing, are you?"

She just smiled.

"It was twenty years ago."

"So you're about thirty-six now, aren't you?"

"Yeah. Is it important?" Crawford nuzzled the area behind her ear.

"I just wanted to know," she murmured. "Who is Colby?"

"Nobody."

"That's your name, isn't it?"

But he didn't answer.

"Crawford," she said. "Talk to me."

"OK. Let's talk about mojo man."

He hadn't meant to bring it up. Maybe he didn't want to know.

"He's just another nobody," she replied tartly. She stood up and went into the kitchen.

Now he was sure he hadn't wanted to know.

Chapter 29

In her frustration with Crawford, Chloe stalked out of the living room into the small, functional kitchen. There wasn't much there, but if she wanted to explore the rest of his miniature apartment, she would have to stalk back through the living room, and she wasn't ready to deal with Crawford just yet.

The kitchen was as impersonal as the remainder of the unit. Crawford didn't invest much of himself in his surroundings.

Then she noticed the clock. It wasn't standard issue. It was a work of art.

The round, metal clock face showed a painting of Crawford's cabin. The jagged ridge line of the Silver Peak Mountains loomed in the background. The lonely cabin was little more than a shed at the end of a dirt road. The base of the one-story building was fieldstone. The sides were unpainted, weathered wood. The roof was sheet metal. There was no path to the door of the remote structure, which was surrounded by desert scrub.

The painting showed a small red fox lazing on the doorstep. The slanting sun lit up one side of the cabin, but left the other in a triangle of shadow. Chloe could sense the encroaching darkness.

Crawford was an artist. This time he had used the clock dial as a medium to capture a moment in time. But that's all it was — a moment. The viewer was aware that it wouldn't last.

The earth was continuing its orbit around the sun, just as the hands of the clock were circling the dial. The clock and the sun did what they were supposed to do. They didn't ignore the mechanical process and natural order in which they operated.

Before meeting Crawford, Chloe had done the same. She had followed the rules. She didn't want to end up like her parents, living in a netherworld half removed from and always in conflict with society.

Ronald and Mandy Mathews had lived on a derelict property in western Kansas, and had refused to pay taxes until the government reformed itself, which, of course, never happened. They had ignored state laws requiring driver's licenses and vehicle inspections. They taught Chloe at home, boycotting the local school. The county curriculum covered creationism. They wanted Chloe to study evolution.

It wasn't only evolution that Chloe had learned at home. Her father, an avid geologist, had expounded on the ancient history of Kansas and the Western Interior Seaway, an ocean that once covered much of the Midwest United States.

Geology had become Chloe's passion. She had known the difference between limestone and sandstone by the time she was five years old. She had collected fossil crinoids, which were sea lilies, and the bones of plesiosaurs or marine reptiles with her father. And she knew more about the Cretaceous Period than she did about life outside own her small world. Chloe's interest in geology had eventually turned into a life-long hobby.

As an adult, Chloe read about geology in her spare

time and seized every opportunity to visit caves, cliffs, canyons, and craters. She toured volcanos and water-falls, explored sand dunes, and tramped across the dry lakes, known as playas, of the desert. It was a lasting reminder of what she had shared with her father.

Chloe's mother had contributed her own interests and passions to her young daughter. Mandy Mathews, who had majored in Buddhist and Hindu mythology, often regaled Chloe with fantastic tales of ancient kingdoms and faraway peoples. One of Chloe's favorite legends had to do with the *nagas*, a mythical serpent people who lived in underground kingdoms. The men were the guardians of treasure chambers, her mother had said, and the serpent princesses were particularly beautiful. *Nagas* were wise and wonderful creatures. They could appear out of nowhere and disappear just as suddenly. They were magicians, able to revive the dead.

"The *naga* venom can burn like fire," her mother had whispered. "Like a flame of lightning. But don't worry. *Nagas* bite those who are evil, not little girls. So you only have to watch out for real snakes."

As a child, Chloe had seen streaks of lightning hit the Kansas prairie. One had burned down a shed. Another had charred a windmill. She had imagined it was the *nagas*, spitting fire as they flew above the earth.

When she was seven years old, Chloe's parents had died in a fire that destroyed the ramshackle homestead in which they were living.

Chloe hadn't witnessed the fire. She had been playing with a friend, Sunflower Birdwhistle, who lived a few miles down the road.

Rebecca Birdwhistle, Sunflower's mother, had been the one to tell Chloe that her house had burned and her parents were dead. Becca Birdwhistle had refused to let Chloe go see for herself, but that night, Chloe had slipped out the window of Sunflower's bedroom and walked across the fields. She wanted to know what had happened to her home.

It wasn't there. Just the chimney, a pile of smoking ashes, and the smell of burned wood. Chloe had picked up the carved stone *naga* figure, like a snake with a canopy of many heads, which her mother had placed beside the front door, and brushed off the soot.

As she held the small figure, she imagined that the *nagas* had come from their lavish palaces below the earth and taken her parents back with them. The *nagas* could make people disappear as easily as they themselves could.

Chloe had stayed with Becca until her grandmother came to Walnut Creek to pick her up. At the funeral, the caskets had been closed, and Chloe hadn't seen the remains of her parents. It was easy to believe that one day, the *nagas* would bring her parents back.

Grandma Mathews had taken Chloe with her to Wichita. Her grandmother hadn't liked the *naga* figure, but it was the only thing Chloe had been able to salvage from the fire, and Noe Mathews had let her granddaughter keep it.

For years, Chloe had believed that her parents would reappear as suddenly as they had disappeared. But eventually the admonishments and teachings of Grandma Mathews had taken hold. When Chloe was ten years old, she and her grandmother had stopped at Walnut Creek on their way to Colorado, and had placed flowers on her parents' graves. That was when Chloe finally accepted that Ronald and Mandy Mathews were gone. She wouldn't see them again.

"You don't want to end up like your parents," her grandmother had repeated over and over until it had become a refrain.

"*Don't break the law like your parents. Don't make trouble like your parents. Just see where it got them.*"

At times, Chloe had awakened in the night, trying to reconcile her grandmother's admonitions with the memories of her warm-hearted, freedom-loving, unconstrained parents. But the memories hadn't stood up against the cautionary messages. In the end, Grandma Mathews had the final say.

For most of her life, Chloe had followed the rules. She liked rules. They brought stability and order to a chaotic world. Games had rules. So did life.

But today she had hitched a ride with the operator of a chop shop. She had helped Crawford rescue would-be burglars.

"Aberrations," Chloe muttered to herself. "The game and the rules are still the same. I'll get things back on track tomorrow."

When she looked up, the cabin pictured on the clock face was engulfed in shadow. In the darkness that covered the cabin door, she could no longer see the fox.

Surprised, Chloe moved closer, wondering if she

had imagined the setting sun. Perhaps it had been a hallucination. Then she saw a small mechanism that aimed a beam of light on the face of the clock. It followed the hands as they circled the dial.

If she walked into the kitchen in the morning and looked at the painting, she would see sunlight hitting the east side of the cabin. It would be morning in the high desert. Tomorrow evening the sun would set again. Each day, the pattern would repeat itself.

Was that what Crawford, the artist, was saying? That in the microcosm of a minute or an hour, nothing stayed the same? But in the macrocosm of a day, there was a pattern?

What about a week or a month or a lifetime?

Was there a pattern in her life? In that of her parents? In Crawford's?

Right now she was angry with him, but that wouldn't last. It would tick away along with the seconds on the clock. When she calmed down, she would ask him about the artist's message.

But when Chloe returned to the living room, Crawford was gone. No explanation. All she found was a note in his distinctive, angular handwriting telling her he would stop by her apartment in the morning.

Chapter 30

"We're in," Sid said as he cut the lock on the shipping container. Crawford had already oiled the door, which swung open on its hinges without a sound. It was just after two a.m.

"How do we know which of these bags is the right one?" Crawford asked. He and Sid were wearing black pants and sweaters. Black ski masks covered their faces. Both had on gloves.

They climbed into the overflow evidence locker of the McCullough Sheriff's Office and closed the door behind them. The container was lined with metal shelving, every possible space filled with a cardboard carton or brown paper bag, each labeled with a sheet of white paper on which someone had placed names, dates, and case numbers.

"They found the car in November," Sid told him, turning on his flashlight. "The evidence might be stored according to date. But it could also be by the arresting officer's name or the name of the owner of the car."

The two men were searching for a pair of shoes and a baseball cap belonging to Carter Allenby. The sheriff hadn't yet determined to whom they belonged. But Carter's DNA would be on both. When the sheriff's deputies started looking, they might be able to trace the evidence to Carter and arrest him for grand larceny of a motor vehicle, Nevada's answer to grand theft auto. But even with a different name, it was still a felony that could result in imprisonment and a fine.

Crawford hadn't had time to hack the sheriff's office's evidence handling system. He started down another row of shelves, checking each set of items. Not all of the packages were sealed. There weren't any drugs, guns, or cash. He assumed those were maintained in more secure surroundings. But he found license plates, tools, knives, towels and pillow cases, small appliances, and samples of hair and blood. At the end of the row were bicycles, tires, two bumpers, and a mattress. "Got anything?" he asked Sid.

"No," Sid grunted, his head in a box.

"Did they confiscate anything else?"

"The car. It's out there on the lot."

"There'll be DNA in that, as well," Crawford commented. "I'll get rid of it when we leave."

"How?" Sid asked with interest. "Going to drive it away?"

"Set it on fire," Crawford said mildly. "We'll send the owner an anonymous donation."

"The bastard wants to press charges," Sid complained.

"Can't blame him."

"Yeah," Sid muttered.

After twenty minutes of shuffling bags and boxes, Crawford found the package they were after. "Got it," he said, handing the brown paper sack to Sid. "Let's get out of here."

Chapter 31

"Simon Lang knows who you are," Crawford told Chloe.

He had been attempting to dissuade her from returning to LB Freight. Yanko might have provided Simon Lang with a description of the gun moll he met in the warehouse last night. Chloe's purple and orange hair was as conspicuous as the red Audi.

But deterring Chloe from an activity she wanted to undertake was like riding into the wind. Now he had something that would convince her.

"No. I don't think he does," she replied.

"Read this," he said. She came to stand behind him, looking over his shoulder to peer at the message on the computer screen.

It was a communication between Simon Lang and Graciela Martín. "I'll be out of the office today," Simon had written. "Keep an eye on Ms. Reynard-Mathews."

"Damn," Chloe snapped.

She paced the floor a few turns before returning to the chair in which Crawford was sitting.

"How did you get that message?" she demanded.

"We're intercepting LB Freight's emails, Sweet Cheeks. You know that."

"That was a personal email between Simon and Graciela. It didn't go through the LB Freight system."

"I'm intercepting the personal emails too."

"You don't have permission to do that," she reminded him.

"I don't need permission."

Chloe moved slowly, with almost exaggerated calmness, to sit in the chair on the other side of the table.

She might look calm, but her eyes were an electric blue, sizzling and sparking.

"You . . ." she sputtered. But she ran out of words. Her mouth opened and closed several times. Then she pressed her lips together and stared at him.

She was remarkably skilled at staring him down. No one else could do it like she did. In fact, very few people ever tried.

But this time it wasn't working. Crawford was determined to keep her safe. He wasn't going to apologize for doing what he thought was best.

"You can't go back to LB Freight. But we can work from here."

"Doing what?" She was still mad.

"You can read the rest of these emails. You might pick up something I would miss."

"You want me to read illegally obtained emails?"

"That's the way this operation is going to work from now on."

Chloe muttered something, but it was probably just as well he couldn't make out her words.

Chapter 32

"I don't have any leads on who might have been following you," Tom Jefferson said. *At least none that he wanted to talk about.*

He knew Mathews was going to ask him the same questions again, so he changed the subject. "What do you know about Enrique Castellanos?"

"Pretty much what you know. He's a boss in the Bosqueros syndicate. I've never met him."

"He had a sister named Fay Courtney," Jefferson told Chloe. "A while back, Jerónimo Torres sent Fay to Colombia to recruit for the Bosqueros. Castellanos wasn't happy about it. Then Fay disappeared."

"Why happened to her?" Chloe asked.

"The Colombian authorities recently found her body. Bullet to the head."

"Does Castellanos know?" Chloe asked.

"No. The authorities don't know how to reach him."

"Torres is still in prison, isn't he? Do you think Castellanos will seek revenge once he finds out?"

"Probably," Jefferson muttered. But he wasn't greatly interested. Torres was in an Arizona prison. Whatever happened wouldn't occur on Jefferson's watch. "Let me know if you hear anything?"

"Sure," Chloe replied.

"What else is happening?" he asked.

"Simon Lang knows who I am."

Jefferson was so startled he forgot to brace his chair against the wall. When he leaned back, the chair tilted abruptly, causing him to spill coffee on his shirt. The jelly doughnut he had been eating fell to the floor, but not before leaving a trail of raspberry jam across his clothing.

"How did he learn that?"

"I don't know," she admitted. "But we found an email in which he referred to me as Ms. Reynard-Mathews."

"What email?" Jefferson was holding the phone in one hand and mopping up spilled coffee with the other. "I didn't see it."

"Perhaps it hasn't come to your attention yet," she said. "I can send you a copy."

"Do that. In the meantime, stay away from LB Freight. Work with Crawford. I'll get back to you."

Jefferson wiped up the coffee, sponged off the jam, changed his shirt, and sat down gingerly in the creaky chair. If Simon Lang knew Mathews' real name, he might know everything. The whole investigation could topple at any moment. Then it would be more than coffee and jam that was spilled.

He recalled the meeting at Bruno's Pizza when he had recruited Mathews to work with him and Crawford. At the time it had seemed like a good idea. The two of them had made an excellent team when dealing with the

Bosqueros. Mathews had seemed the perfect inside person – someone who could hide her reactions and stand her ground. Crawford could handle the technical aspects.

But now Crawford had been picked up for carrying an unregistered SBR. He had a lot to explain. So for that matter did Mathews.

Chloe Mathews was on loan to Jefferson's office. She had made a name for herself when the Phoenix office asked her to infiltrate the Bosqueros. Not only had she obtained the information they were after, she had uncovered evidence that one of the Phoenix agents was accepting bribes from the Bosqueros.

That agent was dead. But now there were rumors that Mathews was taking bribes. Maybe she had seen a good thing and decided to get in on the action.

When Jefferson had asked the techs to check out the story, they had discovered a bank account in Mathews' name in the Dominican Republic. The account held $500,000. The techs had said the money appeared to come from the Bosqueros.

Jefferson had told Mathews to continue with the investigation. If she was working with the Bosqueros, that would keep her in town until he could gather more information. In the meantime, he would make some inquiries.

He picked up the phone.

Chapter 33

"What did you find," Crawford asked Freddy.

Sid had dropped him off at Freddy's Auto Service to pick up Chloe's car. He and Sid had taken a load of supplies to Diego and his wife, Ximena, who were getting settled in the safe house. Then Sid had left to drive Harrison to Los Angeles. Now Crawford wanted to know about the GPS.

"What is Dee doing with Fergus Ockleberry's Audi?" was Freddy's response. "He's in prison."

"Yeah, I know. But she wanted that car. Trevor rented it to her. I checked the car. It was clean."

"Trevor served time for counterfeiting and bank fraud," Freddy warned. "He's not somebody you want to have financial dealings with."

Freddy might run a chop shop, but his advice was usually sound. Crawford nodded. "What kind of counterfeiting?"

"Wine labels. Don't think that's in your line." Freddy came as close to smiling as he ever allowed himself. "But while we're on the subject, I could use a little help with a driver's license."

Crawford had been expecting a request of some type. Now he knew what it was. Freddy wanted a fake driver's license in exchange for helping Chloe. "Why not ask Trevor?" he said.

"Trevor's a skilled counterfeiter, but he talks too much. You're the most close-mouthed bastard I've ever met."

Crawford rightly took that as a commendation.

"One-time arrangement," he stipulated.

Freddy didn't argue, and having obtained what he wanted, he quickly provided the specifics. The license would be in the name of Reginald Guthrie. Freddy provided the photo of a man Crawford had seen at the repair shop from time to time. Crawford was pretty sure the man's name was Riley Gillespie. Same initials, he thought. Probably would have been better to alter those as well, but he didn't question Freddy's plan, whatever it was.

Crawford agreed to provide the license in three days. It might take him that long to break into the DMV system and forge the records. Then Diego would print the new license. Crawford would get it back to Freddy by the weekend.

Once that was settled, Freddy returned to the matter at hand. "Somebody must have gotten to the Audi after you checked it out. Fergus is as high tech as you are. He wouldn't have had a tracker in his car."

"Dee said Eugene removed the tracker for her. I want to see what he found."

Freddy contemplated a pile of used tires. "The tracker looked like something the Feds would use, and I didn't keep it. We don't want them snooping around."

"What did you do with it?"

"I had a use for it."

"What?"

"Let's just say the persons who wanted to follow your lady friend will find themselves facing a different kind of opponent."

"Who?" Crawford demanded.

"Enrique Castellanos of the Bosqueros was here this morning," Freddy finally admitted. "I never liked him much."

Fractals, Crawford thought. *Endless complications.*

He hadn't wanted to become involved in Freddy's illegal activities. He had enough of his own.

Chapter 34

Graciela Martín finished double checking the files for left-over material related to the O'Neill supply chain issue. There was nothing in the paper files or on the computer system.

She had known she wouldn't find anything. But Simon Lang was watchful and suspicious, so she was going through the motions. Then she would report back to him that she had found nothing at all related to the matter, that the files were clean.

Gracie had worked her way up in LB Freight. Starting as a financial clerk, she had taken care of minor bribes and payoffs. Then she had graduated to money laundering. Now she was handling it all.

Simon kept the proceeds from his sports betting operation and escort services separate from the LB Freight books, but he occasionally relied on her for advice, particularly when it came to the IRS. Gracie was an expert at fixing the books.

It was just part of the job.

So was sleeping with Simon Lang. Simon was using sex as a way to subordinate her and keep her wanting more. It was a belief she carefully encouraged.

It was a strategic business move on her part, Gracie thought.

Nothing personal.

Chapter 35

"What happened to our arrangement?" Uncle Joey growled.

"I couldn't make the meeting," Crawford explained. "I had an encounter with an old acquaintance."

"Huh. What old acquaintance?"

"One-Eye ran me off the road."

"What's he doing back in town? I thought we got rid of that son of a bitch."

"I guess he didn't get the message. Anyway the deal's off," Crawford continued. "We recovered the items we were after."

"Damn," Uncle Joey lamented his lost opportunity. Then he rallied. "I've got other information. It's important and you'll want to hear it. I'll trade it for the merchandise."

"What kind of information?"

"I'll tell you when I see the goods."

"I'll be in touch," Crawford promised. And he meant it. If Uncle Joey said something was important, it would be. The SBR was the only thing Uncle Joey wanted in return for his information. Crawford just had to figure out how to get it back from the detention center. It hadn't been in the evidence storage container that he and Sid had searched. The sheriff must be keeping it inside with the other weapons and valuable items.

He had an idea. He called Diego.

Chapter 36

"Are you going to let me in?" Crawford asked. He was standing at the door of Chloe's apartment.

Chloe looked at him for a few seconds, then she stepped back from the door so he could enter. But she still hadn't said anything.

After learning that he was illegally intercepting personal emails, she had gone out grocery shopping.

"Lock the door when you leave," she had said to him as he sat at the table with his computer.

Now he was standing in the small living room, but he wasn't sure how to begin. Chloe's eyes were no longer simmering and she didn't look angry. She looked determined. He didn't know what that meant.

"Can I sit down?" he asked.

When she nodded, he sat on the sofa. She took one of the chairs. Someone had hand-painted red and white giraffes on the sofa fabric. He didn't think it was Chloe.

It might have been the same person who had painted ladybugs on the chair cushions. They were red with black spots, and they appeared to be headed in random directions. They were still round and robust. None of them had been flattened to form a Mandelbrot set.

Maybe the set of ladybugs was another fractal. Perhaps each ladybug was made up of millions of smaller ladybugs. There could be a hidden, invisible connection there somewhere.

Just as there was between him and Chloe.

The thought gave him courage. Maybe he could get her to talk to him. He had never been good at personal stuff, so he stuck to business.

"I talked to Freddy," he said.

"Did you get a look at the tracker?" she asked. He was relieved that she sounded almost normal.

"No. Freddy didn't want to keep it around. He placed it in another vehicle."

"Whose?"

"Enrique Castellanos. He's the vice president of the Bosqueros. The syndicate, not the motorcycle gang."

When Chloe smiled, he smiled back. Then her chuckle became a whole-hearted laugh.

Crawford leaned back on the sofa and relaxed. "What have you been doing?" he asked.

"I had a strange conversation with Jefferson."

"How's that?"

"He didn't learn anything about who was following me. But he wouldn't discuss it. When I told him that Simon Lang knew who I was, he was angry."

"Huh," Crawford replied.

"But there was something else," Chloe went on. "He wouldn't talk about the investigation. He just told me to stay away from LB Freight. I got the idea he didn't trust me."

"There's no reason for him not to trust you," Crawford said.

INTO THE WIND

Jefferson had plenty of reason not to trust Crawford, but Chloe was a different matter.

"Something is going on," Chloe said, "and I want to find out what it is. I'm going to the FBI office. I'm no longer undercover, so there can't be a problem with being seen there."

"No." *So much for relaxing.*

"I'm my own boss, Crawford."

"No."

"Does 'no' mean you're worried about me?"

"Damn straight."

"I'm worried about you, too," she said. She moved over to sit beside him on the sofa. "But you just came back from Freddy's. You're still holding your keys. Where are you going now?"

"To meet Diego. I'll ask him to find out what's going on with Jefferson."

She was frustrated and annoyed. He reached out to push her hair behind her ears, but it was too short to stay in place.

"When I come back, let's go for a ride."

"Your bike is in the shop," she reminded him.

"I'll borrow Diego's."

"I thought we were going to stay out of sight."

"We'll be discreet. You can drive," he offered. He wanted to cheer her up, but he didn't know how.

"Sure," she answered, but without any real enthusiasm.

118

"I'll see you in a couple of hours," he said. "I'll bring lunch."

"I'm going to have lunch with Patty."

"OK," he agreed. "Look out for One-Eye."

"I know how to take care of myself, Crawford. I'm a pro. You keep forgetting that."

"I don't want anything to happen to you." He gave her a quick kiss and started to get up, but she put a hand on his shoulder to stop him.

"What's your stake in this?" she asked.

"In the investigation?"

She nodded.

Chloe knew Simon Lang had taken over Lang Brothers Metal Works, but Crawford didn't think she knew everything Lang had done to gain control. He gave her a brief history.

"That's appalling. How many people have died because of Simon Lang?" she asked.

"So far we know of thirty-eight. There are probably more. And others are sick. You met Luis."

A few weeks ago he had taken her to see Luis Gonzalez, who was hospitalized in San Bernardino.

"He's one of your men, isn't he?" she asked. "What about the others? Sid? Carter? Barney? Harrison? Diego? You? Are you sick?"

"No," he assured her. "Not me. None of the ones you've met."

"Who then?"

"Darius Taylor. He's in Hawaii. He wanted to visit the islands before . . ."

"Before he got any worse," she guessed.

"Yeah. You should go back to Buffalo. Simon is a killer."

"No," she replied. "I've got a stake in this too."

"What?"

"I made a commitment," she told him. "I'm going to see it through."

Chapter 37

When Crawford showed up at the door of the safe house, Diego and Ximena invited him to lunch.

"But first," Ximena told him, "I want you to pick up some *epazote*. Diego and I moved so quickly I didn't have a chance to pack everything I needed."

"What's that?" Crawford had asked.

"It's an herb." She wrote down the name and gave him the address of a store that carried it.

"What are you going to make?" he asked.

"*Guiso de Flor de Calabaza*," she replied.

He hadn't asked anything more.

While Ximena was preparing the meal, Diego was trying to locate Wesley Bernard.

"We think he's in a beach town on the Pacific coast of Mexico," Diego told Crawford. "I can't reach him by telephone, but I've got a man on his way to warn Bernard."

"Who did you find to do that?" Crawford asked, but he already knew. Diego would have sent one of his many relatives.

"My nephew," Diego replied. "He knows it's a rush job. He'll be there tonight."

While Diego was taking steps to prevent the murder

of Wesley Bernard, Crawford unpacked and set up computers, faxes, and printers. Diego's office, even in the safe house, formed the communications center for the Squad.

Then the two men joined Ximena for a lunch of vegetable stew and tortillas. Afterward, Crawford and Diego got down to the business of retrieving the SBR.

"Which relative are you going to bring into this affair?" Crawford asked.

"Humberto, but we're just going to use his name. We'll find someone to pretend to be him. And it won't be you," Diego added.

Crawford knew Diego's cousin, Humberto, was a police officer in Phoenix.

"Why not?" Crawford asked. "I can do a Hispanic accent."

"He doesn't have a Hispanic accent. Humberto's from Boston."

"I can sound like a Bostonian," Crawford assured him.

"No, you can't," Diego insisted. "But I know someone who can."

"Who?"

"Connor. He lived there for a few years. I'll call him."

Connor Jackson was another former employee of LB Freight. He had originally been a bystander to the takeover, paying little attention to Simon's activities. But after he was accidently exposed to the toxic chemicals, he had become a convert. Now he was a member of the

Squad.

Crawford waited in silence as Diego made the call. Before Chloe had come into their lives, none of the Squad had argued with Crawford's decisions. Once in a while, Sid might question his actions. But Sid would bring up a matter, make a suggestion, and leave it to Crawford to decide what he was going to do. Now Diego was beginning to follow Chloe's lead.

Things were changing and Crawford wasn't sure how he felt about it.

"Connor's working at a casino on the Strip," Diego reported a few minutes later. "He'll come over when he gets off."

"We need to talk about your wardrobe," Ximena said from the doorway. Crawford took one look at her determined face and decided it would be easier to go along than to resist.

When he had the condo, Ximena had been his cleaning lady. Crawford had allowed only a few people to know where he lived, and Ximena had been the only one he trusted with a key.

"You don't have any clothes," she had said to him one day.

"I have jeans and T-shirts," he had replied. "That's enough."

"*Que tontería!*" she scolded. "You're the *jefe*. You have to dress like one."

Ximena was in her late twenties, unabashed and impertinent. She was the only daughter of doting parents, and was used to getting her way. Diego didn't seem to mind.

Ximena and Diego had put off having children until they finished dealing with Simon Lang. "We'll have children in a few years," she had told Crawford, although he hadn't asked. "In the meantime, you're my project."

"Why don't you make Diego your project?" Crawford suggested.

"I already did. He's got a closet full of clothes."

When he considered the matter, Crawford realized that Diego was always dressed for the occasion. Whether Diego was breaking and entering, or masquerading as a businessman, Ximena had provided an appropriate outfit. Diego never worried about looking out of place.

"Huh," Crawford had said. And that was enough for Ximena.

She started bringing Crawford clothing that she had found in thrift shops, and altered it to fit him. Before she was finished, he possessed apparel ranging from designer jeans and expensive sweaters, to stylish suits, to ragged outfits that only a tramp or a miser would wear.

Crawford normally wore khakis and black T-shirts, but when he needed a disguise, there was always something suitable in his closet. She had also supplied wigs, false mustaches and beards, and a pair of crutches.

"Well, you never know," she had said to Crawford. "The more you look like the person you're trying to look like, the safer you and the Squad will be."

He couldn't argue with that.

When he abandoned the condo, Crawford had left most of his wardrobe behind, but Ximena had rescued it. Now she had an armload of clothing and was obviously determined to discuss it with him. He couldn't see the crutches, but she had probably kept those, as well.

"We're just waiting for Connor," Diego said with a grin. "I'll look for George Chaplin while Ximena tells you what she wants you to wear."

"No cowboy boots," Crawford grumbled, thinking of Trevor. Crawford might be a counterfeiter, but he didn't want to look like one.

"Not today," Ximena said, "but that's an idea. You'd look good in cowboy boots. Maybe a cowboy hat, too."

"Wipe that smirk off your face," Crawford muttered to Diego as he pushed back his chair and got ready to follow Ximena. "Or I'll tell her to buy you a Hawaiian flowered shirt and plaid pants."

Chapter 38

"I'll do it," Connor Jackson said a few hours later. "Sounds like fun."

"Humberto said we could use his name," Diego put in, "but only if we make the call and do the pickup at times when he has an alibi."

"OK," Connor agreed. "Give me the timing and I'll take care of everything."

Crawford watched as Connor and Diego discussed their approach. They didn't require his help. He could have stayed with Chloe and avoided the wardrobe consultation. But, he consoled himself, with his newly expanded range of outfits, at least he wouldn't have to do laundry for a while.

"I'll need a fake ID," Connor said, turning to Crawford.

At least they still relied on him for something.

"You know you could be arrested for impersonating an officer," Crawford reminded Connor.

"I'll probably die of cansah anyway onna-conna the frickin chemicals," Connor said. "I like livin' on the edge. Gettin' bagged is naht a prahblem."

"You're making up that accent," Crawford accused.

"Yeah, I am," Connor admitted cheerfully. "But they won't know it in McCullough."

"This is Humberto Galindo with the Phoenix PD," Connor said when he called the McCullough Detention Center. "Tahm Jeffahson of the Vegas FBI tells me you're holding an SBRuh. We wondahed if we could borrow it for a few days. We're plannin' a sting opahration, and it would come in handy."

Diego choked back a laugh as Connor spoke with Sergeant Akers. Crawford rolled his eyes.

"We can't loan it out," Akers told Connor.

"Yeah, you cahn," Connor assured him. "I checked with your attorney. You cahn call him if that makes it any easiuh. Besides we'll have it back to you in a few days. I can come by this aftahnoon to pick it up. I'll leave you a receipt. You'll be helpin' us get this mutha fucka. He's one of them Bosqueros. The FBI ain't doin' shit to catch the asshole. We're gonna show 'em how it's done."

Crawford had told Connor that Akers wasn't keen on the FBI. Evidently bringing up the failings of the bureau helped Akers make a decision.

"We'll need it back by Wednesday," Akers said.

"Of coahse," Connor agreed.

"How did it go?" Crawford asked Connor when he returned from McCullough.

"No prahblem," Connor replied, handing him the SBR and the fake ID. "But they're not gonna be happy when they don't get their rifle back."

"Can't be helped," Crawford maintained. "They've got your picture," he warned.

"They have shots of a man with shaggy hair, a mustache, and a fat face," Connor said as he removed the foam padding from his cheeks. "With the shoe lifts, I looked two inches taller. They won't find me."

Chapter 39

While they were waiting for Connor to return, Diego had traced the license plate number of the vehicle that was tailing Chloe.

"That car you asked about is a rental. The FBI is paying for it," Diego told Crawford.

"Son of a bitch," Crawford replied. "Chloe was right."

"She usually is," Diego said. His matter-of-fact voice held the hint of a smile.

"Yeah. That's what I'm learning. Who was driving?"

"Don't know yet, but I'll keep checking. There's something else that popped up," Diego warned. "Humberto heard rumors about a bank account in Chloe's name in the Dominican Republic. The talk is that she's taking bribes from the Bosqueros."

"Chloe?" Crawford said. "Taking bribes? Not a chance in hell."

"I agree," Diego said. "I got Dave to look into it. He found an account with $500,000 in Chloe's name. He says the money might have come from the Bosqueros, but there's something funny and he's still investigating."

David Huang, the tenth member of the Squad, handled financial issues for the group. He had never worked for LB Freight, but his father had.

Mr. Huang was fired for cause when he opposed Simon Lang's takeover. When he failed to find another job, he had become depressed. Dave had watched helplessly as his father gave up hope and died.

"It's a setup," Crawford said. "I think Jefferson knows about the account. Chloe said he was acting strangely. He's probably investigating her."

"Want me to get rid of the account?" Diego asked.

"Wait until I talk to her. She may have a better idea," Crawford admitted. "In the meantime, I've got a meeting with Uncle Joey. He may know something."

But what Crawford learned from Uncle Joey wasn't about the FBI. Uncle Joey told him that Alice Lang had returned from Mexico.

"Shit," Crawford muttered in a toneless voice. He had known it was going to happen, but he had been hoping he would have a few days before Alice showed up.

"Don't think she'll be coming to Las Vegas anytime soon, if that's what's bothering you," Uncle Joey informed him as he ran his hand across the barrel of the SBR, snapped the side-folding stock into place, and looked through the prismatic sight. Uncle Joey loved firearms.

"We heard she was moving into Lenny's old condo. The one in San Diego," Uncle Joey added. But he wasn't really paying attention. All he wanted to do was admire the weapon.

"That's not the problem," Crawford divulged. "Alice was supposed to carry out a hit before she left Mexico. We tried to warn the guy, but if she's already here, that means we were too late."

"Friend of yours?" Uncle Joey asked.

"Never met the guy."

Crawford had already said more than he should have. He thanked Uncle Joey and left.

On the way back to his apartment, Crawford called Diego.

"Alice Lang is in San Diego," he said. "We might be too late to save Wesley Bernard."

"Chavelo is still on his way to Troncones. I'll let him know, but he will want to make certain."

"Let me know what he finds. And keep looking for George Chaplin," Crawford said. "We have to get to him before Alice does."

Chapter 40

"I've got a lot to tell you," Chloe said.

She looked different. Crawford tried to figure out what had changed. *Alive*, he decided. She had been down in the dumps this morning. Now she looked alive.

"Same here," Crawford replied. He wondered what had happened to pull her out of her funk. "How was your lunch?"

"Great." She walked over to where he was standing and kissed him. He could feel the energy vibrating through her body. Crawford wrapped his arms around the dynamo that was Chloe and pulled her closer. He wanted to absorb her vitality.

She helped him out of his jacket, her lips never leaving his. Then she lifted the hem of his T-shirt and ran her hands across his back.

The sounds of Graham's music swirled in Crawford's head. *Te Vagy a Fény. You Are the Light.*

Chloe was his light, he realized. She always would be.

Crawford sprawled lazily by Chloe's side, liking the way she nestled against him.

When she sat up, he tried to pull her back down beside him, but she shrugged off his hand. "I want to see your face when we talk," she explained.

"What are we going to talk about?" he asked.

"Principles."

Whatever he might have expected, it wasn't a conversation about principles. But if that was what she wanted to talk about, he would give it a try. "OK," he said.

"I've always followed the rules," Chloe remarked. "Well, except for a few aberrations."

"No surprise there," Crawford muttered.

She glared at him.

"What I meant was you're learning that following the rules doesn't always produce the best results," he hastily explained.

"What I'm learning," she retorted, "is that a person can know the rules and not know the game. That's what Regina told me before I left Buffalo. At the time, I thought I knew the game, but I think that's what Regina was trying to say. That I really didn't understand how the system worked."

She was watching him closely, waiting for his reaction.

"What do you think now?" Crawford asked noncommittally.

"Jefferson won't talk to me. He won't let me do my job. I don't know what his game is, but if that's the case, then I don't know what the rules are, either. When the game changes, the rules change. You can't play basketball using the rules of baseball."

"Huh," Crawford replied. He knew that Chloe had always believed in the system. Now she was beginning to doubt it. And he hadn't even told her that Jefferson was having her followed, or that someone had set up a bank account in her name in the Dominican Republic. Those would change the game even more.

"There's something else," Chloe added. "Today at lunch, I told Patty that I was having trouble following the rules. She laughed and said I wasn't born to be a rule follower."

"You like challenges," Crawford put in.

"Yeah. That's what you told me. You also said I was a rebel. Patty agrees with you. She said my lifestyle didn't follow any regular pattern."

Crawford wondered why she would listen to Patty and not to him, but he felt it best to refrain from comment.

"Then she said I should think about the difference between rules and principles. 'Rules control,' she told me, 'and principles guide.' She said I didn't have to give up my principles. Then she said that any moderately intelligent person could find a way to circumvent the rules."

"Sounds reasonable and logical," Crawford admitted. *He had misjudged Patty. She wasn't an airhead after all.*

"Patty's a very logical thinker," Chloe said. "When I first met her, I realized that she deconstructs in order to reconstruct. Do you know what I mean?"

"Not really."

"She doesn't follow a preset pattern. My theory is

that she breaks things down to basics. Then she chooses the elements she wants to keep, puts them together in a way that suits her, and disregards the rest. When I told her that, she said she had never thought about it, but she agreed. Then she said I needed reconstructing."

"You're perfect the way you are," Crawford asserted. He liked having the confident, feisty Chloe back. That much of a change was good, but it was all he wanted.

"Thanks," she said. "We talked about how I don't have to follow the rules just because they're rules. But principles are different. I follow them because I want to."

"Maybe they're the same thing."

"No, they're not. You don't follow the rules, but you have a lot of principles."

"Not so many anymore."

"Yes, you do. You wanted to halt the investigation so we could rescue Diego and Harrison. You look after the Squad. You want to stop Simon Lang from killing more people. Those are principles."

Crawford lost interest in principles. He rolled her over on the bed and watched her eyes sparkle a brilliant blue. He had made a number of drawings of Chloe, but black and white sketches weren't enough. He wanted to paint her in full glorious color. She was a butterfly in orange and purple, emerging from a chrysalis, ready to leave her protective covering behind her. Patty wasn't the only one who could reconstruct. Right now though, he wanted to make love again to Chloe. As he leaned down to kiss her, she met him half way. That was all the encouragement he needed.

Chapter 41

"Alice Lang is back and Jefferson is following me?" Chloe fumed. "Why aren't they following her? What does Jefferson think he's doing?" She was performing maintenance checks on Diego's bike before taking Crawford for a ride.

"He might not know about Alice yet." Crawford stood back, enjoying watching her as she bent over the bike.

Ximena had provided disguises for both of them. Chloe was wearing a shaggy dark-haired wig. Crawford himself was bald. But the disguises weren't really necessary. It was dark, and once they were on the bike, the helmets would cover their heads.

It was chilly and Chloe was wearing an old parka. Crawford didn't think she realized that all of the inside pockets had been designed by Ximena to hold ammunition, explosives, and miscellaneous tools. Ximena, fortunately, hadn't gone into detail. Diego must have warned her.

Crawford was wearing another jacket provided by Ximena. Or rather, two jackets. She had found them at a thrift shop and sewn them together. "Windproof and waterproof," she had announced proudly.

"I'll give Jefferson a call," Chloe said resignedly. "I don't think he wants to talk to me, but it's the right thing to do. That makes it a principle," she added.

Crawford didn't allow his lips to twitch. She wasn't

watching him, but he had to be careful. She always seemed to know when he found something entertaining. She had interviewed a lot of suspects and prisoners in her time, he thought. She had the special ability of many law enforcement personnel to sense what the interviewee was thinking.

"There's something else you should know first," Crawford said. He told her about the bank account in the Dominican Republic.

"So now I'm taking money from the Bosqueros," she scoffed, looking up from the tires, which appeared to Crawford's eyes to be fully inflated. "Why would I do that?"

"You wouldn't. Someone is setting you up."

"Simon Lang might be doing it to get rid of me," Chloe guessed as she checked the fluids.

"The Bosqueros want you out of the picture," Crawford reminded her.

"Nice to have obliging enemies," she remarked. "The bike looks good. Let's go."

"I'll get on first," he said. Diego's bike had a raised passenger saddle with a large backrest. Diego often took Ximena out on his bike, and he had also installed rear-seat armrests. Crawford adjusted the footrests. Ximena might be tall, but she wasn't as tall as he was. When he had settled into the comfortable rear seat, Chloe grasped the handlebars and swung her leg across the bike.

"Diego can get rid of the bank account," Crawford suggested. He settled the helmet on his bald wig and zipped up his jacket.

"Let's leave it for the moment," Chloe said. "We might find a use for it. Hold on to the armrests or the grab bar, and tell me when you're ready."

Crawford would rather have held on to Chloe, but he thought he could work that in later. "Ready," he said. And he was.

Twenty minutes later, Crawford realized he was enjoying the ride. He had suggested it as a way to cheer up Chloe, and it was having the same effect on him. He didn't experience the sense of freedom and independence he normally found on a bike, nor did he feel the rush of adrenaline as he broke the rules. Chloe handled the bike expertly, but she wasn't a grandstander. After a few initial misunderstandings, the two of them had melded into a team. They were communicating and riding the bike as one.

As she took the turns, they leaned to the side in agreeable harmony. Crawford was higher on the bike, with a wider field of vision, and he could see over her shoulder. He occasionally pointed out an approaching vehicle or another hazard, using the same signals they used when she rode behind him.

When she turned her head he could see the smile on her face. He was smiling too.

ANNIE BARET

Chapter 42

Crawford cleared the table as Chloe sat down at the computer. She had agreed to scan the emails and telephone calls – personal and official – from LB Freight.

"Tell me if you run across anything on a man named Ernest O'Neill," he said.

Crawford still hadn't figured out what the supply chain issue was or what Darius had to do with it. Other things kept getting in the way.

"O'Neill as in the 'O'Neill supply chain issue'? Who is he?" she asked.

"I don't know, but he may be able to provide evidence against Simon Lang."

"I haven't found anything with that name, but I did find a telephone conversation between Graciela and a man she called Quino. He's with the Bosqueros. I think it's Ochoto."

That was enough to get Crawford's attention. "Ochoto is the boss, isn't he?" Crawford pulled up a chair beside her.

"Yes. He's a shadowy figure. The FBI has very little information on him, and no photos."

"Graciela manages transfers of funds between LB Freight and the Bosqueros," Chloe continued. "They do a lot of business together. But the conversation between Graciela and Quino was as much personal as it was about business."

"You think there's something going on between them, don't you? But you said Graciela and Simon were lovers."

"I think she's involved with both men. The Bosqueros may have planted her in the LB Freight organization, or Simon Lang may be using her for information on the Bosqueros," Chloe theorized.

"Or she could be in it for herself," Crawford suggested. "Whatever is happening, she's playing a dangerous game."

"Yes, she is," Chloe agreed. "Gracie is in the center of whatever is going on. That means she could be the key to taking out Lang. I'll have to think of a way to work that angle."

Chloe had met Graciela Martín during her one work day at LB Freight. Make that a half work day. She had spent the afternoon meeting Crawford, retrieving the Audi, and getting rid of the person who was tailing her. Then she and Patty had arranged to meet Robbie at Les Trois Épices. Chloe hadn't gone back to the office, and the next day she had learned that her cover had been blown. So much for her career as an administrative assistant.

Gracie, the chief financial officer of LB Freight, had made it a point to introduce herself to the new employee, Agnes Reynard. Chloe had been sorting the drivers' log books she had taken from Robbie's office, arranging them by date and vehicle, when she looked up to see an attractive woman in her forties standing in the doorway.

"I'm Gracie Martín," the woman had said with a smile. "I trust all is going well."

Everything about Gracie was gracious and dignified. She wore a refined, well-tailored suit. Her hair was styled in a short, sophisticated bob that framed her face. Gracie could have taken her place in any of the world's fashionable cities. Chloe could imagine her dining with the elite in Paris, Rome, or Rio.

She wondered about Gracie's ties to Las Vegas. The city had life and energy, but Gracie looked like someone who would be drawn to culture and elegance. There wasn't much of that in Vegas.

"Yes, thanks," Chloe had replied. "Robbie asked me to take a look at the log books. But I think some of them are missing. I'll check with the dispatcher to see if he has them." Robbie had given Chloe a whirlwind tour of the building and had pointed out the dispatch office.

"I'm sure they'll turn up," Gracie said. "Have you worked with truckers before?"

"I helped out in an office in the Midwest," Chloe said. She didn't tell Gracie she had been a police officer at the time, gathering evidence in a fraud case. That was when she discovered that the information contained in vehicle log books was generally as chaotic as Crawford's fractals. Except that there was some system to the fractals. Logbooks tended to be a complete fiasco. She didn't think LB Freight's would be any different.

Gracie was still hovering, and Chloe looked at her expectantly.

No, Chloe decided. *Hovering was the wrong word.*

Gracie didn't hover. She had something on her mind and she was going about it in her own, self-possessed way.

"LB Freight is a large operation," Gracie said. "Nothing personal, but do you think you can handle the pressure?"

"I'm certain I can," Chloe replied.

"Well, good luck, then," Gracie had said before leaving Chloe holding a log book from which several pages were missing.

Chloe stared at the empty doorway for a few seconds. If she wasn't mistaken, Gracie had just given her a warning. Whose side was Gracie on?

Chapter 43

Sylvia Blackshear watched the Lexus SUV pull into a parking lot in the Valley of Fire State Park. The driver was Enrique Castellanos, one of the Bosqueros. But this man wasn't just another biker. Castellanos was not only on the board of the Bosqueros syndicate, he was one of the vice-presidents.

Two days ago, Sylvia had lost contact with Chloe Mathews, but then the text messages from the tracker appeared again. Only now they were randomized, not every ten seconds, as they had been before.

Someone had found the tracker and placed it in another vehicle. That same person must have screwed with the mechanism to change the timing of the signals.

Sylvia had picked up the signal from a location in North Las Vegas, but before she got there, the next text message showed her quarry in Sandy Valley. She had followed, but by the time she arrived, the text messages had ceased.

Then the signals appeared again, this time leading her back through Vegas to the state park east of town. She thought she had caught up with Mathews, only to find she was following Castellanos.

What was the connection between Castellanos and Mathews?

Sylvia didn't have an answer, but the boss was always interested in the activities of the Bosqueros' leaders. She parked a few spaces away, turned off her engine, and took out her camera.

Several hours later, Sylvia was again following Castellanos. She had tried to record the transaction in the Valley
of Fire, but hadn't come up with much. Castellanos had
extended his arm out the driver's window of the Lexus,
a manila envelope in his hand. Someone in the gray van
parked adjacent had taken the envelope and handed
over a briefcase. Neither party had waited long enough
to open the packages.

A lotta trust there, Sylvia thought. Probably been in
business together for a long time.

She had recorded the license number of the van.
Then she had tailed Castellanos.

Now she was at Willy's Truck Stop, an out-of-the-
way meeting place not far from the California border.
Castellanos took the briefcase into the station, returned
without it, gassed up his Lexus, and left.

Sylvia knew she could find Castellanos again. She
pulled out her phone. If she was right, there were drugs
in Willy's safe.

Special Agent Jefferson would want to know.

Chapter 44

Yanko felt out of place in Simon Lang's opulent office. He remembered when the old man ran the business. Isaiah had used a battered wooden desk and it was always piled with papers.

The desk Simon Lang had chosen was an imposing arrangement of stainless steel and Russian birch. Yanko had read the shipping label when the crate arrived, but he hadn't seen the desk until now. There wasn't a paper in sight.

Isaiah's desk chair had been something he brought from the old country. Simon's chair resembled the inside of a Cadillac.

Lang offered Yanko a seat on an expensive looking sofa, but Yanko preferred to stand.

"You're sure the man was Colby?" Lang asked as he leaned back in the Cadillac chair. He stared out the large window at the Las Vegas Strip.

"Yes. I recognized the kid, even without the ring in his nose."

"He always was a troublemaker," Lang replied. "I thought we were rid of him, but he keeps coming back. This time he won't get away. I'm going to kill that *dadengero.*"

Chapter 45

Gazsi Yanko was uneasy as he drove home. Young Colby was trouble, all right, but he wasn't a *dadengero*, a bastard. Mike Colby, his father, had been a good man.

Yanko had captured Gutierrez and Knight and held them, fully expecting Lang to call the police after they found out who had sent the two men. Now Yanko wasn't sure that would have happened.

He had reported young Colby's activities to Lang. Then Lang had threatened to kill Colby. Yanko didn't want to be the cause of anyone's death.

When Yanko and Colby had been together in the warehouse, Colby could have killed him, but he hadn't even tied him up.

Then there was the gun moll. Yanko liked her, even if she did have orange hair.

What was Colby up to? He had rescued his friends. Then he had asked Yanko about the O'Neill supply chain issue.

Yanko remembered Ernest O'Neill. He had come to the company as a day hire. Then he had moved up through the ranks. By the time he died, he was the supply chain manager.

Yanko also remembered Frida, the widow of Ernest O'Neill. She was a plump, comfortable woman, always baking something. Her long hair had been a deep auburn in color. He wondered what she was doing now. He knew where she was living.

He hadn't intended to make a detour by her house, but he found himself turning at the next intersection and heading west on Sahara Avenue.

Frida not only remembered him, she had changed very little, Yanko thought complacently. And she was still baking things. She offered him a chair and brought him coffee and cookies.

"It's good to see you, Gazsi," she said. "How have you been?"

She and Yanko spoke of the deaths of their spouses. Then they compared the accomplishments of their children and grandchildren.

After several cups of coffee and a half dozen kiffles, Yanko was ready to come to the point of his visit. "I recently heard something about a supply chain issue," he told her. "Did Ernest ever talk about that?"

"You still work for Simon Lang, don't you?" Frida asked.

"Yes. But I'm not asking for him. This is a personal matter."

"How do you come into it?" she asked suspiciously.

"Do you remember Mike Colby?" he asked.

"Of course. He was a friend of Ernest."

"This has to do with his son."

"His son died."

"I don't know what happened, but he didn't die," Yanko told her. "I talked to him the other night."

"Then you talked to a *chovihano*, a ghost," she said. "I went to his funeral."

It wasn't until after dinner that Frida finally told Gazsi about the supply chain issue.

"Metalworking fluids are expensive and are often recycled," she said. "Ernest used to tell me how it was done. When the fluids are mixed with oils and stored for long periods of time, the components can interact to become carcinogenic."

"You sound like you know a lot about it," Yanko noted.

"Ernest talked about it often. He believed Simon Lang was using unsafe chemicals, and he threatened to expose the company's practices. In fact, he sent a packet of material to OSHA, but nothing was ever done. Ernest said Lang paid off OSHA to shelve the file."

"People died, Gazsi," she continued. "Mike Colby died. Aurelio Alejandro Gutierrez died. Clarence Watson died. And there were more. Ernest was sure it was because of the chemicals."

"What kind of information did Ernest gather?"

"He had names and dates. He documented instances when the unsafe chemicals were used."

"What happened to his notes?" Yanko asked.

"I don't know," she replied sadly. "They disappeared when he died."

"His death was an accident, wasn't it?"

"That's what they told me. It was Lenny Lang who

called to say that Ernest had a heart attack when he was returning from the warehouse. He crashed the truck and was killed."

"Did you identify the body?" Yanko asked.

"No. They said it was too mangled and didn't want me to see it. Lenny identified it for me."

The next morning, Yanko sent a message to the email address Colby had given him. "I may have something for you," he wrote. "Call me."

Chapter 46

"First you wanted to borrow her. You insisted she was the only one who could help you. And now you're telling me she's in trouble," Regina Bentley berated Jefferson. "What have you done to my agent?"

Jefferson had called Buffalo, New York, to obtain additional information on Agent Mathews. It appeared he had stirred up a hornet's nest.

"I need to know more about Mathews' background," he admitted. "What can you tell me?"

"One would think you would have asked that question in the beginning," Regina said, "not now. What's going on?"

"We've discovered an account in Mathews' name in the Dominican Republic," Jefferson told her. "It contains half a million dollars. It appears the money came from the Bosqueros."

"So you think she's on the take, is that it?"

"Looks that way."

"Well, you're wrong," Regina's voice snapped like the sting of a hornet. It also carried more than a bit of venom.

"Agent Mathews would be the last person to accept illegal money. She was responsible for the arrest of at least a dozen Bosqueros, and she brought in enough evidence to convict them. It could be revenge on the part of the Bosqueros. You've also got her involved in another undercover operation that you wouldn't tell me about. Maybe your targets have discovered who she is."

"They have, actually," Jefferson admitted.

"Well?" Regina demanded.

"I'll consider every angle," Jefferson assured Regina. He recognized that he was backpedaling. "But if I'm going to figure this out, I need to know more about Agent Mathews."

"You want it from kindergarten or just from the time she joined the agency?"

"Start from kindergarten." He could hear Regina issue a long beleaguered sigh.

"She grew up in Kansas," Regina said. "Her somewhat offbeat parents died when she was a child. After that she went to live with her grandmother in Wichita. From what Chloe says, the grandmother was very strict. Chloe graduated from high school and college, served as a police officer for several years, and then joined the Bureau. Her record is spotless. Or it was until she became involved with you."

Jefferson ignored the jibe. "Tell me about the offbeat parents."

"They were environmental activists."

"Eco-terrorists?"

"Both had arrest records for things like vandalism, trespassing, and unauthorized assembly."

"How did they die?"

"There was a fire, according to Chloe. Look, for what it's worth, I don't know a more straight-forward person than Agent Mathews. I can vouch for her honesty."

"You may have to," Jefferson told her. "What have you heard from her lately?"

"She asked us to ship some clothing and a few personal effects," Regina said. "One of her coworkers took care of it. She also asked us to ship her Fatboy."

"What's a Fatboy?" Jefferson asked.

"Her bike. She emailed me that she received it yesterday."

Jefferson put down the phone and stared out the window at the parking lot. So Agent Mathews had a motorcycle. He wondered if she planned to ride with the Bosqueros.

Regina Bentley considered her reasons for agreeing to send Chloe Mathews to the Wild West. Granting favors to other regional offices was, of course, good politics. But it had been more than that. Chloe's black-and-white version of life hadn't been working well in Buffalo. Chloe, who knew every rule in the book, had applied each regulation as a dictum in its own right. It hadn't gone over well with her associates.

Regina had tried to advise Chloe, telling her that rules couldn't cover every possibility, but Chloe had always found something – a law, regulation, order, statute, or isolated incident – to justify her decisions.

Regina thought she knew why Chloe was so damn set on following the rules. It all went back to her misguided parents and her dogmatic, overly protective grandmother. But Chloe was an adult. It was time she learned how the rest of the world functioned.

When all else failed, Regina had volunteered Chloe for an undercover assignment. Chloe, intrigued with the idea, had agreed. It was a risk, Regina conceded, but it was also a possibility. Becoming familiar with undercover life might alter Chloe's world view, let her discover the conflict between reality and the rules.

The first undercover assignment had been in Buffalo, where Chloe had inserted herself into a female biker group suspected of narcotics trafficking. Chloe had come back with the evidence needed to bring charges.

Then the Phoenix office, searching for a female biker, had asked for Chloe's assistance. Both Chloe and Regina had agreed. Again, Chloe had been successful.

Now Chloe was involved in an assignment that Jefferson refused to discuss.

Whatever it was, it appeared that Chloe and the real world were discovering each other.

That was what she had wanted, wasn't it? Regina asked herself.

Chapter 47

"The Bosqueros received a shipment of drugs," Crawford told Diego. "If we steal them, we can make it look like the Langs did it."

"How did you learn about the drugs?"

Diego never used to ask for details. Now he wanted to know everything.

"I figured out a way to tap into Enrique Castellanos' personal phone," Crawford admitted.

"You want to start trouble between the Langs and the Bosqueros, don't you?"

"Yeah."

"Why?"

"Haven't been able to come up with anything better."

Crawford parked the van just off a dirt road not far from Willy's Truck Stop. It was the interim distribution point for Bosqueros drugs now that Virgil's Roadhouse was temporarily closed.

"You got everything?" Diego asked.

Crawford nodded. He had wrapped a bandana around his face, and was wearing the LB Freight T-shirt he had found in the warehouse. He had removed part of the logo from the T-shirt, but had left enough of the lettering for the name to be recognizable.

"Did you check the cameras?" he asked.

"Yeah. The only one remaining is the one by the back window," Diego assured him. "It's filtered and partially blocked. Keep your back to it as you go in."

Crawford nodded at Barney and Diego, and silently slipped into the desert, making his way among the boulders and low mounds of burro bush. He could smell the pungent, resin-scented odor of creosote, said to be the oldest living plant in North America.

Willy's wasn't as popular a meeting place as Virgil's, but there was enough activity to provide cover for the Bosqueros drug trade. Bikers dropped by when they were in the area. Long-haul truckers often stopped to use the showers and eat at the small café.

Now, at nearly three a.m., the place was almost deserted. Several semis were parked in the overnight lot. The drivers would be in the sleepers behind the cabs – too far away to hear any sounds that Crawford might make. There were miscellaneous trailers, a pickup, and two sedans in the long-term storage lot that Willy maintained. But there was no visible activity. Barney, who was serving as a lookout, would signal if anyone appeared.

Breaking into the station wasn't difficult. The Bosqueros had only recently moved their operation to Willy's and hadn't yet installed heavy-duty security equipment. They likely planned to return to Virgil's as soon as it reopened.

Crawford jimmied the back door and entered a small office that held a metal desk and two straight chairs. Miscellaneous tools and spare parts were scattered around the room. Against one wall under a faded pin-up calendar was a mid-sized safe with an electronic lock.

The lock wouldn't pose a problem. Crawford had already hacked into Willy's computer system. The combination to the safe was in his pocket.

There was no security camera in the office. They were all in the public area.

Crawford knelt in front of the safe and examined the lock for trip mechanisms. Finding nothing obvious on the outside, he entered the combination and let the door swing open.

He moved back and counted to one hundred while he waited. He had occasionally encountered safes with tear gas canisters and explosives, but this time, nothing happened.

The passing headlights of an eighteen-wheeler flashed across the window, but the trucker didn't stop, barreling down the highway toward California. When there was no other movement, Crawford took out a flashlight and looked inside the safe. There were no booby traps.

Inside the safe were plastic bags of cocaine, meth, ecstasy, heroin, and other tablets he didn't recognize. He swept them all into the reusable grocery bags he had brought.

The safe also held a sizable amount of cash. The stacks of bills were fastened with rubber bands. A self-respecting burglar would hardly leave them behind.

Crawford added those to his stash.

He didn't bother to close the safe or remove signs of his entry – he wanted the theft to be discovered.

Leaving the back door slightly ajar, he returned to the van where Diego was waiting. They picked up Barney as they left.

The three men took a roundabout route back to Vegas. When they reached a secluded location, they stopped the van and walked a short way into the desert. They emptied the drugs on the sand, poured water on the contents, and stirred the mixture into a white paste. Then they buried the concoction in the sand.

Crawford kept the cash. He would turn it over to David Huang to add to the Squad's coffers.

Chapter 48

It was Joaquin Ochoto himself who called Gracie to ask about the drug theft. When the one functioning security camera at Willy's revealed that a man – and a not very intelligent one at that – had stolen a supply of drugs while wearing an LB Freight T-shirt, Ochoto had delegated Castellanos to look into the matter. But Ochoto had his own source of information.

Gracie and Ochoto had met several years ago at the wedding of his sister, Angela. She and Gracie had gone to school together. Ochoto had told Gracie that his name was Bartolomeo Joaquin Reyes. His sister called him Quino, so that's what Gracie called him.

"I haven't heard anything about a drug theft," Gracie told him.

"That shipment of drugs had a street value of a million dollars, and the thief was wearing an LB Freight T-shirt."

"Those T-shirts are easy enough to come by," she replied. "Maybe he found it at the Salvation Army."

"We've got it on tape."

"It doesn't prove a thing, Quino. You know that."

Gracie had been attracted to Quino the first time they met. She liked a man who was in charge. He reminded her of her husband, a professional gunman whom she had left in Colombia.

The night of Angela's wedding, Gracie had felt the electricity in the air and seen the fire in his eyes each time Quino approached her. Her response to him had been equally strong – effervescent and sparkling with sexual energy.

When the reception eventually ended, he had taken her to one of his houses in Flagstaff, where they had torn off each other's clothes, and spent what remained of the night in a frenzy of heated sex. After that they met as often as possible. She would travel to Flagstaff, or he would come to Vegas and they would go to a hotel.

Gracie hadn't realized at first that Quino was with the Bosqueros. He had told her he ran an import/export business called Mesquite Traders.

But she suspected that he was more than just a man dealing in imports and exports. He traveled by private plane, had security backup, and didn't talk about his business activities. It didn't bother her that he might be into something shady – many of her activities weren't legal, either.

The second night they were together, Gracie had listened as Quino spoke to someone on the phone. "*Cada muerte de obispo*," he had said. Literally, each time a bishop dies. In English, it meant almost never.

Which was about as often as she had heard anyone incorporate that particular, somewhat outmoded, phrase in a conversation. Almost never.

Yet Enrique Castellanos of the Bosqueros had used the same expression only that morning. He had been quoting his leader.

"You're the boss, aren't you?" she had asked Quino. "You're Ochoto."

"I'm not the boss," he had said. But a year later he had taken over when his brother, Basilio, died.

Now Quino really was the boss. She was having an affair with the *jefe* of the Bosqueros.

Chapter 49

Sylvia Blackshear showed Jefferson the photos of the activities at Willy's Truck Stop.

"Last night – actually it was about 3:00 this morning – I watched as a group of three men took out all but one of the cameras. Then one man forced open the door and entered the building. A bit later he came out carrying several grocery bags. I tried to follow, but lost them when they took a cutoff into the desert. If you want me to continue to work with you, I'll need a four-wheel drive, something that can take the mountain roads."

"It was Crawford, wasn't it?" Jefferson asked.

"Yes, I think so. The man moved like he does – quiet, precise, deadly."

Jefferson tapped his pen against his desk. Enrique Castellanos had taken a briefcase that likely contained drugs to Willy's Truck Stop. Now Crawford had broken in to the place and left with several bags full of unknown items. He must have taken the drugs. But how had he known about the drug buy? And what was he planning to do with the Bosqueros' drug shipment?

Jefferson had planned to set up a raid on Willy's, hoping to gather evidence to prosecute, but there was no reason to do so now. He turned to another question that had been bugging him.

"How did Castellanos end up with your tracker?" he asked.

She shrugged. "That's a mystery I haven't solved."

After Sylvia left, Jefferson thought about Crawford. Several nights ago, someone had broken into the shipping container holding evidence for the McCullough Sheriff's Office. The security cameras had been blacked out, but one camera on an adjacent building had obtained a fuzzy image of the perpetrators. The McCullough Sheriff's Office had sent the image to other law enforcement agencies in the area. Jefferson pulled out the photo and studied the two figures in dark clothing, ski masks on their heads. Then he compared the image to the one from Willy's Truck Stop that Sylvia had brought.

He was almost certain that one of the men who had broken into the evidence container was the same man who had been at Willy's. It was Crawford.

What kind of imbroglio had he gotten himself into? Jefferson worried. He had recruited Crawford and Mathews to work on his investigation. Now Crawford was stealing drugs and breaking into evidence lockers. Mathews could well be on the take, in spite of what that harridan, Regina Bentley, believed. Crawford and Mathews were key figures in his investigation of Simon Lang. Their escapades could destroy everything Jefferson had worked for.

Then there was Arthur Blackcotton, otherwise known as One-Eye. The man had shot at Crawford and Mathews in the Lazy Lake Casino, but after that, he had disappeared. The black Sierra had vanished, as well. Jefferson hadn't forwarded the identity of the shooter to his superiors. An inquiry into the happenings at the Lazy

Lake could reveal activities that were better left sub-rosa.

When it came to One-Eye, Crawford and Mathews would have to look out for themselves.

Chapter 50

"Alice Lang is back from Mexico," Chloe told Jefferson. "We think she's in San Diego."

"How do you know?"

She had guessed it wouldn't be easy to talk to Jefferson. She wasn't going to tell him Crawford had obtained the news from Uncle Joey. She kept her answer brief. "Information received."

"You sound like Crawford," Jefferson complained. "Tell him I want to talk to him."

"You tell him," Chloe said. "I know about the bank account in the Dominican Republic, but I had nothing to do with it."

"We're investigating it," Jefferson said, but he didn't sound as if he thought it would get him anywhere.

"I also know you had someone following me," she told him. "If you want to know what I'm doing, why don't you ask me?"

"We have to conduct an investigation. You know the routine."

"No, I don't. I've never been investigated."

"Yeah. Agent Bentley told me," he admitted. "What do you have to report?"

"We've got some ideas," Chloe replied.

"Meaning you don't have squat."

Chloe didn't deny it.

Chapter 51

Alice Lang came from a lineage of women who were demanding, ruthless, and efficient. She was no exception. The one area in which she might have varied slightly from her forebears was in her calling. She was a hit woman.

Alice stood in the hallway of the San Diego condo that had belonged to her late brother, Lenny, and studied her reflection in the large rococo mirror. Lenny had always enjoyed looking at himself in mirrors, but she didn't particularly care for them. She had removed all but this one in the entryway. At certain times of the day, it caught the flash of sunlight off the Pacific Ocean. She found the shimmering reflections satisfying in some unaccountable way.

In addition to mirrors, Lenny had collected a number of pre-Columbian artifacts. The ornate and exaggerated statues of humans, animals, and gods disturbed Alice, just as the mirrors did. She had banished all of them to a dusty corner of the San Diego warehouse.

Alice regarded the image before her. She was tall. Athletic. 30ish. But other than that, her body and facial features were unremarkable. Her high cheekbones, a trait that showed up from time to time in the Lang bloodline, were the only clear identifier.

Alice was adept at the art of invisibility. She could blend into any setting and virtually disappear in plain sight. She had made a career of erasing herself.

There was nothing mystical about it, just common

sense to ensure that no one remembered her. Alice rarely made eye contact with others, and she didn't say much. She avoided scents and used makeup to create lines and shadows on her face. She could change her walk and alter her posture. She could virtually adopt the shape of her surroundings. She usually wore hoods or caps, along with nondescript clothing in muted colors that fit her surroundings. She drove the most common make, model, and color of vehicles.

On occasion, Alice took on specific identities. Once she had masqueraded as a homeless woman. Another time she had driven a utility vehicle and pretended to be a female construction worker, complete with hard hat, reflective vest, and boots.

For Alice, misdirection had begun about the time the McCauley brothers had realized she was growing up. The descendants of Isaiah Lang's second wife, Lizzie McCauley, didn't carry the Lang bloodline, but they existed on the fringe of the Lang clan. Simon Lang had often included the pair of miscreants in family gatherings, and he had ignored his daughter's request to banish them from Lang social activities. Alice later learned the reason – the brothers worked for her father, doing odd jobs no one else would take on.

Alice had been twelve years old when Robert McCauley tried to rape her. He thought by doing so, Simon Lang would force him to marry Alice. That would be his entrée into the Lang family.

Alice had escaped by pulling a knife and slicing Robert's hand. Jameson McCauley had backed away as Alice threatened to do the same to him. Then both young men left, vowing to get revenge.

Venetia Lang, Alice's mother, refused to listen to her daughter when she told her about the McCauley boys. Venetia liked the two young men. But Venetia decided that Alice was mature enough to drop out of school and stay home. It was what most young Romany women did.

For Venetia, the only future for Alice was in an early marriage to a successful Roma man. Venetia was already discussing bride prices and potential husbands, planning to arrange a marriage for Alice by the time the girl was sixteen years old.

Simon Lang had left Alice's upbringing to his wife. Alice knew he wouldn't listen to complaints against the McCauleys.

Lenny was the only one who had paid attention to her story. At Alice's request, he had taught her how to shoot a gun.

Alice didn't want an arranged marriage, and she didn't want to run away from home. When she was sixteen, and her mother told her a marriage had been settled with the parents of a man she had never met, Alice decided to take charge.

On the pretext of going shopping, she drove her mother to one of the LB Freight warehouses, telling her that a new shipment of gowns had arrived. Lenny, who knew of Alice's plan, had made certain the warehouse was deserted.

Alice had escorted her mother into the warehouse, and had given her a quick and efficient demonstration of her shooting ability.

"Do not try to marry me off," Alice had said as her mother gaped at her, too startled, for once, to speak. "I will shoot either you or the prospective groom. Maybe I'll shoot both of you."

"I want your agreement that the subject will never come up again," she demanded.

Venetia Lang was a strong, opinionated woman. When she began to argue, Alice had calmly shot the bow off of her mother's hat.

"I wouldn't mind shooting you now," Alice had said, and her mother had given in.

From that point on, relations between Venetia and Alice were strained. Alice avoided her mother whenever possible, and when she and her mother were in each other's company, Alice faded into the background. Making herself unnoticed was so successful that she began to do the same when her mother wasn't around. Alice had always been a loner. She liked being ignored.

Now, as she looked at herself in Lenny's mirror, Alice altered her image by changing her expression, making faces at herself. She could appear stubborn, pathetic, friendly, or hostile, merely by slanting her eyebrows or puckering her mouth. The only thing she couldn't change were those damn cheekbones.

It didn't matter, she told herself. Whatever she looked like, she was still deadly.

Enrique Castellanos of the Bosqueros had recognized her abilities, and he frequently employed her. They had had numerous business dealings with each other, but it was an uneasy alliance, strewn with misunderstandings, half-truths, and one or two unexplained deaths.

Just this morning, for example, Castellanos had accused LB Freight of stealing drugs from the Bosqueros. As if the Langs couldn't find their own source of street drugs.

But Alice hadn't responded with anger. She had merely told Castellanos she would look into the matter. She wasn't ready to cut him off. He was a valuable contact.

He was more than that, she admitted to herself. She and Castellanos occasionally met for a drink. They didn't say much about their work. Mostly they talked about baseball. But he was a kindred spirit, and she didn't have many of those.

Still, it was dangerous. If the Bosqueros turned out to be enemies, she might have to kill him. And she might hesitate to shoot a friend. In her business, even the slightest misgiving could be fatal. Alice took one last look at her reflection in the mirror.

Deadly, she reminded herself.

Chapter 52

Alice Lang hadn't planned on going into assassination as a career field. But she hadn't turned down the opportunity, either.

Alice had been close to her brother, Lenny, and had been angered by his death. Shortly before he was shot, Lenny had texted her saying that FBI Special Agent Art Wilson was playing a double game. Wilson hadn't fired the gun that killed Lenny, but Alice blamed him for Lenny's death.

The day after Lenny's funeral, Alice had tracked down Wilson and shot him in the chest. "That's for Lenny," she had told him as he died. Then she had disinterestedly watched Wilson's body slump to the ground, hoping he was suffering as Lenny must have suffered.

Alice had been lonely after Lenny's death. Simon wouldn't talk about the loss of his oldest son and heir. Venetia Lang had never stopped talking about what a wonderful boy Lenny had been. Robbie, who had looked to Lenny for guidance, now came to Alice, but she didn't have any sage counsel for the woebegone Robbie. She had told him to buy a parrot if he wanted to talk to somebody.

Wilson was the first man Alice had killed. When her father learned of it, he recruited her for another assassination. Then several others followed. The man who never had time for his daughter finally realized her usefulness and welcomed her into his business.

Before leaving Mexico, Alice had found Wesley Bernard living in the small beach town of Troncones on the Pacific coast. Bernard was in his fifties, but he had evidently believed he still possessed the vigor and agility to take up surfing. She had left his body lying next to the surfboard, one bullet hole in his chest.

There were two more men her father had asked her to take out. Darius Taylor was vacationing in Hawaii. He wouldn't be a problem. She would go after him when he returned.

Then there was George Chaplin. He had no fixed address, but he was usually somewhere in Las Vegas. He had recently been held in the McCullough Detention Center on drug charges. She had contacts in McCullough. She would be able to find Chaplin.

Chapter 53

"I've got some information for you," Yanko said. It was what Crawford had hoped to hear.

"What is it?" he demanded.

"You're so damned pushy," Yanko complained. "Whatever happened to common politeness?"

"Skipped my generation," Crawford told him. "What have you got?"

"You're a *dadengero* after all. I want to talk to the gun moll."

"I'll get her."

"But not on the phone," Yanko stipulated. "I'll meet her tonight."

"She's not going back to the warehouse," Crawford stated. Chloe was leaning against his shoulder, trying to listen to what Yanko was saying. Crawford punched the speaker phone button so they could both hear. But Yanko wasn't ready to talk about O'Neill.

"No. I don't want to go to the warehouse, either. I'll meet her at the Peregrino RV Resort. In the back."

"Never heard of it," Crawford told him.

"You need to get out more," Yanko replied. "It's across from Trevor's Rental Car."

"Do you know Trevor?" Crawford asked, surprised.

"He's my cousin's boy. He said the gun moll had rented Fergus' Audi. That bent-eight can agitate the gravel. I'll tell her what I know if she gives me a ride."

"She'll take you for a ride, all right," Crawford replied, looking at Chloe.

"Yeah, and the car only seats two, so you can't chaperone," Yanko snorted.

Crawford was losing this battle, but he didn't know how to turn things around. He handed the conversation over to Chloe.

"Yes, Gazsi," Chloe said. "I hear you'd like a ride in the Audi. I call it Vayu, like the Hindu god of the wind."

"Because it goes like the wind," Yanko guessed.

"Yes, exactly."

Crawford gazed at Chloe. She hadn't told him about Vayu. Just Yanko. And she and Yanko were carrying on as if they had known each other for years.

"Get him to set a time," Crawford mouthed to Chloe. She nodded.

But it took several more minutes before Chloe and Yanko agreed to meet at ten o'clock that evening.

That afternoon Crawford picked up his bike, which Sid had restored before leaving for Los Angeles. Then he took the carefully reproduced driver's license to Freddy, who had immediately handed it to Eugene, saying "Tell him to get out of here."

Eugene had nodded and left to deliver the license to the newly christened Reginald Guthrie. Crawford wondered what the man had done to merit such a hasty exit.

"We're even now," Crawford announced.

Freddy nodded. "But I'll keep you in mind if anything comes along."

Crawford hoped nothing came along. It was best to maintain a respectable distance from Freddy, even if the man did take part in church plays.

Chloe pulled into the parking lot of the Peregrino RV Resort, agitating the gravel slightly as she brought the Audi to a stop with a generous spin of the wheels. Crawford knew she was doing it on purpose.

Yanko had a broad grin on his face as he climbed out of the passenger seat. He looked over the top of the Audi at Chloe. "Nice ride. Thanks. You and me, we could go out dancing one night," he suggested.

"That sounds like fun, Gazsi," Chloe replied. "Maybe Frida would like to go, too. We could arrange a double date."

Frida? Crawford thought. *Double date? What was going on?*

"You'd better watch your step," Yanko warned Crawford.

"Yeah, I know," Crawford replied.

"What did he say?" Crawford asked Chloe as she drove them back to her apartment. "Who's Frida?"

"Frida O'Neill is the widow of Ernest," Chloe replied. "Yanko likes her."

"How did she get involved?"

"Simon Lang made the mistake of saying he wanted to kill you. Gazsi didn't like the idea, so he talked to Frida to see what he could learn."

Chloe repeated what Yanko had told her.

"What's a *dadengero*?" she asked.

"A bastard."

"That's what Simon Lang called you," Chloe said. "Is that a Roma word?"

"Yeah."

"You know the Langs are Roma, don't you?"

"Yeah. But how did you know?"

"Robbie told me."

Crawford didn't respond. Chloe waited a few minutes before speaking again. "Is that all you have to say?" she asked. "Nothing?"

"I'm going to pay Frida O'Neill a visit," Crawford divulged. "She may know more than she told Yanko."

"Are you going to use common politeness when you talk to her?" Chloe asked.

"I haven't figured out what it is."

"That's what I thought. I'm going with you."

Chapter 54

Chloe drove Crawford to Patty's house, where he picked up his bike. He had told Chloe he was going back to his apartment, but that held no appeal for him. He would have spent the night with Chloe, but she hadn't invited him in.

Crawford was restless, frustrated, and uncertain. He hadn't felt that way since he was a teenager. He rode his bike aimlessly for a while, without a particular destination in mind. It was Saturday night and the streets and highways of Vegas were busy.

When he passed where One-Eye had knocked him off the road, Crawford pulled over and examined the site, reliving the moment when he had tumbled through the air. When he saw the book in the ditch, he got off his bike and picked it up.

"The Pilgrim's Progress
From This World to That which is to come
Delivered under the Similitude of a Dream"

Flipping randomly through the pages, Crawford came to the section in which Apollyon was attempting to destroy Christian. "When I fall, I shall arise," the protagonist promised, giving Apollyon a deadly thrust of his sword.

Christian had encountered no real problems slaying

Apollyon. But that didn't help Crawford. He might have risen from the dead, but he was still fighting his own version of the destroyer.

Crawford closed the book and placed it in the pocket of his jacket. Then he headed toward Lake Mead, searching for something, but he didn't know what.

He had told Chloe they had to slow down the investigation of LB Freight. He hadn't meant they had to bring it to a standstill.

Crawford had thought that working with Jefferson and Chloe might bring progress in the conviction of Simon Lang, but nothing was happening. Jefferson's approach wasn't working. Neither was his own. He had to do something.

Crawford remembered the old days, when he operated on his own. He had been the instigator and creative director of his one-man operation. His harassment of Lang had been visionary. He had stolen trucks, embezzled funds, disrupted operations, blown holes in warehouse walls, and started fires in company facilities. And he had answered to no one.

Then he and Sid had formed the Squad. Under Sid's guidance, they had made the Squad into a superb tactical unit, one that operated with almost military precision. They were organized, efficient, and, due to a spectrum of lucrative, illegal activities, well-funded.

But it wasn't as satisfying as his former approach. Not only that, the Squad really didn't need him anymore. All they required from him was an occasional foray into counterfeiting.

Crawford plunged through the solitary night on the roads that bordered Lake Mead. There were no Saturday night crowds here. As he came to a turn, he counter-steered and kept the throttle smooth. The horizon point, where the two sides of the road met around a curve, moved away from him at a steady pace, beckoning him forward into the unknown. Then the corner opened up and he began to accelerate.

He revved the engine slightly, with no other purpose than to hear the brrrooomboom sound echo into the night. The ride was all that mattered, flying into the wind. Creating thunder.

He and the bike were one, living in the moment. As he sped downhill, he took it airborne for a few seconds, reveling in the sense of complete freedom.

A large insect hit his helmet, rocking his head back. Waves of heat flowed from the engine. He might have been riding a hellhound, trailing fire and brimstone, singeing the earth.

Fires, he thought, as he brought the bike under control. He had always enjoyed the chaos they created, although he usually left before the real excitement began.

What he needed was a good fire.

A few hours later, Crawford stood outside the LB Freight main office and watched smoke curl from a fourth-story window.

Earlier today, he had downloaded LB Freight's complete security profile, along with an architectural plan of the building, but until his thrill ride on the bike, he hadn't decided what to do with his newly-acquired information.

Removing his computer from the bike's panniers, he had used his access to the security system to disrupt the cameras and modify the guard orders, reassigning all of those at the main office to other locations.

With the building to himself, Crawford had entered through a back window and made his way to the file room.

Once Chloe had inserted the thumb drive, Crawford had been able to penetrate all of LB Freight's digital records. He had previously examined the personnel files for Wesley Bernard, George Chaplin, and Michael Colby. Their names came toward the beginning of the alphabet and their files had already been scanned into the computer.

There was nothing useful in the three files. Nothing on the supply chain issue.

He had discovered that Michael Colby had been let go for allegedly stealing tools from the maintenance shop. His father hadn't ever said why he had been fired. His intestinal cancer had been particularly aggressive. By that point, he was already dying.

"I know you didn't steal anything, old man," Crawford had said to the memory of his dad that afternoon as he studied the computer screen. "You weren't doing anything but collecting evidence against Simon Lang. But don't worry. I'll get the bastard."

The files for Ernest O'Neill and Darius Taylor were still in paper format. This evening, he had found them in the file room. There was nothing of interest in those, either.

Crawford had returned the files for O'Neill and Taylor to their former locations. After checking to make sure that no one was left in the building, he had opened the small window in Lang's private bathroom.

Then he dropped a lighted match into the discarded paper towels in the gold-plated executive wastebasket.

Chapter 55

"Damn," Chloe muttered. The black GMC Sierra behind her was traveling too fast. She watched in the mirror as the front grille and headlights of the large pickup bore down on her Audi, completely filling the rear window.

The Sierra was going to hit her.

Traffic was heavy and she was in the center lane of the freeway – there wasn't much room to maneuver. Chloe always drove with both hands on the steering wheel. She tightened her grip and braced herself for the impact.

When the Sierra rammed her left fender, the Audi jerked forward and swerved to the right. Chloe was prepared, but she barely managed to pull the car out of the way of an oncoming tanker. She heard the long wail of the trucker's horn as he cleared the right side of the Audi.

She took a breath and checked the mirror. The driver of the Sierra was still behind her. She had been expecting him to pass her, maybe flashing a finger as he went by. But he wasn't finished. He was bearing down on the Audi again.

Chloe had aced the precision driving course in the academy and finished at the top of her class. She could easily force another vehicle off the road. This time someone was after her.

But who was it? The Sierra had tinted windows. She couldn't see who was driving.

Eugene had removed the tracker from the Audi, and Freddy had placed it in the vehicle driven by Enrique Castellanos of the Bosqueros. Maybe Castellanos had figured out what happened and was angry.

It probably wasn't Jefferson or one of his crew. The person Jefferson had sent after her hadn't been trying to cause an accident. He – or she – had merely been tailing her.

But it didn't really matter at the moment, Chloe thought as the Sierra again bashed into the rear of the Audi. What did matter was preventing an accident that could kill or injure someone.

She struggled once more to keep the Audi in the center lane. There was no escape. She was boxed in on the three-lane section of the freeway and traveling over sixty miles an hour. To her right was a large semi-trailer that bore the name of a popular soft drink. A fast moving SUV came up on her left. Ahead of her was a white van. She focused on controlling the Audi, waiting to see what the Sierra would do next.

Just then the driver of the semi-trailer slowed and flashed his lights. He was either warning her or letting her know that he had seen what was happening. Either way, it meant that he was paying attention. He would be able to react quickly.

Chloe hit the turn signal, sped up, and changed lanes, edging her car into place directly in front of the semi.

The driver of the semi gave one short friendly tap of the horn and closed the distance between his vehicle and the Audi, leaving no room for the Sierra to hit Chloe from behind.

Having regained a modicum of control, Chloe took a breath. She could easily get away from the Sierra. That was no longer a problem, thanks to the alert driver of the soft drink truck. But she wanted to find out who was driving the Sierra.

And she wanted to stop him.

The Sierra, temporarily blocked in the center lane by the slow-moving white van, was a short distance behind the semi.

Chloe was in a section of the city that was under development. She wasn't familiar with the area, but she thought the next exit led to a side road. At a slower speed and with less traffic, she would be better able to take out the Sierra.

She hit the turn signal some distance ahead of the exit, hoping the driver of the Sierra would see what she was doing and follow her.

As she moved onto the exit ramp, Chloe waved to the trucker, who honked his horn and continued down the freeway. Then she watched in the rear view mirror as the Sierra crossed the right hand lane without signaling and swerved on to the ramp.

She ought to arrest him for failing to signal before changing lanes. Maybe she would. The other driver hadn't realized it yet, but she was in control now.

They were on a two-lane road leading to an unfinished development and there were no other vehicles. A concrete V-shaped drainage ditch – utilitarian but definitely lacking in esthetics – paralleled the right side of the road. It was just what she needed.

Chloe allowed the Sierra to close the gap between them. Then she abruptly slowed down and swerved to the right. The other driver, who hadn't been expecting her to decrease her speed, pulled ahead.

Chloe spun the Audi back on the road. Now she was behind the Sierra.

She pulled out as if to pass the Sierra on the left. When her front wheels were just behind its back wheels, she sped up and steered the Audi into the side of the larger vehicle. The Sierra skidded, spun out, and rolled over, coming to rest on the spillway.

Chloe kept her vehicle under control, jumped the curb, and came to a stop thirty feet behind the Sierra.

She called in the accident.

Then she took her Glock 23 out of the lock box and inserted the magazine.

Chapter 56

Chloe held the gun on One-Eye as he crawled out of the wrecked Sierra. He staggered a few steps, then sank to the ground. He had a head wound and his right arm appeared to be broken.

"What the fuck?" he said. "You ran me off the road."

Chloe didn't confirm or deny his accusation. She didn't want to get into a discussion. She would save it for the highway patrol.

"I called 911," she told him.

Now that she knew who had been in the vehicle, she was eager to get moving. She had been on her way to meet Crawford, who was planning to drop in on Frida O'Neill. Chloe wanted to be sure Crawford adhered to common politeness in his discussion with Frida.

But Chloe didn't have any politeness, common or otherwise, for One-Eye.

"How well do you know Fergus Ockleberry?" Trooper Reinhart asked Chloe. She watched as the emergency medical personnel loaded One-Eye into an ambulance.

"Aren't you going to send an officer with One-Eye?" she asked.

"One-Eye?"

"Arthur Blackcotton. He tried to run me off the road."

"We'll send a trooper to speak with Mr. Blackcotton

in the hospital," Reinhart said. "What about you and Ockleberry?"

"I don't know Fergus Ockleberry," she said. "What does he have to do with this? He's in prison. That's where One-Eye should be."

"Mr. Ockleberry is in the Carson City Correctional Center," Reinhart said.

Reinhart hadn't reacted to Chloe's comment about One-Eye. Maybe he hadn't read One-Eye's arrest record.

"So I heard," Chloe said. "I rented the car from Trevor Jones."

"Not a good idea," Trooper Reinhart advised. "Jones is a known counterfeiter. Served time for bank fraud, too."

"He wasn't wearing a sign around his neck. I didn't know," Chloe replied. "Look, I'm working undercover at the moment and this has nothing to do with Fergus or Trevor."

She had shown Reinhart her FBI credentials when he first arrived. He hadn't seemed impressed.

"I'm working with Special Agent Tom Jefferson in the Las Vegas office," Chloe said. "You can call him. I'd like to get out of here. I don't have much time. I was on my way to meet a contact."

"You were driving a vehicle with a suspended registration," Trooper Reinhart told her.

"I have a copy of the registration certificate. It shows that everything is up to date."

"Mr. Ockleberry was sent a notice informing him

that his registration was suspended because the vehicle wasn't covered by liability insurance."

"I don't know about that, but I'll show you the documents I have," Chloe said. She pulled the paperwork out of the glove compartment and handed it to him. Reinhart took the folder and went back to his car.

Chloe looked at her watch. She was late for her meeting with Crawford. She called him to let him know what had happened.

"Are you OK?" Crawford asked. "I'll come get you."

"I'm fine," Chloe told him. "I'll call Freddy and ask him to send someone to tow the Audi. I'll get a ride with them."

"It's best not to get too involved with Freddy and his outfit," Crawford said.

"Why? Do I still owe him for the last time?"

"No. You're paid up."

"That's OK, then," Chloe replied. "But I'm going to be here a while. Why don't we visit Frida tomorrow?"

"No," Crawford told her. "I'll talk to Frida without you."

"You should wait for me," Chloe said.

"We've had another death. I want to get this thing settled."

"Who died?" Chloe asked. "Not one of your men?"

"No. You don't know him. I didn't know him, either."

But even though Crawford hadn't known the man,

she could tell by the sound of his voice that he was troubled by the death. She didn't argue with him. Maybe Frida would talk to him, even if he did ignore social niceties.

"OK," Chloe agreed. "Trooper Reinhart is taking his time with the paperwork."

"Trooper Reinhart, huh?"

"Yeah. You know him?"

"We've met." Crawford didn't add anything further.

"What, Crawford?"

"Trooper Reinhart is probably in touch with Jefferson."

"A set up?"

"Yeah. Let me know what happens. And if you need to get out of jail, I can help."

She didn't know if he was joking or serious. But then, Crawford rarely joked.

Chapter 57

"Let's see, we've got driving a vehicle with a suspended registration. That's a fine of $300, but after you add in the court costs and other fees, it's a total of $415." Trooper Reinhart seemed to be enjoying himself.

"It's the responsibility of the owner to keep the registration up to date," Chloe objected.

"The renter has an obligation to make sure the paperwork is in order," he told her. "In addition to negligence with regard to the registration, there's the fact that you were driving on a highway marked as closed. That's an offense totaling $305."

"I didn't see a sign saying the road was closed," Chloe protested.

"Right there at the end of the exit ramp," Reinhart said. "Hard to miss."

"One-Eye was trying to run me off the road," Chloe said angrily. "He was trying to kill me. I didn't have time to look for a sign saying the road was closed."

"Do you have witnesses to Mr. Blackcotton's alleged attempts to run you off the road?"

"The driver of a semi-trailer tried to help me." Chloe described the soft drink truck.

"Did you get his license number or the number of the truck?"

"No. I was too busy avoiding One-Eye."

"Without a witness, it's your word against his," Reinhart advised. "Mr. Blackcotton said you forced him off the road."

"I was trying to stop him before he injured someone."

"A clear case of road rage on your part," the trooper admonished. "I'll sign you up for a class on aggressive driving. They will give you suggestions on how to avoid getting angry behind the wheel."

"And you really should be more careful about the vehicles you rent," he added.

Chloe was angry and didn't answer.

It wasn't road rage, but it came close.

Chapter 58

It was Eugene who dropped Chloe off at her apartment. He hadn't had to tow the Audi. Trooper Reinhart had confiscated it. "It's going to need a front end alignment when I get it back," she told Eugene. "That's assuming the highway patrol returns it."

"They will," he said. "We'll take care of the alignment and repair the dents. You'll need a couple of new tires, as well. And we can provide another vehicle until then."

"I won't need another rental, but thanks anyway, Eugene," Chloe replied. "I've got something else in mind."

"Tell Crawford that Riley sends his thanks for the new license," Eugene mentioned as Chloe got out of his truck.

"Why is that?" she asked. "What did Crawford do?"

"Oh, well, you know, he sort of helped Riley with the paperwork," Eugene mumbled. "I thought you knew."

"No. I don't know about Riley," Chloe said. She thought Eugene had a strange look on his face, but she didn't know what it meant. Crawford had said it was best not to get too involved with Freddy's outfit. She wondered if Crawford had followed his own advice.

"I can get you another vehicle," Trevor said when she called to tell him the highway patrol had taken possession of the Audi. He hadn't sounded surprised to hear that the car had been picked up.

"I won't be needing another vehicle, Trevor," she said. "I really like driving the Audi. I don't mind waiting for the highway patrol to return it. But in the meantime, I want you to take care of the insurance and clean up the registration. Got it? And I expect a discount to cover the cost of the fine."

Trevor assured her that he would take care of the details.

Chloe changed clothes and went to Patty's garage to get her Fatboy. She had been wanting to take it out for a run.

She wiped off a smudge and checked the items on her list. Brakes. Fluids. Cables. Lights. Tires. Suspension. The bike had traveled across country in a custom-made pallet. She had also insisted on a closed trailer. It had been worth it. Her Fatboy looked good.

Chloe made certain her New York motorcycle license was in her biker purse. She donned her helmet, goggles, and gloves. She was wearing leather riding gear, along with a protective vest and knee guards.

She always wore protective clothing when riding the bike. It was one of her rules.

Or maybe it was a principle.

She set it aside to think about later. Right now she wanted to catch up with Crawford.

Chapter 59

"I thought you were dead, Chase Colby," Frida O'Neill told Crawford. "I went to your funeral and took flowers. Who did they bury if it wasn't you?"

"Damned if I know," he said. "And my name is Crawford now. Tell me what you told Yanko."

"Just because I talked to Gazsi, doesn't mean I'm going to talk to you."

Crawford evidently wasn't using common politeness. Chloe had said he should wait for her. He should have listened.

But Frida had information that could save lives. He took a deep breath and tried again.

"Frida, we think you can help us."

"You and who else?" she asked.

"What do you mean?"

"You said we. Who else is involved?"

Crawford didn't want to reveal the names of the Squad. Frida appeared to be close-mouthed about what her husband had learned, but she might gossip about other things.

"There's a group of us," he said. "We work in secret. We believe Simon Lang is guilty of criminal acts. We want to convict him."

If even that much information got around, Simon Lang would know that Crawford was involved. And he would start looking for the Squad. Lang already knew the names of Darius Taylor, Diego Gutierrez, and Harrison Knight. It wouldn't take him long to find the others. But it couldn't be helped. Crawford needed the information that perhaps only Frida possessed.

Crawford wasn't good at reading people, and he couldn't tell what Frida was thinking. He wished again that he had waited for Chloe. She had a way of getting people to talk. Or if Sid had been in town, he could have brought him. People liked Sid.

For some reason, Crawford thought of his soon-to-be-brother-in-law. Paulo Simoneaux always seemed to know what other people were thinking. That was one of the reasons Crawford tried to avoid him. Then there was the fact that Crawford just didn't like him. That made two reasons to avoid Simoneaux.

Crawford thought Frida was upset. She might be angry that she had taken flowers to his funeral and he hadn't stayed dead. Or maybe she had dinner on the stove and he had interrupted her. That sort of thing used to exasperate his mother.

Right now, Frida was cooking meat stew with paprika and onions. He could smell it.

"You're fixing *pörkölt*, aren't you? My mom used to make it." Yesterday he had thought of his father. Today the scent of paprika brought back more memories.

"My grandkids are coming for dinner," Frida told him with a smile. "They like the old Hungarian dishes."

"Then I won't keep you long," he said. "Are you willing to tell me about the supply chain issue and what Ernest was doing?"

Maybe the thought of *pörkölt* convinced Frida she could trust him. Maybe she had been fond of Belle Colby. Whatever it was, she invited him to sit down. "I'll tell you what I can," she said simply.

But a half hour later, Crawford had little more than what Gazsi had told Chloe. It wasn't enough.

"Did your husband leave records?" he asked.

"What kind of records?"

"Notebooks, loose papers, computer disks or files?"

"Gazsi asked me the same thing. We threw out Ernie's old computer. The kids said it was too outdated to be useful. I've never found any papers."

"I'm trying to get in touch with George Chaplin," he told Frida. "Did you know him?"

"He's homeless, poor man," Frida said. "He shows up now and then. I let him store clothing and blankets in the shed back there." She pointed to a small building in her backyard. "Sometimes I give him a meal. He knows he can use my washing machine to launder his clothing. And he turns the hose on when he wants a bath. But that's usually in the summer. It would be too cold in the winter."

"Do you expect him to come by anytime soon?"

"No. He doesn't have a regular pattern. Sometimes it's months before he shows up again. He's got a problem with alcohol, you see. Drugs, too."

"Yeah, I heard," Crawford muttered. He was trying to be polite, but he didn't know how, and social situations sapped his energy.

He found long conversations exhausting, like trying to stay awake during an opera or attending meetings in the military. He wanted to be outside. He wanted action.

"Maybe Gus knows what happened to the notes," Frida said.

"Who's Gus?" Crawford asked drowsily.

"George Chaplin," she said. "People call him Gus. Isn't that who we were talking about?"

"Yeah, it is." All at once Crawford was wide awake and able to concentrate. "Tell me what Gus looks like."

"I have a photo," Frida said. She got up, went to the bureau, and pulled out a snapshot. "It's Ernie, Gus, and Wes," she said. "That's Gus in the middle."

And it was Gus. The same Gus who had been in the McCullough Detention Center with Crawford. Gus of Pilgrim's Progress. Gus with the blanket.

"Frida, we need to find Gus," Crawford said urgently. "Of the men in that photo, he is the only one left alive. Simon Lang wants to kill him."

"Wes is still alive. He's living in Mexico."

"Wesley Bernard was killed a few days ago. Can you help me find Gus?"

"Did Simon Lang kill Wes?"

"His daughter did."

Frida's eyes were shiny, but she blinked back the tears. "You're right. We have to stop it. Gus sometimes hangs out in Huntridge Circle Park. That's a good place to start looking for him."

Chapter 60

Just as Crawford walked out of Frida's house, Chloe arrived on her motorcycle.

"Are you OK?" he asked, checking her over. He saw no sign of injuries.

She sat easily on her bike with a contagious buoyancy. He wanted to join her, but he was driving Carter Allenby's old Ford pickup.

"I'm fine," she assured him.

"I've got a lead on Gus," he told her. "I'm going to Huntridge Circle Park."

"Gus?"

"Turns out Gus is George Chaplin "

"What are you talking about, Crawford?"

He realized that he hadn't told Chloe anything about either Gus or Chaplin. "It's a long story," he said. "Something to do with Pilgrim's Progress. But there isn't any time to lose. If I found Gus, Alice can as well. She plans to kill him."

"Alice killed the other man, didn't she? The one you said had died," Chloe guessed.

"Yeah."

"I don't understand what Gus has to do with Pilgrim's Progress, but if Alice is involved, we need to get moving. I'll meet you at the park," Chloe told him.

Crawford was relieved that Chloe would be with him

when he looked for Gus. She seemed to have a way with cantankerous old men, himself included.

Before he left, Crawford had warned Frida to be careful. "You might want to go away for a while," he told her. "The, uh, stuff is about to hit the fan. If Simon Lang thinks you know something, he won't hesitate to send Alice to kill you."

"Why would they want to kill me? I'm an old woman," Frida protested.

"And Wesley Bernard was an old man," he reminded her.

She nodded. "I see what you mean. Well, I can take the *pörkölt* and *nokedli* to my grandkids just as easily as they can come here."

"Better go further than that," Crawford advised. "Not to a family member. Go somewhere Alice Lang won't know about."

She looked at him with worried eyes. "She won't hurt my family will she?"

"I don't know, Frida. But it's you she'll be after. I think they'll be safe if you're not with them."

"What about Gazsi?" she asked. "If I'm not safe, he's not safe, either."

"Could be," Crawford muttered. He wasn't sure about Gazsi Yanko's loyalties, but he didn't think the man would do anything to hurt Frida.

"I'll go to Dollywood," she decided. "Maybe Gazsi will go with me."

"Dollywood?"

"Yeah, Dolly Parton's amusement park. I've always wanted to see it. Visitors can tour Dolly's trailer and see the Southern Gospel Museum."

"Huh," Crawford replied. He had never heard of Dollywood, but it sounded like a good place for Frida. "Yanko knows how to get in touch with me. I'll let him know when it's safe for you to come home."

She reached out to shake his hand, and Crawford willingly took it in his. "Be careful, Chase," she said.

"You too, Frida."

Crawford wasn't wearing a disguise, and he didn't want to take the time to go back to his apartment to get one. He would go as he was. But to make sure he found a parking place, he took out the handicapped parking permit Carter always carried and hung it from the rear view mirror.

Then he called Darius, who was still in Hawaii. Bucket list or not, Crawford had to warn him. He didn't want Darius returning to Las Vegas just yet. In fact, it might be better if Darius stayed in Hawaii. Alice Lang wasn't likely to search for him there.

"We'll go to Seattle," Darius told him when Crawford explained the situation. "My wife has family there."

"Better fly to the mainland and drive from someplace else," Crawford warned. "Alice will be checking with the airlines. And stay away from the rental car agencies. She'll be watching those, too. Sid is in L.A. with Harrison. If you fly there, he can fix you up with a car."

"You're taking this seriously, aren't you?" Darius said. "But I don't want to stay in Seattle. Once my wife is safe with her relatives, I'll come back to Las Vegas. I want to help."

"If you come back, you'll have to stay out of sight."

"I can do that," Darius said.

"OK," Crawford agreed. "There's something else. Did you know a man named Ernest O'Neill?"

"Yeah. He died of a heart attack. At least that's what Lenny Lang said."

"Did you believe Lenny?"

"No. It didn't sound right and there was never an autopsy. I think the Langs arranged the accident that killed him."

"We'll get around to dealing with that. Do you know about the records he was keeping on the supply chain issue?"

"Yeah. Both O'Neill and I had some records – dates and names and test results on the different chemicals Lang was using."

"What happened to them?"

"I never got a chance to ask O'Neill, but I think he turned them over to a man named Michael Colby."

Son of a bitch, Crawford thought. He was going in circles.

Crawford had been baptized as Chase Colby, the only son of Michael and Belle Lang Colby. His parents were dead. The house in which they lived had been sold. Crawford's sister, Claire, was living in Texas.

Whatever information Michael Colby might have gathered hadn't been found in the effects he and his wife left behind. Crawford had no idea where his father might have kept the information, or even if he had.

Another bootless errand.

Chapter 61

Alice Lang had used her contacts to track George Chaplin. She discovered there were several locations in Las Vegas in which he liked to spend time between rounds of drinking and drugs. He often turned up at the rescue mission, which provided hot meals to anyone requesting them. He sometimes slept there, as well. Chaplin occasionally used the laundry and shower facilities at the homeless shelter. He also liked to hang out at the Goodwill Store on West Sahara Avenue. And, as a number of other homeless persons did, he frequented Huntridge Circle Park.

"Chaplin seems to spend his time in Vegas," Alice mentioned. "How did he get to the McCullough Detention Center?"

"LVPD sent him. McCullough often takes prisoners from the surrounding areas," her contact said. "It's a way of bringing in revenue to pay for the facilities."

Alice had the mug shot of Gus from the McCullough Detention Center. He was an old man with white hair and a grizzled beard. As far as she could tell, there was nothing distinctive about him. Medium height, medium weight, no facial scars, no significant injuries. Just an anonymous homeless man who had an issue with drugs and alcohol.

Alice had staked out the rescue mission last night, but no one who looked like Chaplin had shown up. She would watch for him again this evening, but they didn't start serving dinner until five o'clock. In the meantime, she would search elsewhere.

She checked out the Goodwill Store, but he wasn't there. Then she went to the homeless shelter. Not there, either. That left the park. It was a pleasant, sunny afternoon, and people were outside enjoying the improved weather. Perhaps her luck would improve, as well.

Alice parked her car in a nearby shopping center and walked a few blocks to the park. The three-acre park wasn't shaped like a circle. It was more like an elongated tear drop.

She found a bench and sat down in the shade. Her disguise consisted of a blonde wig and sunglasses. She was wearing running shoes, her footwear of choice when making hits, dark slacks, and a T-shirt of no particular color. The gray scarf around her hair partially hid her face.

Alice had a good view of the section where the homeless people tended to concentrate. She leaned back and began to scan the area.

Chapter 62

"That's Alice," Crawford whispered to Chloe.

"How do you know?" Chloe asked.

"Cheekbones," he said. "I'd recognize her anywhere. If she's here, that means she hasn't found Gus."

Chloe studied the slender woman with the sculpted cheekbones. The sharply defined ridges were similar to Crawford's, but elegantly striking, like those of a fashion model, while Crawford's were strong and angular.

Alice was negligently watching a group of children kick a soccer ball. Chloe had seen Alice running from the scene of a shooting, but had never come face-to-face with her. She was curious about the infamous hit woman.

We're polar opposites, Chloe thought. *I want to make things right. Alice is a killer.*

If that was why Chloe had become an FBI agent, why had Alice become a hit woman? To gain favor with her father? Simon Lang would be a difficult man to live with. What would he expect from a daughter?

But that was where Chloe's train of thought came to an end. Crawford had sighted Gus.

"I'll go get him," he said.

"What about Alice?"

"I don't think she'll take a shot from that distance. There are too many people around."

"You think she planned to identify Gus and then

walk right up to him? Take a point-blank shot?" Chloe said. "That means she has a silencer."

"Yeah," Crawford replied. "She's probably got the gun in that shoulder bag she's carrying. She could shoot him through that."

Alice's shoulder bag was muted in color, but timelessly chic in its cut and design. *Classy*, Chloe thought. *Looks like something I would choose.*

Maybe she and Alice weren't polar opposites, after all.

That was a disconcerting thought.

"You look after Gus," Chloe told Crawford. "I'm going to report a sighting of Alice. There's a warrant for her arrest. Then I'll keep an eye on her. I don't want her to shoot you or Gus."

Crawford nodded and walked toward a small cluster of men. Chloe called Jefferson to report that Alice Lang was currently in Huntridge Circle Park.

"What's she doing there?" Jefferson asked.

"Seems to be enjoying the sunshine," Chloe reported.

"What are you doing there?"

"Enjoying the sunshine." Crawford hadn't explained who George Chaplin, aka Gus, was, but Chloe knew he was important to Crawford in some way.

She and Crawford had no proof that Alice intended to shoot Gus. If Crawford was able to get Gus out of the line of fire before backup arrived, there was no need to mention either of them.

"Alice has blonde hair today. She's wearing sun-glasses, a gray scarf, dark slacks, and a sort of green-gray-tan T-shirt. She's carrying a shoulder bag.

"Don't approach her," Jefferson warned. "Wait for backup."

Chloe walked at a moderate pace, taking a circui-tous route that would place her slightly behind and to the right of Alice. If Alice tried to shoot anyone before backup arrived, Chloe planned to disable her right hand.

That way Chloe wouldn't have to shoot at and pos-sibly destroy the shoulder bag that held Alice's gun.

Chloe didn't believe in the senseless destruction of works of art. It was one of her principles.

Chapter 63

As Crawford bent over the recumbent form of Gus, he had his back to Alice, but he knew she had seen him. She would know he was removing her target.

"Gus," Crawford said as he shook the man's shoulder, "we have to get you out of here."

"Why?" Gus mumbled.

"Remember Simon Lang? He sent his daughter to kill you. I'll explain it all later. Right now, we're going to leave."

"That makes us even," Gus mumbled.

"Makes who even?"

"I've been trylng to get rid of Simon Lang for years," Gus said.

"What did you do?" Crawford asked. He and Gus thought alike. They should have joined forces a long time ago.

"I sent Apollyon an email," Gus claimed. "Told him I knew what he had done to O'Neill."

So Gus had sent the email that started Lang's latest trail of violence.

"I want to find out what you know about O'Neill," Crawford said. "But first, we need to get you out of here."

Gus's eyes were closing and he didn't answer.

"He's on the nod," another man told Crawford. "You won't get anything out of him for a couple of hours."

Heroin users often experienced an initial euphoria followed by a state of drowsiness in which their limbs felt heavy and their mental functioning was impaired. They could become alternately sleepy and wakeful. Evidently Gus was entering one of the drowsy periods.

"Shit," Crawford muttered. The only thing to do was carry Gus out of the park. He lifted him up and slung him over his shoulder.

"Crap," the other man muttered as he struggled to his feet. "You can't just grab Gus and carry him off like a bag of trash."

"He's in danger," Crawford said. "I want to get him out of here."

"You're not taking him anywhere."

But the man hadn't done anything to stop him, and Crawford wasn't willing to argue. He turned toward the parking lot and walked away, setting as brisk a pace as he could manage. Gus was heavier than he looked.

The other man followed, yelling at Crawford to stop. Four more men joined the procession. Now they were all shouting.

Well, that should take care of Alice, Crawford thought as he maintained a steady pace at the front of the small cavalcade. It was unlikely she would shoot into a group of homeless men. But he had to figure out a way to prove to Gus's friends that he didn't intend any harm. And he had to do it before they attracted the attention of the police.

When Crawford reached the pickup, he gently lowered Gus to the ground and patted his shoulder. "Gus," he said. "Wake up."

Gus's self-appointed guardians gathered around, watching intently. Crawford knew they were prepared to attack him. One of the men was grasping a set of brass knuckles. Another had a stick with a sharpened point. Crawford didn't bother to see what the remaining men were carrying. Gus was the only one who could save him.

"Gus," Crawford tried again. "You have to wake up."

"I'm awake," Gus said, but his voice was blurry.

Crawford reached for the bottle of water he had stuffed into his pocket. When he pulled it out, the book came too. Crawford left the book on the ground and handed him the water. Gus's mouth was probably dry, another symptom of being on the nod.

"Gus," Crawford said. "Simon Lang wants to kill you. I'm going to take you to a place where he can't find you."

"Why would you do that?"

"I'm Michael Colby's son. Lang has killed enough men. I don't want him to kill you."

"Shit," Gus muttered. "I thought you were dead."

"Yeah, I get that a lot. Look. Frida told me where to find you. She's gone into hiding. Now we have to get you someplace safe, too. Tell your friends here that it's OK."

Gus gazed at the faces of his companions, all of them staring down at him. "What are you guys doing here?" he asked.

"We thought he was kidnapping you. We was gonna to stop him."

"Naw, Marty. I knew his dad. Colby wouldn't kidnap me."

"Are you sure?" Marty asked. "You was using that new stuff. You're probably out of your senses about now."

Crawford picked up the book and handed it to Gus. "I brought this for you," he said. "I thought you'd like to have it."

"Well, damn. It's my copy of Pilgrim's Progress," Gus chortled. He wiped a smear off the cover.

The copy of Pilgrim's Progress seemed to satisfy Marty and the other men. "He's been looking for that," Marty said. "Where'd you find it?"

"In the ditch."

"Well, damn," Marty echoed.

Crawford helped Gus into the truck. Then he turned to the men.

"If you need anything, here's how to get in touch with me."

He wrote the address of his encrypted email account on a piece of paper and handed it to Marty. "If anyone asks about Gus, it would be better not to tell them anything."

"Nothing," Marty replied. "We won't say nothing."

Crawford wondered how long that would last. The men were probably addicts. All Alice had to do was offer money, alcohol, or drugs.

But he was one step ahead of Alice. That was enough for now.

Chapter 64

A frustrated Alice Lang watched from a distance as the Ford pickup pulled out of a handicapped parking space near the perimeter of the park. Crawford was driving and George Chaplin was in the passenger seat.

Alice hadn't found an opportunity to take a shot at Chaplin, and she couldn't follow Crawford. She had left her car a few blocks away.

How had Crawford known she was after the man? She hadn't asked for Chaplin at any of the locations she had searched.

Alice wasn't particularly concerned about not taking down Chaplin. A homeless man in Vegas would show up again. She would find him. But she was furious that Crawford had intervened. He had already caused enough trouble for the Langs, and getting rid of him had long been one of her objectives, a goal that had been superseded when other more urgent matters arose. Like the warrant for her arrest.

However, she now had the license plate number of Crawford's vehicle. She would recognize the pickup if she ever saw it again.

Alice was preparing to cross the street when she saw a black SUV. Out of habit, she ducked out of sight into the trees at the edge of the parking lot. Then she sighted two more plain black SUVs.

What the hell, she murmured. She knew a Fed vehicle when she saw it.

Alice always had an escape plan. Under cover of the trees, she took the gun from her bag and tucked it into her waistband. She dumped the contents of the bag on the ground and turned it inside out. Now it was khaki colored with brown stripes.

She removed the blonde wig and scarf from her head, leaving her dark hair coiled in a bun, placed a faded baseball cap on her head, and slid her arms into a man's leather jacket, softened with age. She had placed a skirt in the bag, but she left it there. She might have to run, and it wasn't easy to run in a long skirt.

Dumping everything but a small tool kit into the bag, Alice picked up her belongings and walked to a bicycle stand. She cut the chain of a sturdy looking bike and got on.

Alice rode quickly, the bag over her shoulder, into the residential neighborhood that surrounded the park. It was a middle-class section of town. The city blocks were long, but only two lots wide. There were no alleys, and the generally one-story houses had small yards surrounded by fences.

She slowed momentarily and took the time to push the wig and scarf into a storm water drain. If they were ever found, any DNA would be so mixed with the detritus of the drain that they would be useless.

The neighborhood wasn't an ideal place in which to disappear, so she kept going.

A few blocks later, Alice got off the bike, lifted it over a fence, and left it. Then she walked down a neighboring driveway and tossed the tool kit into a trash barrel, before making her way through the back yard. Seeing a clothes line, she draped the skirt over it. Now all she had left was the bag.

She looked around. Before her was a high concrete wall.

Lenny had been on the track team in high school, and Alice had often practiced with him. Steeple chase, pole vault, high jump. She had done them all. She still knew how to get over an obstacle.

But this time she made a slight misjudgment. As she topped the wall, the bag slid from her shoulder and became stuck on a protruding piece of metal. Alice landed on the pavement without the bag.

She left it behind. Someone would eventually find it. There was nothing in it. On the off chance it held some of her DNA, such as a strand of hair, the Feds couldn't pin anything on her. She had found the bag in a bin at the back of the Goodwill store. Anyone could have donated it.

Alice was in the unloading area behind a drug store. She considered going into the back entrance and walking through the store, but decided against it. Too many security cameras.

She walked around the store to the front parking lot and found the silver-gray Toyota Camry she had left there. She hadn't succeeded in shooting George Chaplin, but the afternoon hadn't been a complete loss. She had found Crawford.

Chloe ran after Alice Lang as she rode away from the park on a stolen bike. She managed to keep her in sight for several blocks, before admitting that it was a lost cause. She called in the information, telling Jefferson that Alice was now a brunette, wearing a baseball cap and a leather jacket.

Chloe blamed herself for losing track of Alice. She thought of all the things she should have done. She should have called in the sighting earlier, should have had her bike closer, should have stayed closer to Alice, should have tackled Alice when she stopped to adjust her wardrobe. But she had been following orders not to approach the suspect.

"Damn, damn, damn," Chloe mumbled as she searched the neighborhood, one street after another. She stopped an FBI vehicle circling the block, talked to the agents, and turned down an offer to ride with them.

"I might be able to see more on foot," she explained. One of the agents climbed out of the SUV and accompanied her. More agents arrived, spreading out over the area.

An hour later, one of them found the bike, and Chloe was able to identify it. Twenty minutes later, they spotted the bag caught on top of the wall. One of the agents climbed up to retrieve it.

"That's the bag she was holding," Chloe confirmed. "She turned it inside out."

Jefferson took charge of the bag. The FBI techs would check it for fingerprints and DNA.

Chloe wanted to talk to Jefferson, ask him about

Trooper Reinhart, find out if he had learned anything about the money in the Dominican Republic, and discover whether he was still investigating her.

But Jefferson was in a hurry to get the bag to the lab. Then he wanted to look at footage from security cameras in the area. He said he didn't have time to talk to her.

It was just as well, Chloe thought. Jefferson would want an update, and when it came to evidence against LB Freight, she and Crawford still didn't have squat.

Chapter 65

Patty agreed to accept Gus as a temporary visitor. After seeing Gus safely inside her house, Crawford left him with Chloe and Patty and went outside to make phone calls.

"Is this a big secret?" Patty asked Chloe.

"It would be better not to say anything about Gus," Chloe told her. "He's in trouble. We need a place where he will be safe until we can get him to a treatment facility. And he will likely sleep for a while."

"No prob," Patty replied. "There's room in the basement. Gus can stay as long as he wishes. He looks like my grandfather."

She smiled at Gus, who smiled back. "Cool house," he told her. "Blast from the past."

"You better believe it," Patty confirmed. "My mother's a fanatic. She said a mid-century house had to have a mid-century style, and there was no holding her back." Patty handed Gus a blanket decorated with atomic age designs, UFO symbols, and space ships, before leading him downstairs.

"The casino boss who owned this house used the basement for private meetings with persons he didn't like," Patty said, as she showed Gus the downstairs area. "I think he killed them," she whispered in an aside to Chloe.

"Now, the only thing we keep down here is the waterbed. My Aunt Sophie used to sleep on it. She thought it was exotic, but I think it's sloshy."

Patty gave Gus a pillow decorated with 1958 Ford Edsels and told him to make himself comfortable.

"I don't have a pillow anymore," he said, as he admired the design. "Someone took it."

"You have one now," Patty told him. "It would make me happy if you kept this one."

"Great-Heart," Gus said to Patty. Then he must have agreed with Aunt Sophie because he settled down on the bed, wrapped himself in the blanket, hugged the pillow, and closed his eyes. He had a smile on his grizzled face.

"Did you hear about the fire?" Patty asked as she and Chloe left Gus to sleep off the effects of the heroin. "The one at LB Freight last night?"

The thing about Patty, Chloe thought, *was that if you remained silent, she could carry on an entire conversation by herself.* Patty continued without waiting for Chloe to answer.

"It was on the morning news. The fire occurred in the executive suite. That was where you were working, wasn't it?"

"Yes," Chloe managed to interrupt Patty's monologue. "Was anyone injured?" She was thinking of Yanko.

"No," Patty said. "There was a sprinkler system and the fire was contained to a small area. They're investigating to find out what caused it."

Chloe considered the matter. The LB Freight office was a smoke-free zone, so no one left cigarette butts around. The fire might have stemmed from the electrical system.

The executive suite had a kitchen with various small appliances, and she had noticed that one of the electrical sockets was overloaded. She was going to suggest to Peggy that the Fire Department wouldn't approve, but she hadn't had time.

The receptionist, Alicia Armstrong, had used a space heater to warm her desk in the cavernous entry lobby. Perhaps she had forgotten to turn it off. Space heaters were probably another violation of the fire code.

There might be any number of reasons for a fire in the building. It was probably an extraneous event, unconnected to the investigation.

But all the same, Chloe decided to ask Jefferson about it.

Chapter 66

That afternoon, Chloe watched from the sidelines as the Squad took care of business. There was no wasted time or effort. They were as organized and disciplined as a Special Forces unit.

Diego found a drug rehabilitation center near Reno that would accept Gus. Chloe and Crawford would take him in the morning. That required a larger vehicle than the pickup, and it wasn't long before Carter showed up with a Land Cruiser.

"Alice Lang saw us leave in the pickup. Might want to change the plates," Crawford warned him. "Maybe a new paint job."

"Got it," Carter said. "Sid called. He's coming back tomorrow."

By evening, Gus was installed in one of the Squad's safe houses, a two-bedroom, second-story apartment in a former motel a few blocks east of Las Vegas Boulevard. Gus had showered and eaten dinner. Then he had examined the clean clothes provided by Barney Watson, put on his new pajamas, and fallen asleep with his arms wrapped around Patty's pillow.

But keeping an eye on Gus and observing the Squad in action hadn't required Chloe's full attention. She had found time to think about the other things on her mind.

Crawford had said they had to slow down the investigation of Simon Lang, but that hadn't been necessary.

The sluggish and haphazard enquiry into Lang's activities had already been going nowhere.

So was she. And she was allowing extraneous events to get in the way of her mission.

Like One-Eye, for example. Chloe had spent an entire morning dealing with his attempt to ram her car, time she should have spent finding evidence against Simon Lang. Now she was slated to attend traffic school.

Chloe had interviewed Yanko, but other than learning more about Lang's use of unsafe chemicals, she had nothing to show for her efforts, no solid evidence.

Then Crawford had wanted to rescue Gus. Chloe was uncertain how Gus fit into the picture, or if he did. But now that he was safe, it was time to think about what she was doing.

Jefferson didn't trust her. He had even had her followed. Then there was the bank account in the Dominican Republic.

Chloe had tried to contact Jefferson to ask about the fire at LB Freight, but he was busy chasing Alice Lang and wouldn't return her calls.

Chloe was committed to pursuing the conviction of Simon Lang. At the same time, she was determined to restore her reputation. Nobody else was going to do it for her.

But how? She was involved with a man who lived below the radar and a supervisor who had lost interest in his investigation.

"I have to take control," she thought, "get tougher.

I have to start finding answers." She couldn't do much about Jefferson until he consented to talk to her. But she would push the sphinxlike Crawford for information.

Who was Crawford, anyway? What did he do when he disappeared into the night?

Crawford would have to talk to her, tell her what was going on. She had a right to know.

Tomorrow she would begin her search for answers. Crawford held some. Then there were the answers that only she could provide.

Crawford had said they couldn't have a relationship, that they were too different.

Why, then, was she drifting aimlessly in a non-relationship with an unforthcoming man who rarely told the truth and who tossed out aliases like they were confetti?

She already knew the answer to that one.

Because it would hurt too much to let him go.

Chapter 67

"Do you think he will stay?" Chloe asked. They had left Gus, his pillow, and the copy of Pilgrim's Progress in the determinedly cheerful cafeteria of the rehab center, and promised to return in a few days.

"For a while," Crawford told her. "I don't think Gus is interested in curing his addiction. But at least he's out of Vegas."

Gus hadn't provided any useful information. He would speak of Simon Lang as the devil. Then he would have to be reminded who Lang was.

"What do you know of Ernest O'Neill?" Crawford had asked.

"Good man," Gus said. "Liked goldfish."

"Was he investigating Simon Lang?" Crawford queried.

"Who?"

"O'Neill. Was he gathering information on Simon Lang?"

"How would I know?"

"Frida said you and O'Neill were friends."

"Yeah. He was a good man. Liked goldfish."

At that point Crawford became frustrated, and Chloe had stepped in to take over the conversation.

"What else?" she asked.

"Frida," Gus recalled.

"Yes," Chloe prompted, "she remembers you. She said you left some things at her house."

"I did?" Gus asked. "What did I leave there?"

"Clothing. Anything else?"

"Blankets," Gus recalled. "It gets cold in the winter."

"Yes, I know," Chloe said with a smile. "What kind of drugs are you using?"

"Synthetic," Gus admitted. "Thought it would give me a beautiful rush."

"Did it?"

"I had a dream," Gus said. "I was being carried through the park."

"That was real," Chloe said gently. "Crawford was making sure you got away from Alice Lang."

"Why?" Gus asked.

"She wants to kill you," Chloe warned him. "It's important. Try to remember."

"OK," Gus mumbled.

He looked around the rehab center as if surprised to find himself there. Then he turned to Crawford. "Listen to the Interpreter," he said. This time his voice was clear and distinct.

"Do you know what that means?" Chloe asked Crawford.

"Probably something else from Pilgrim's Progress," Crawford said. He should have read the book before he returned it to Gus.

"I don't think there's any use asking the same questions again," Chloe said. "We can talk to him after he's been clean for a few days, unless the drugs and alcohol have fried his brain permanently."

But Gus had been coherent enough to send an anonymous message to Lang. Crawford was hoping that his brain wasn't completely fried.

Chapter 68

"Alice will be too busy avoiding the FBI to try to find Gus," Chloe commented. "Anyway, you gave the rehab center a false name and paid in cash."

"Huh," Crawford replied. His dark green eyes were wary and alert as they scanned the highway. She knew he was watching for anything unusual that might signal an ambush or an attempt to force the Land Cruiser off the road.

But even though he was worried, Crawford was taking her sightseeing. They were headed northeast out of Reno on Interstate 80. The desert sky stretched overhead like a bright blue dome. A few wide, straight bands of white clouds marked the way to the stratosphere. The desert landscape was stark and forbidding, nothing but parched earth and somber mountains. Chloe was fascinated by the land around her. It was a dramatic change from the lakes and waterfalls of Buffalo or the wheat fields of western Kansas.

"Where are we going?" she asked.

"I thought you'd like to see Sand Mountain."

"Ooh, yes," she breathed softly, staring at Crawford in delight.

He hadn't attempted to disguise himself today, and she liked looking at what she thought of as the real Crawford, even more than she enjoyed seeing the desert. His long hair was tied back in a ponytail, revealing a lean face with a strong jaw. Then there were those amazing cheekbones, as stark and forbidding as the desert around them. There was nothing soft about Crawford.

"Do you know about Sand Mountain?" he asked.

"The dunes make sounds," she said. "Like kettle drums or thunder."

Crawford knew of her interest in geology. He was doing this for her.

He was upbeat today, like a man anticipating a successful outcome to his ventures. *He's on a roll,* Chloe thought. *He found and rescued Gus. Things are going well for him.*

She didn't have the heart to bring up the difficult questions she wanted to ask. She put them off until later.

"Like fog horns," he told her, referring to the dunes.

"We'll see which one of us is right," she said.

"Told you," Chloe stated as they returned to the Land Cruiser. "Kettle drums."

The dunes, often overrun by all-terrain vehicles, had been almost deserted. She and Crawford had climbed to the top of one of the smaller peaks and had slid down, listening to the sand.

"It only works when the sand is dry," she told him. "And the grains have to be rounded. The sound occurs when the grains roll over each other and vibrate."

"Is that right?" he asked, a half smile on his lips.

"You already knew that, didn't you?"

"Yeah, but I like to hear you say it."

"What's next?" she asked.

"We'll stop for lunch," he said. "Then we'll hit Pyramid Lake."

Chapter 69

The two short, blonde women in their early twenties greeted Chloe with smiles and hugs as she came out of the restaurant. They also called her Dee. Crawford wasn't the only one who spread aliases around the countryside like confetti.

Chloe had met both women at the Bosqueros gathering. After she had given Trixie Lawson a lesson in self-defense, Trixie had proceeded to punch out her abusive boyfriend. Then she and Jolene Rogers, who had been living with another Bosquero, had set out on their own. Chloe hadn't seen either of them since.

"What are you doing now?" she asked.

"We're living in Reno," Trixie told her. "I'm working at an animal shelter and Jolene is an event organizer. We're doing fine without Woody and Spider-Man."

"Have they made any attempt to find you?" Chloe asked. She was concerned that one or both of the male bikers might be upset that their women had left them.

"No." It was Jolene who replied. "Woody is on a downhill slide from drugs. And Serge is too busy being road captain. Now that I'm not there to take care of the details, he has to do everything himself."

Chloe knew the road captain arranged events for the motorcycle gang. Before she walked out on the man she had lived with for three years, Jolene had done most of the work.

Both Woody and Sergio, also known as Spider-Man,

had arrest records. Chloe believed the two women had made a wise choice when they left to start a new life.

"And I'm taking more lessons in self-defense," Trixie added, determination in her voice. "Just in case Woody tries anything."

"Glad to hear it," Chloe replied. "Do all your new activities leave you time to ride?"

"Yeah. We've got our Hondas," Trixie answered. "They're in the parking lot. What about you? Are you still with Ghost?"

"He's putting gasoline in the Land Cruiser," Chloe told them. "I've got my Fatboy with me in Vegas."

The women spent a few minutes discussing their bikes. Then the conversation turned back to the Bosqueros.

"After the arrests, Gina Hernandez became the new treasurer," Jolene told Chloe. "It's the first time a woman has been an officer."

"And Otto, her husband, is vice-president," Trixie added. "But Gina does most of the work."

"Otto is lazy," Jolene said. "But Gina is different. She's ambitious and ready to move up. She wants to participate in the syndicate and take over the position held by Jerónimo Torres. He used to be Ochoto's deputy until he was arrested."

"Did Gina tell you that?" Chloe asked in surprise.

Jolene grinned. "We went out drinking with her one night, and everyone got a little loose. Trix and I don't attend Bosquero events, but we stay in touch with the women."

When Crawford joined them, Trixie and Jolene greeted him politely, but didn't hug him or offer to shake hands. Chloe thought they were a little afraid of the man they knew as Ghost.

"Are you ready?" he asked. She nodded, said good-bye to Trixie and Jolene, and promised to stay in touch. Then she and Crawford returned to the Land Cruiser.

Chapter 70

Chloe and Crawford spent the remainder of the after-noon visiting Pyramid and Walker Lakes. The two bodies of water were remainders of the once immense Lake Lahontan, which dated back to the Pleistocene epoch.

"The tufa mounds were formed when calcium from spring water combined with carbonate already dissolved in lake water," Chloe informed Crawford as they looked at the numerous strange formations around Pyramid Lake. There were pillows, branches, pendants, and nod-ules of tufa. In some places, the limestone spheroids re-sembled enormous intricate flowers. In other places, the spires rose from the earth like abandoned towers.

"How long have they been here?" Crawford asked.

"Some are as old as 26,000 years," she answered happily. "The youngest are probably 13,000 years old. After that, the springs may have dried up."

"There were animals around, too," she said. "Mam-moth, cheetah, horse, camel, lion, and giant sloth."

When Chloe appeared ready to begin searching for fossils of the ancient, long-departed animals, Crawford took her hand and led her back to the Land Cruiser.

He drove south to Walker Lake, where they parked the SUV and walked to the overlook.

Chloe studied the blue-green water, sparkling in the afternoon sunshine. Barren mountains surrounded the oval lake. "No tufa formations," she noted.

"No," he agreed. "But people have reported monsters."

"Like the Loch Ness monster?" she scoffed.

"It's an old lake that has never dried up," he reminded her. "The locals say it's inhabited by a giant water snake that eats people."

"Right," she said, with obvious disbelief in her voice. "I think it's time to go home. It's been a wonderful day, but we should get back to business." This time she led him to the SUV. "Do you want me to drive?"

"No," he told her. "I'm good. I'd like to go to the cabin."

They had already spent one night in Reno. Now, they would be away from Vegas for a second night. Chloe wanted to know what was happening – whether Jefferson had caught up with Alice or gathered more information on the bank account in the Dominican Republic. She wouldn't be able to find out from the cabin, where cell phone service was sporadic to nonexistent.

But Crawford loved the cabin. When he was there, he relaxed and became, for Crawford, almost talkative. He had just spent a day doing what she wanted to do. She would do the same for him. Besides, she might be able to get answers to her questions.

"OK," she agreed. "I've got an idea about the investigation. We can discuss what to do next."

"Yeah," Crawford replied, a smile curving the corners of his mouth. "That, too."

Chapter 71

Chloe sank into the warm water of the hot spring, leaned back to rest her head on the ledge, and watched as the sun slid below the horizon.

On some nights, the sunsets in the high desert were spectacular, but tonight there were no clouds and the light was fading rapidly. Stars were already appearing, bright sparks of white in the dark blue sky. The approaching night was mysterious, ethereal, and romantic.

Crawford stood at the edge of the pool formed by the spring and opened the bottle of wine. His body was lean and hard and perfectly sculpted. In the twilight, he looked like the chieftain of an ancient culture, poised nude above a sacred body of water, prepared to make an offering to the gods. Or maybe he was the god come down to earth.

Crawford handed her the bottle, which had been chilled in the cold spring, located on the other side of the hill behind the cabin. Then he stepped into the pool and sat down beside her.

"Did you bring the glasses?" she asked.

"It's a man thing to drink from the bottle," he replied, closing his eyes and sinking lower in the water.

So much for being the romantic god of an ancient civilization.

"It's a woman thing to drink from a wine glass. Why do you think I gave you those glasses?"

"You can go get one," he murmured.

But she didn't want to leave the comfort of the warm water to walk back in the chilly air to the cabin amid rocks, cacti, and possible scorpions and snakes. She took a sip of the wine – it was sweet and crisp – and passed the bottle to him.

He gulped down several mouthfuls and handed the bottle back to her.

"Crawford!"

"Sweet Cheeks!"

"That's expensive wine," she remonstrated.

"The faster we drink it, the sooner we can get to the good part." He ran one hand along her thigh and left it there. "Have another drink."

Crawford had been unusually convivial all day, but he had unwound even more as soon as they arrived at the gate to Azariah's house. He had greeted the old man cheerfully, unloaded a stack of groceries for him, petted the dogs, and taken the time to chat.

"Dee and I are spending the night," Crawford had told Azariah.

"Good to see you again, ma'am," Azariah told her. "But Jim, here, didn't tell me you was comin'. The cabin ain't been swept out."

"Don't worry, Azariah. We'll take care of it," Chloe said.

"And where'd you get that Land Cruiser?" Azariah asked. "Don't tell me you got rid of the pickup?"

"The pickup is at home," Crawford said. "I borrowed this from a friend."

Crawford's beloved Toyota 4x4 pickup was being stored in Barney's garage. After he abandoned his condo, Crawford had decided to take the pickup off the streets for a while.

Azariah believed Crawford's name was Jim Whistler. Chloe didn't know what other stories Crawford might have spun for the old man.

Crawford depended on Azariah to look after his cabin when he was away, which was most of the time. In return, Crawford routinely brought food and household supplies to Azariah, along with cases of dog food for Orville and Wilbur.

The two dogs, a mixture of Border Collie and cattle dog, guarded the perimeter of Crawford's and Azariah's land. They were litter mates, beautifully marked in black, white, and tan. The major difference between the two was in their ears. Orville had drop ears, while Wilbur's were semi-erect.

Orville and Wilbur had passed by the hot spring on their evening rounds, lolled on the rocks while Chloe rubbed their ears, and then slipped away into the dusk. They were working dogs, diligent and well trained. They had a job to do.

Chloe felt the cool surface of the wine bottle as Crawford rubbed it against her upper arm. When she turned toward him, he placed his lips, warm and inviting, where the bottle had touched her skin.

She took the wine bottle from his hand before he could drop it in the spring, and stood up.

"What?" he asked.

She set the wine on the rock ledge and lowered herself back into the water. "I've got a better idea," she said, as she ran her hands across his chest. "We'll save the wine for later and go straight to the good part."

"You're my kind of woman." When he smiled, there were glimmers of fire in his eyes.

"Just don't go all romantic on me," she cautioned. "I wouldn't know how to handle it."

"Yeah, you would," he reassured her as he pulled her closer. "You can handle anything."

Chapter 72

"What was this place called?" Chloe asked. They were in the midst of a small ghost town – a few fieldstone walls with empty windows, some rusted metal machinery, and the boarded up entrance to a tunnel that led into the hillside.

"End of the Road," Crawford told her. "The miners were after gold. The town got started in the early 1880s, but most people had left by 1890."

"How many people lived here?" she asked.

"About two hundred at its height. They even had a post office for a short time."

"What happened?"

"Gold ran out."

"But Azariah still finds gold."

"A little, but it's mostly leftover bits and pieces."

Orville and Wilbur had accompanied them to the remains of the small settlement. Now they were pawing at the entrance to the tunnel, trying to dig under the wooden partition. A chain held the door closed. A shiny padlock was attached to the ends of the chain.

"What's in there?" Chloe asked. "They must smell something."

"Probably a dead animal."

"What if it's something else? Maybe we should notify the sheriff's office."

Crawford called to the dogs, and they came bounding toward him, forgetting whatever it was that had momentarily attracted them to the old mine.

"It's probably nothing more than a few bones," Crawford assured her. "The entrance is secured. Nobody can get in. Do you want to go up to the ridge for lunch?"

"Lunch sounds good," she agreed. "I'll drive."

They let the dogs out as they passed the gate, and started up the mountain.

"You've got some explaining to do," Chloe said as she took a bite of her roast beef sandwich. She washed it down with a swallow of water.

Crawford knew he had a lot of explaining to do, but he didn't want to go into it now. The sky was bright blue with a few puffy white cumulous clouds. The Silver Peak mountains spread out around them, their summits edged with snow. He and Chloe were near the watershed. The streams to their back ran east. The water from the river in front of them would eventually make its way into California and perhaps as far as the Pacific Ocean.

"Is your name really Colby?" she asked.

"Yeah," he mumbled, chewing on a piece of his sandwich. He swallowed and took another bite.

"Talk to me, Crawford," Chloe insisted.

The last time he had avoided the question of his name, she had stalked into the kitchen. If he didn't tell her, she might stalk back to the Land Cruiser and take off, leaving him stranded. She had the keys.

Besides, Jefferson had already discovered Crawford's real name. If Jefferson knew, there was no reason not to tell Chloe. He might as well give her the information she was after and get it over with. Otherwise, she would keep asking until he did.

He put down the sandwich and looked at her.

"My parents named me Chase Colby. My dad was Michael Colby. He worked at LB Freight and tried to gather information on Simon Lang's activities. He was exposed to toxic chemicals and died of intestinal cancer. Is that what you wanted to know?"

"Wow," Chloe said softly. "When you unload, you really unload. What about your mother?"

"She's dead, too."

"What happened?"

"Simon Lang sent someone to kill her."

"Holy shit," she murmured.

"Yeah."

"Can you prove any of that?"

"Why? Don't you believe me?"

"It doesn't matter whether I believe you or not. Although, as it happens, I do believe you. What matters is whether we can get the evidence to try Simon Lang in court."

"I'll get what I need."

"Yes," she said thoughtfully. "I believe that, too."

Chapter 73

"You said you had an idea," Crawford said, proving that he really did listen to her. "Want to tell me what it is?"

They had said very little as they drove back to the cabin. Chloe had glanced at Crawford from time to time, but he stared out the window, his posture stiff, and his eyes as remote as those of the hawks that circled the desert sky. He had been wearing his biking jacket, the one with the name "Ghost" on the back. Perhaps he was seeing ghosts.

Chloe had concentrated on her driving. When they came to a crossing on the unpaved roads that spread across the mountains, Crawford would say "Go right" or "Turn left." That had been the extent of their conversation.

Crawford had prepared dinner, heating up a can of soup and setting out the last of the roast beef. He had also toasted the remainder of the French bread. Chloe had gone to the cold spring to retrieve the unfinished bottle of wine. They hadn't gotten around to drinking it last night.

Somewhere between the soup and the roast beef, Crawford had come out of his dour mood, and they had eaten the meal in companionable silence. Now he was ready to talk.

"Remember Biker Babe?" she asked.

"The woman who promised to provide information against the Bosqueros?"

"The woman who did provide information. I'm pretty sure she was Gina Hernandez."

"But you thought she might be a man."

"I made up that rumor to throw everyone off track," Chloe admitted. "I didn't want any of the women at the gathering to become targets for revenge."

"If the Bosqueros learn she was the one who recorded their meetings, they'll go after her," Crawford said.

"I don't plan to tell anyone but you."

As she poured wine into the glasses, she glimpsed the trace of a smile on Crawford's face. He lifted his glass, swirled the wine gently, and took a polite swallow. Then he set down the wineglass and waited for her to continue.

"Trixie and Jolene told me that Gina is the new treasurer of the Bosqueros. Otto is now vice-president."

"Heard that somewhere," Crawford remarked.

"They also said that Gina wants to move into Jerónimo Torres' position in the syndicate."

"That's something new," Crawford admitted.

"I have information that would be of interest to Gina," Chloe said. "In return, she can tell me if the Bosqueros had anything to do with the bank account in the Dominican Republic."

"You're going to try to make a trade."

"I learned from the best," she said with a grin. "If the Bosqueros didn't set up the bank account, then our most likely suspect is Simon Lang."

"Yeah, but we can't prove he set it up."

"At least we'll know where to look. During my one day at the office, I met Gracie Martín, and I think she was trying to warn me about Lang. If he established the account, she'll know about it. Hell, she would have been the one to do it. Lang doesn't get into the details of the finances."

"You think Gina will talk to you?"

"I don't know, but it's worth a try."

"That might give us an answer about the bank account, but that doesn't leave us any further ahead with taking out Lang. We haven't found information from the wiretaps to convict him. I tried to start trouble between the Langs and the Bosqueros, but nothing came of that, either."

"What did you do?" Chloe asked.

"Raided a Bosqueros' drug shipment. Made it look like LB Freight operatives had done it."

"You love to challenge the norms, don't you?" Chloe said in exasperation. "You're like a trickster who disdains convention. A mischief-maker."

"Most conventions are pretty useless," he replied. He picked up the wine bottle and refilled their glasses. "And norms are a form of social control."

"Norms and conventions are a historical social legacy," she insisted. "They encourage consistency and cooperation."

"Not all of them are valid," Crawford reminded her.

"They help people avoid mistakes."

"I like to make my own mistakes," he asserted. "I'm an out-of-the-box thinker."

"I can think out of the box," she insisted.

"Prove it."

"Trading information with Gina is out of the box," she argued.

Crawford made a pretense of genteelly sniffing his wine before he took another drink. "But you said you learned how to make trades from me. That's called transfer of learning, the application of knowledge gained in one problem-solving situation to a different context. What about an original idea?"

He tipped back his chair, kicked off his boots, and waited for her response. His eyes were unreadable in the soft glow of the Coleman lantern, but she knew he was baiting her.

"Here's what we have in our investigation," Chloe said. "A summary, if you will. Gracie Martin is having affairs with both Ochoto and Simon Lang. No one outside the Bosqueros, with the exception of Gracie, knows what Ochoto looks like. The Bosqueros think the Langs stole their drug shipment. Alice is on the run. That leaves Lang without family backup."

"You forgot the parrot master," he said dryly.

"Robbie Lang is a sweet, innocent nonentity."

"He's the son and brother of killers."

"OK. That leaves Lang with only Robbie as family backup. Does that make you happy?"

"Sure." He finished his wine and twirled the glass in

his fingers. "Was that your idea?"

"I'm providing background, so you'll understand the context," Chloe said, "in case you have to do a little transfer of learning yourself. Lang is shorthanded and under pressure. We might be able to get him to do something out of character."

"He's not that shorthanded. He has Gracie."

"We're not sure of Gracie's loyalties, remember? She has a relationship with Ochoto. She may have tried to warn me off."

Chloe paused for a moment, waiting to see if Crawford would interrupt, but he was watching the gleam of the lamp through the bottom of his glass. He didn't even look up.

"I'm thinking we could arrange a meeting between Lang and Ochoto," Chloe continued. "Get them to throw a few accusations at each other, remind each other of past favors, that sort of thing."

"Ochoto would never attend a meeting. He doesn't go out in public," Crawford reminded her.

"He doesn't have to attend," Chloe said. "All we have to do is make Simon Lang believe he's talking face-to-face with the real Ochoto."

Crawford was silent for a few moments. "Damn," he murmured. "You really can think out of the box. You think if he's pushed, Lang will say something to incriminate himself."

"You've already set the scene by stealing the drugs," Chloe reminded him. "Lang is probably angry that the

Bosqueros don't believe him when he says that LB Freight had nothing to do with the raid."

"You're right. That should make him eager to meet with Ochoto and set the record straight," Crawford acknowledged.

"There's one problem, though," Chloe remarked. "What if Gracie finds out about the meeting? She'll know there is something wrong."

"It's a risk we have to take," Crawford decided. "I'll send an email to Lang from Ochoto requesting a meeting. I can make it sound like I'm keeping it a secret because of a suspected leak in the Bosqueros organization. I'll also insist that Lang not tell anyone else about the meeting. Maybe I will include a threat, as well."

"We'll have to find someone to play Ochoto," Chloe said.

"Sid could do it."

"We don't know what Ochoto looks like, but I doubt if anyone believes he's African American."

"Darius, then. He wants to help," Crawford told her.

"He could be putting his life on the line. There's no guarantee that Simon Lang won't have Alice standing by ready to shoot him."

"I'll remind him, but I already know what he'll say. It's what any of the Squad would say."

"What?" Chloe asked.

"Put me in the same room with that bastard and I'll take him out."

"There will be no killing, is that clear?" Chloe stated.

"We're only after information."

"Can we rough up Simon Lang a bit before we let him go?"

"No."

"Spoilsport," Crawford complained.

Chapter 74

"Now that I know your real name, what do you want me to call you?" Chloe asked as they packed to return to Vegas. "Chase? Or Colby?"

"Neither. Call me Crawford. Chase Colby is dead."

"You had better explain that," she said, pausing to look up at him.

"Simon Lang was getting too close. He offered a reward for the death of Chase Colby. I killed the guy off." Crawford lifted his duffel bag and started toward the door.

His hand was on the latch when Chloe spoke again. "That's why you called yourself Ghost when you rode with the Bosqueros, isn't it?"

"Seemed appropriate."

He continued out the door toward the SUV.

Before returning to Vegas, Chloe and Crawford traveled to Reno to check on Gus. He was alert and clean shaven, and his hair had been trimmed. But Gus's recent memory was a blank.

"Don't remember you," he said to Crawford.

"Do you remember Ernest O'Neill?" Crawford asked.

"Not sure. I've got fog in my brain. I'm not sleeping and I could use some whiskey." Gus yawned and looked hopefully at his visitors.

"Not today, Gus," Crawford said. "We'll check on you again next week."

As Crawford and Chloe turned to leave, Gus spoke up. "The broad parchment will record the sum of your ways," he called to Chloe.

"Thank you, Gus," she replied. "I'll remember."

"What did he mean?" she asked Crawford as he held the door for her.

"No idea," Crawford replied. "He probably doesn't know either."

Chapter 75

Chloe pulled her Fatboy into the parking lot of the small bar and casino that bore the name Rum Raisin. Behind the bar was another establishment owned by the same individual. It was a licensed brothel. The Rum Raisin was located northwest of Las Vegas in Nye County, one of eight counties in Nevada that allowed prostitution.

Chloe had run a check on the Rum Raisin before leaving her apartment. It was owned by Otto Hernandez, Gina's husband. That meant Gina ran the place. Jolene had been right – Otto was lazy.

But Otto and Gina were a team, and the Rum Raisin exemplified their symbiotic relationship. Otto had been Gina's entrée into the Bosqueros, formerly an all-male organization. Gina, who ran a chop shop out of Laughlin, Nevada, provided the income to maintain Otto's lifestyle. She wouldn't have been able to pass the background check required to operate a brothel. But Otto, who was too laid back to get into trouble, had been able to qualify. He might have been arrested, but he had never been charged. All that would have remained would have been payments to local officials for the necessary permits. Gina would have taken care of that.

The Rum Raisin's adobe-style architecture, with its rounded corners, wooden beams, and stuccoed walls, was set amid desert mesquite, bursage, and saltbush. Chloe scanned the parking lot – a few bikes, four dusty pickups, and a battered Jeep. That was all.

When Chloe turned to go into the bar, Alicia Armstrong, the receptionist at LB Freight, met her at the door.

"Good afternoon. I'll take you to Gina," she said.

"Alicia?" Chloe uttered, too surprised to say more.

"Yes. I work part time here," Alicia told her.

"In the bar or the brothel?" Chloe couldn't help asking.

"The brothel," Alicia said with a smile. "It pays better than LB Freight and I work half the hours."

"You're a prostitute." Chloe said.

"We prefer to be called independent contractors," Alicia told her, as she led Chloe through the bar and into the back offices.

And when I went to LB Freight, I thought I was the only one with a private, unrevealed life, Chloe mused to herself. *What else have I been getting wrong?*

When she contacted Gina, Chloe had identified herself as Dee Atkins. That was the name she had been using when she met Gina.

"I've got information you might find useful," Chloe had stated. "I'd like to make a trade."

"What do you want in exchange?" Gina asked.

"I want to know whether there's a relationship between the Bosqueros and a certain bank account in the Dominican Republic. You deal with Bosqueros finances.

If you don't have the answer immediately available, I believe you may be able to find out."

"What's the name on the bank account?"

"Chloe Mathews."

"Figures," Gina said. "How do I know the information you have will be of any value to me?"

"It has to do with Jerónimo Torres," Chloe replied.

It had taken Gina only two seconds to come to a decision. "Meet me at three o'clock at the Rum Raisin. Come on your bike and come alone."

She told Chloe how to find the place and ended the call.

She doesn't want to talk about Jerónimo Torres on the phone, Chloe thought. Probably a wise decision qiven Gina's ambitions.

"You're not going by yourself to meet Gina," Crawford had argued.

"Why not?"

"She runs a chop shop. She's got criminals working for her."

"I'm not in danger from Gina. Besides, you can't go with me. You have a meeting with the Squad."

"The Bosqueros want your blood," Crawford reminded her.

"I'm a pro, Crawford. I keep telling you that. I know how to meet contacts. And I know how to look out for myself."

Chloe had traveled to the Rum Raisin by herself, but she wasn't certain that Crawford wasn't having her followed. She hadn't met all the members of the Squad, and there were some she wouldn't recognize. One or more of them could be driving the pickups or bikes parked in the lot.

She checked the sky for drones, something else Crawford and Diego might use to keep an eye on her, but saw nothing unusual.

Crawford had wanted her to wear a covert listening device, but she had refused.

"Girl talk," she had told him. "We might say something to embarrass you."

Chloe had met Gina Hernandez at the Bosqueros run in Boulder City. At that time, Gina had worn her long hair in a leather hair glove to protect it from the wind when she rode her bike.

Now the sleek look was gone. Her hair was definitely tousled. Shaggy, in fact. Not only that, the formerly black tresses were currently auburn with blonde tips at the ends.

Chloe wasn't the only one who experimented with hairstyles and highlights. But that was where the similarity ended.

Chloe thought of herself as mundane and moderate. The word for Gina, she decided, was vivid. Gina was wearing hand-tooled black leather pants with a design that swirled across her buttocks. A sultry black corset was somewhat muted by a stylish fuchsia blazer. Open-toed sandals with three-inch spike heels completed her outfit.

Gina was magnificently brash with an exaggerated sexuality. She was, in a word, stunning.

Chloe, on the other hand, was dusty and windblown after her ride. The molded chest and spine protectors on her vest restricted her movements, making her feel clumsy. She hadn't looked in a mirror, but her cheeks were probably red and her nose shiny. The bike helmet would have flattened her hair. She brushed the strands back from her face and smoothed them into place with her fingers.

Gina pushed a bottle of water toward Chloe, who opened it and drank thirstily. Then she sat down at the table Gina indicated.

"Your meeting," Gina said. "Talk."

Chloe looked around to make certain they were alone.

"We won't be interrupted," Gina said. "But you already know that. You wouldn't have come without doing your homework. Otto owns this place and I manage it."

"Nice establishment," Chloe commented. "I see you hired Alicia."

"Yes. She's an old acquaintance of yours, isn't she, Ms. Reynard?"

"An acquaintance that lasted a day," Chloe noted. "If you're here, who runs the operation in Laughlin?"

Gina smiled. "Freddy and I are joining forces," she said. "Eugene will take over the Laughlin setup. He told me he had helped you out a few times."

Gina had no qualms about mentioning her illicit activities to an FBI agent. She would know that Chloe had stepped over the line in dealing with Freddy and Eugene.

Chloe got down to business. She didn't want to wear out her welcome before she gained the information she needed. "Did you find out anything about the bank account?" she asked.

"Only that it's there," Gina said with a small, satisfied smirk. "Must be kind of unnerving, huh, Dee? To wake up and find yourself with half a million dollars you didn't even know you had."

"Tell me about it," Chloe said, taking another swallow of water. Riding the bike always made her thirsty. "What do you know about Fay Courtney?"

"She disappeared," Gina replied.

"She's the sister of Enrique Castellanos," Chloe added. "Jerónimo Torres sent her to Colombia to recruit for the Bosqueros."

"Yeah, I know that much," Gina said.

"A few days ago, the Colombian authorities found her body. She died from a bullet wound. The information hasn't been made public. I understand there's been a delay in notifying her next of kin, possibly because the Colombian police don't know how to reach Castellanos. Is he the only relative?"

"Yeah," Gina said. "The parents are dead and there were no other siblings."

"Was Castellanos fond of her?"

"Yeah. They were close."

Gina had a thoughtful look on her face. Chloe took another drink of water as she let Gina ponder the information she had provided. She wondered if Gina would consider it good value received, and would tell her what she wanted to know. Nothing to do but ask.

"Did the Bosqueros have anything to do with the bank account in the Dominican Republic?"

"Hmm?" Gina murmured.

Chloe waited patiently.

"No," Gina finally said. "The Bosqueros did not put $500,000 into a bank account in the Dominican Republic."

"Thanks," Chloe said. She stood up, getting ready to leave.

"You think you know who did, don't you?" Gina asked, standing up as well.

"Now that you've eliminated the Bosqueros, yes."

"How do you know I'm telling the truth?" Gina asked.

"What's in it for you if you don't?" Chloe replied.

"Nothing. You still with Ghost?"

"Yes. And you're still with Otto."

"Otto and I have an understanding," Gina said wryly.

Chloe grinned at her. "I would expect nothing less. Thanks, Gina."

"Should I call you Chloe?" Gina asked. "Or maybe Agnes?"

"Should I call you Biker Babe?"

Gina laughed. "No. I think we'll stick with Dee and Gina."

"Goodbye, Gina," Chloe said as she picked up her helmet and gloves. "Thanks, again." Gina showed her to a side door that opened directly onto the parking lot.

"Take care, Dee," Gina said from the doorway.

It wasn't a warning, Chloe thought. It was the kind of remark that anyone might say to a companion. The chop-shop-diva-turned-brothel-madam was treating the undercover FBI agent as she would a friend.

"You too," Chloe said.

Chapter 76

"Don't start overacting," Sid warned Darius.

"I can handle myself," Darius replied as he moved his weight from side to side and made jabs with his fists like a boxer warming up for a fight. "Make a list of the topics you want me to cover in the meeting with Simon Lang. Include details so I can get the names and dates right. This is going to be a great show." His feet danced on the carpet as he circled Sid, jabbing and retreating from his pretend foe.

"He's already overacting," Sid complained to Diego.

"But why are we going to all this trouble? Why can't I just shoot Lang?" Darius asked. He still hadn't stopped moving, his mock punches darting through the air.

"Too hard to get rid of the body," Diego replied. "Besides, Chloe doesn't want us to kill him."

They turned to look at Crawford, who was sitting with his chair propped against the wall.

"Haven't met Chloe," Darius remarked. "But I'm looking forward to it."

"She wants to meet you, too," Crawford told him. "But she has to start traffic school this evening."

"Why doesn't she do it online?" Diego asked. "For that matter, why don't I do it for her?"

"Chloe wants to prove a point," Crawford said. "She can only do that in person."

"I'd like to see her take on the DMV," Diego said.

"Might be worth showing up at traffic school just to watch the fun."

"Save it for the court," Sid advised. "Traffic school is run by a provider."

"When will you schedule the meeting with Lang?" Darius asked Crawford. "I want to get started."

There was no other word for it, Crawford thought. Darius was pumped.

"When do you go back for treatments?" he asked.

"Not until late next week," Darius replied.

Really pumped, Crawford amended. The thought of chemotherapy hadn't fazed Darius. He was still smiling.

"We'll try to set it up before then," Crawford replied. "But we've still got to get Simon Lang to agree."

"How will you do that?" Sid asked.

"Send Lang an email, ostensibly from Ochoto. I think Lang's relationship with the Bosqueros is important enough to him that he will go along with a meeting."

"He won't turn down a chance to meet Ochoto," Diego put in. "The man never appears in public."

"We've still got that video of Alice Lang killing FBI Agent Carson-Burleigh," Sid reminded Crawford. "Maybe we could use that, too. Tell Lang the Bosqueros have a copy."

"I'll do two emails," Crawford decided. "One will be from Ochoto, asking for a meeting. The other will be anonymous and will say that the Bosqueros have a copy of the video. Lang will think Ochoto wants to meet in order to blackmail him about the video."

"Screw the bastard," Darius said.

There wasn't a man in the room who disagreed with him.

Chapter 77

Gracie Martín listened as Simon Lang spoke with Alice.

"Things are happening," Lang told his daughter. "It appears the Bosqueros have a video of you shooting Carson-Burleigh."

"If they do, it had to come from Crawford," Alice claimed. Her voice sounded croaky. *Probably from being on the run*, Gracie thought. *Must cause a lot of tension. Or maybe she's ill and doesn't know how to get help.*

"I saw Crawford the other day when he grabbed George Chaplin," Alice added. "I've got the license plate number and have sent out some feelers. Trouble is, the license plate is registered in the name of Carter Allenby. My contacts say he's just a mechanic who loans out his truck now and then. And they don't know how to find him."

"Crawford can wait," Lang advised his daughter. "Chaplin is the man you need to find."

"He's disappeared," Alice said. "He hasn't shown up at his usual haunts, and the other homeless men haven't seen him for a few days. Crawford is hiding him."

"Did you try bribery?"

"Of course." Alice gave a brittle laugh. "I've distributed several thousand dollars. All I learned was that Chaplin reads Pilgrim's Progress, leaves some of his things with a woman named Frida O'Neill, and told his friends that Colby wasn't a kidnapper."

"That must be Ernest O'Neill's widow," Lang fumed.

"What does she say?"

"She's disappeared."

"Crawford probably had something to do with that, as well," Lang growled.

He's very irritated, Gracie thought. *He knows he's losing control of the situation.*

Then she sat back in surprise as Lang changed the subject. She had to remind herself not to make a sound.

"Ochoto wants to meet," Lang said.

"About the video?" Alice asked.

"Could be. He didn't say."

Gracie held her breath, waiting for Lang to reveal the details. She knew Quino had refused meetings in the past. Evidently he had been the instigator for this one. And Quino hadn't said anything to her about it. Normally, he would have contacted her. He would have asked her to arrange it.

Gracie listened as Simon and Alice discussed the proposed meeting. Either Quino wasn't telling her everything, or Simon Lang was being set up. Either way, it was a signal.

Apollyon the destroyer had warned her. The wheels were in motion. She was ready.

Chapter 78

When Gracie Martín became the chief financial officer of LB Freight, Simon Lang turned all of the company's financial affairs over to her. At first, he or Lenny had monitored her operation, but after a few weeks, no one had questioned her activities. Her books were always detailed and well organized. She had a clear and concise answer to any question that arose, and was willing to provide whatever backup material might be requested.

Her books looked good, even to Gracie. They brilliantly concealed her retirement scheme. Gracie routinely over-invoiced LB Freight's shipments to Mexico, passing the additional funds to the shipper, who, in turn, took his profit and forwarded the remainder to an agent in Bogota.

Gracie was a rich woman, but she wasn't finished with amassing a retirement fund.

All it took was five minutes to drain the LB Freight bank accounts and employee retirement fund, forwarding the money to a series of discreet off-shore banks.

She thought about the half million dollars she had placed in the bank account in the Dominican Republic in Chloe Mathews' name. She removed that as well. Chloe should have taken the money when she had the chance.

It was early evening on Friday, and Gracie was the only one left in the office. By the time Simon Lang came in on Monday morning and discovered what she had done, Gracie would have moved the money several more times. Lang and his IT staff wouldn't find any of it.

Gracie's assistant, Leo Worth-Ingham, was on leave next week. That would make it even more difficult for Lang to discover what had happened.

Gracie wiped the hard drive on her computer. After that, she went to the IT storage room and destroyed the backup tapes. The techs would guess what had happened to the money, but they would be unable to prove it.

Finally, Gracie broke into Simon's safe. She knew the combination. She also knew that, over the years, he had gathered material with which to blackmail her for her contributions to LB Freight's success. Unfortunately, Simon wasn't as organized as she was. She couldn't tell what might apply to her and what wouldn't. She took everything.

Gracie turned on the disintegrator and inserted all the papers, disks, and thumb drives that she had found. She had convinced Simon to buy the machine, telling him that LB Freight should bring its records up to date and get rid of anything that might be used against them in a court of law. It would be easy, she had told him. And it was.

Gracie was a long-range planner, and not an impulsive person. But for once, she acted on a whim. She printed the word "Apollyon" on a sheet of paper and left it on Simon's desk.

Might as well give credit where it's due, she thought.

Gracie had no vendetta against Simon. It was merely

business to her. But her feelings about Quino were different. The sex had been, well, stimulating, and certainly enjoyable. And she liked and admired him.

Gracie knew that Quino wouldn't let her end the relationship. That was the problem with having an affair with a drug lord. He worried when someone knew too much about him. She would have to disappear quickly, before Quino found out what she was doing. Still, she would let him know what he meant to her, and wish him well.

Gracie had multiple sets of identification and the accompanying disguises. She had been preparing for this eventuality for a long time. Ever since Quino became head of the Bosqueros, in fact.

At one time, Gracie had thought Alice Lang might be a problem. Alice was skilled at tracking people. But Alice had a lot on her plate just now. Gracie didn't think Alice would have the freedom to search for her.

When she finished her business at LB Freight, Gracie went to her apartment. She would leave almost everything. The furniture was leased and she had acquired only a few personal items. She regretted the loss of her wardrobe, but it couldn't be helped. She had cash, outfits, and disguises stashed in several cities in the United States, as well as overseas. Clothing wouldn't be a problem.

An hour later, Gracie left her apartment building carrying only a shoulder bag. She walked a few blocks down the street and entered a busy casino. The proximity to the casino was one of the reasons she had chosen that particular apartment building. Casinos were hubs of activity. She wouldn't stand out.

Gracie knew that her exit from her apartment building and her entry into the casino would be recorded by security cameras. So would her entry into the women's restroom. But, with any luck, her departure would be less visible.

In the restroom, she altered her hair style and color with a wig. She changed into slacks and a light-weight pullover. Then she removed the batteries from her cell phone and dropped everything in the trash. She stashed the shoulder bag containing her used clothing in the bottom of a cleaning cart.

Gracie waited until a group of women attending a convention entered the restroom. When they left, she did, as well.

Gracie now had only a purse with a prepaid cell phone, a sizable amount of cash, three false passports, an assortment of credit cards, passwords and keys, and a letter to Quino.

She had known what she was going to write to her lover before she picked up the pen. She told him goodbye, that the time with him had been special, and that what she knew of him would remain private.

"You will always be the man I dream of," she had written. "Someone like you comes along rarely. Almost never, in fact. *Cada muerte de obispo.*"

She knew that Quino would protect himself and the Bosqueros organization, and that he would send men after her, but she also knew she could get away.

The letter was a way to honor their relationship. And

besides, it wouldn't make it any easier for him to find her.

Gracie mailed the letter and went to McCarran International Airport, where she took a flight to L.A. She left Los Angeles International Airport and traveled by taxi to a large hotel. She walked through the hotel, out the side door, and down the street to a self-storage facility. It was open 24 hours a day.

The woman who left the storage facility might have been an eighty-year-old retired school teacher from Paris. Her gray hair was pulled back in a bun, severe but stylish, and she was wearing an elegant, but modest, dark gray suit.

In her new disguise, and with a new name, Gracie flew to Chicago, where she took an Amtrak train to St. Louis. Then she traveled on to Houston and Miami. At each stop, she switched identities.

Each year she had added and changed the number and types of storage units she rented, always keeping them stocked with money and clothing, spare credit cards, and disguises. She always paid for the storage units in cash.

Gracie had known this day would come. She was going to Colombia. She would look up her husband, Mateo. It was time to settle down.

Chapter 79

"He's in," Crawford told the group. "Simon Lang agreed to the meeting."

Sid passed out beers and they drank a toast.

"Screw the bastard!" they repeated one after another. Darius' words had become the unofficial slogan of the Squad.

They might as well have been shouting "One for all and all for one," Crawford thought. He, Sid, and the Squad had worked for years to find a way to convict Simon Lang for his crimes. Now it seemed they might finally achieve their goal. Before, they had had a purpose. Now they had a plan. And not only that, Lang had bought into the plan.

They had managed to assemble most of the group. Luis was too ill to attend, Connor was scheduled for medical tests, and Harrison was still in California, but all of the others were present.

They spent a few minutes congratulating themselves before Sid called the meeting to order and turned the proceedings over to Diego.

"I think we should schedule the meeting on Tuesday," Diego said. "We don't want to allow too much time for rumors and second thoughts. But that will give us a chance to make arrangements. The new kitchen equipment has been installed at Virgil's Roadhouse. The only reason the place isn't open yet is that Virgil isn't back from Mexico. We can use it as the meeting site."

"How will we get in?" Dave asked.

"I'll take care of it," Crawford said. Gina Hernandez would have a key. The videos she turned over to Chloe, the ones that had resulted in a number of arrests of Bosqueros personnel, had been filmed at Virgil's. All it would take would be a slight hint of blackmail, and Gina would agree to loan him the key. Or maybe she would give it to Chloe. The two women seemed to have reached an understanding.

"Diego and I looked the place over," Sid added. He showed them an aerial photograph of the location. The roadhouse was on a side road off US 15, a few miles south of Vegas.

"Virgil's is sheltered from the highway by a *bosque*, a stand of mesquite," Sid told them. "To the back of the roadhouse is a dry river bed. The parking lot is in front and to the north of the roadhouse. There's nothing to the south but desert."

"Lang will probably arrive from the north," Diego said as he took over the briefing. "We can have Darius already in place before he gets there."

"Won't Lang be suspicious?" Dave asked. "He might think it's a trap."

"We could always have 'Ochoto' arrive by helicopter after Lang does," Crawford suggested.

"Yeah," Darius said. "Ochoto is an important *jefe*. He wouldn't want to travel by road. Besides, I've never been in a helicopter."

Crawford added a helicopter to his list, which also

included the name of Special Agent Tom Jefferson, followed by a large question mark. Chloe was determined to notify Jefferson, but Crawford was concerned that the FBI would want to control everything. If that happened, the whole scheme could go up in smoke.

He decided to spring it on Jefferson at the last minute.

"How can we make sure no one else tries to enter the truck stop while the meeting is going on?" Carter asked.

"We could haul in some construction equipment," Sid said to his brother.

"Yeah," Carter replied. "If we place it in front of the roadhouse and string a lot of yellow construction tape around, it would keep most people out."

"Tape is a good idea," Dave said. "It's not like a barricade. Lang will believe he can leave any time he wants to."

"Will Lang have a driver or a bodyguard?" Darius asked. "Will I have a bodyguard, for that matter?"

"We'll have to make sure that any bodyguards remain outside the meeting room," Crawford said. "It won't surprise Lang that 'Ochoto' doesn't want to be seen."

"What if Lang wants to examine the meeting place ahead of time?" Diego asked.

While the others were discussing how or whether they would agree to a request to search the premises, Barney Watson, who hadn't spoken other than toasting the demise of Simon Lang, slipped quietly from the room.

"What's with Barney?" Crawford whispered to Sid as the others continued to make plans.

"He's thinking about his brother," Sid explained. "Clarence died two years ago today."

"Christ," Crawford muttered.

"Yeah," Sid agreed. "It never ends."

"This time it will," Crawford vowed.

Chapter 80

Chloe sat down on one of Patty's mother's atomic age chairs and idly picked up the newspaper that Graham had left. She was alone this morning. Patty was at work and Graham was practicing with his band.

Crawford and the Squad were making last minute plans for the meeting between the fake Ochoto and Simon Lang. They had everything under control.

She hadn't met with them on Saturday to go over the details.

"They're in a raunchy mood," Crawford had told her. "You probably don't want to be there."

Chloe hadn't argued with him. She would be at the scene tomorrow when the meeting between Darius Taylor and Lang occurred, watching from a van parked behind the *bosque*. She would be able to see and hear everything.

Crawford wanted to wait to notify Jefferson until a few hours before the meeting. "We don't want him doing anything to screw it up," Crawford had said. "The fewer people who know about the plan, the higher the chance of success."

Chloe, who disagreed with Crawford, had tried to contact Jefferson to let him know about the meeting. Plus, she still wanted to ask him about the fire at LB Freight. But Jefferson was frantically pursuing Alice and wouldn't return her calls.

Chloe considered other matters. She wanted to talk

to Gracie about the bank account in the Dominican Republic.

If Lang had planned to use the account to discredit her, Gracie would know about it. And if Gracie had mixed loyalties, she might be willing to talk.

Chloe had tried without success to reach Gracie over the weekend. This morning she had spoken with Peggy Lincoln, who said that Gracie hadn't come in to the office yet, but Peggy had promised to let Chloe know when Gracie showed up.

For the moment, Chloe was waiting. She checked her email and leafed through the newspaper. It was a Midwestern paper with Midwestern news. Graham had grown up in Oklahoma. His mother had probably sent the paper.

Chloe read about wheat and oil prices, drought conditions, basketball scores, and arguments for and against abortion and the death penalty.

She turned a page and found herself looking at a photo of Judge Blankenship. She hadn't seen him in almost twenty-five years. Not since she was seven years old and living in Walnut Creek, Kansas. The judge had the same mustache and slicked back hair, now gray, that he had then.

"*District Judge Sam Blankenship convicted of accepting bribes from OKKAN Oil and Gas,*" the headline announced.

The article stated that the judge had dismissed a lawsuit brought against OKKAN for placing oil waste pits too near the town water supply, and for lying about the approval process. Judge Blankenship had said that state officials approved the pit, but that particular pit hadn't been lined, as pits in Kansas were required to be, and the permit had been backdated.

Over the years, the judge had evidently accepted more than one million dollars from OKKAN, mainly in campaign contributions. He was now facing fifteen years in prison and fines of $250,000.

Serves him right, Chloe thought. *But that's not much for a lifetime of corruption.* Intrigued, she looked up the judge on the Internet.

She found that in Coronado County, district judges were selected by partisan vote to serve four-year terms. Blankenship had been in office for thirty years before being sent to prison.

Chloe found a five-year-old article describing irregularities in the judge's treatment of his friend, Sheriff Rod Benson. Chloe remembered Sheriff Benson. Old Baldy, her father had called the sheriff, because of his lack of hair. Her parents hadn't been fond of the sheriff. Or of the judge, Chloe remembered as she thought about it. "The judge is as crooked as a corkscrew," her father had said.

Ronald and Mandy Mathews had been right about Benson and the judge. Perhaps her parents had been right about other things, Chloe thought. Maybe they weren't as black as Grandma Mathews had painted them.

Chloe had set aside her family background, and rarely spoke of her parents to others. They had not been upstanding citizens, but she treasured their memory. Their legacy to her had been a lifelong interest in geology and mysticism. That, and a determination to avoid their mistakes.

Judge Blankenship and Sheriff Benson had been in office when the fire occurred that killed her parents. Chloe wondered if either of the two corrupt officials had filed a report.

She logged into a national database and found a two-paragraph, hand-written summary of the fire. In the report, Benson stated that Ronald and Mandy Mathews had died in a fire caused by freebasing cocaine. He indicated that they had dissolved the cocaine in water and used ether to crystallize it. Then they had heated the crystals with a propane torch to vaporize them.

"The suspects misjudged the potency of the chemicals they were using," Benson wrote. "The ether fumes, which hadn't fully dissipated, spontaneously exploded. The resulting fire destroyed the house and killed the occupants."

"That's a crock of shit," Chloe murmured to herself. "They never used cocaine. And Dad didn't have a propane torch."

Admittedly, she had been only seven years old, but she had been aware of what was going on. Her parents often smoked marijuana, sitting on the front porch on the long summer evenings. But that was the extent of their drug activity.

Chloe recalled listening to her parents as the windmill, pumping water from the well, creaked and groaned.

There was never a lack of wind in western Kansas.

Her mother would talk about mysticism and her father about geology. They had no electricity, but her father had installed a wind-powered generator. There was solar heat in the winter. Her mother cooked on a wood-burning stove.

"Don't be late," her mother had said the morning of the fire as Chloe left to visit Sunflower Birdwhistle. "I'm fixing vegetable soup and cornbread for supper."

Those had been staples, Chloe remembered. Mandy and Ron Mathews were vegetarians. They raised and ate local produce, baked their own bread, and generally abstained from alcohol. But not from marijuana.

Chloe read on to find that at the time of the fire, the daughter of the Mathews had been with a friend, Rebecca Birdwhistle, and was being cared for by that same individual until her relatives could be notified.

Sunflower's parents had been good friends of the Mathews and equally ardent environmentalists.

"Why did your folks name you Sunflower?" Chloe had asked her friend.

"Even though we live in the Nineties and the Millennium is coming, my mom thinks she's a hippie," Sunflower had replied. "When I get old enough, I'll change my name to Jane or Susan or Mary or Betty. Something ordinary."

Chloe wondered what had happened to Sunflower. She had never seen her again after the fire.

Setting aside her memories, Chloe searched for

more articles on Sheriff Benson. She found that he had been in prison for the last ten years for arson and murder. Twelve years ago, Rebecca Birdwhistle had died in a fire on her property. Sheriff Benson had been found guilty of setting the fire.

Two explosions and two fires. Three people dead, and all of them environmentalists. And Benson and Blankenship both connected to OKKAN, an oil and gas company not known for its sensitivity to environmental issues.

Chloe leaned back in the turquoise accent chair with its curved arms and swooped back – once thought to be the perfect blend of form and function – and pondered what she had learned.

It might very well have been the judge and/or the sheriff – not freebasing or the *nagas* – who started the fire that killed her parents. Then years later they had done the same with Becca Birdwhistle.

If so, it was a wrong Chloe wanted to set right.

But it would have to wait until she finished her current assignment. For the moment, she had other priorities.

She picked up her phone and called Peggy Lincoln to ask if Gracie had arrived yet.

Chapter 81

On Monday morning, Bartolomeo Joaquin Reyes, otherwise known as Ochoto, studied the letter that Gracie had sent him. Ochoto paid the postal service well to handle his mail expeditiously. Anything that came for him was placed in his box early in the day before the carriers began their routes. One of his men had picked up the letter and brought it to him.

Gracie had mailed the letter on Friday, Ochoto thought as he slapped it against his palm. That gave her a two-day head start, but it wouldn't do her any good. He would find her.

Ochoto was vigilant, crafty, and arrogant. He was a descendant of Montezuma from a liaison with a royal concubine, and he believed his inheritance proffered certain rights and privileges. His ancestors had been wise and bold warriors, and Ochoto prided himself on being the same kind of ruler.

Ochoto's face was short and broad, with high cheekbones. His eyes were deep set and almond shaped, and his nose was flat and prominent. His skin was coppery. When he looked at himself in a mirror, he saw a face that had come down through history. His ancestors had built an empire that extended from the Pacific to the Gulf of Mexico, with a population of fifteen million people – the most powerful Mesoamerican kingdom of all time. Ochoto himself guided another empire.

Ochoto had taken over leadership of the Bosqueros

organization upon the death of his brother. He had already survived several takeover attempts, not to mention investigations by the FBI. His syndicate earned $10 billion annually through the sale of drugs and weapons, and he was expanding operations throughout the Western Hemisphere.

The notorious Mexican drug cartels used extortion and intimidation to achieve their ends, but Ochoto preferred simple corruption. It wasn't as profitable as violence, but it was much easier and it attracted less attention from the Feds.

Even so, the federal government had been after Ochoto for years, without success. They hadn't been able to gain a foothold in his organization. They didn't know who he was or what he looked like. He wanted to keep it that way.

Ochoto could walk down any street in the United States without attracting notice. And he occasionally did.

Ochoto was fond of Gracie, but he wouldn't let that influence his actions. She was one of the few people who knew his real identity. Most of his family members thought he managed the import/export business called Mesquite Traders. He did, in fact. But it was a front for his Bosquero activities.

Ochoto assigned two men to go to Las Vegas to search for Gracie. "What do you want us to do when we find her?" Delgado asked.

"Get rid of her. Do it quickly. And if you find anyone with her, take care of them as well."

"We'll be in touch," Espinoza said. He managed the logistics. Delgado handled the weapons. Both men were cold and pragmatic. They would carry out his orders competently and without emotion. When they found Gracie, they would kill her and get rid of the body.

Ochoto assigned one of his technical staff to track Gracie, but he didn't think the man would find anything. Gracie was too street-wise to use her credit cards. She was either traveling with a new ID or had gone into hiding. But sooner or later, he would find a trace of her. Then he would clean up the loose ends.

Ochoto had sworn on his brother's deathbed to guide and protect the Bosqueros. He would do what he had to do to keep his promise.

He looked at the letter one last time. "It was nice while it lasted, Gracie," he said with a twisted smile. "A rare treat. *Cada muerte de obispo*, indeed. But it's over now."

Chapter 82

Simon Lang had tried to contact Gracie over the weekend, but had been unable to do so. He wanted to talk to her about the meeting with Ochoto. She often dealt with the Bosqueros, and might have heard rumors. Lang wanted as much information as he could gather on what Ochoto had in mind before he attended the meeting on Tuesday.

Lang had been perturbed that she wasn't available. She was usually at his disposal whenever he called, no matter if it was personal or official. He would have gone to her apartment to look for her, but Venetia, his wife, had scheduled multiple social events over the weekend, and had insisted that he attend. He couldn't get away.

Lang couldn't send Alice to find Gracie. Alice had gone to ground in Phoenix.

When Lang arrived at the office on Monday morning, he found everything in turmoil. The techs were complaining that the backup tapes were missing. The safe in Lang's office was open and empty. He found the note on his desk saying "Apollyon."

Lang blamed Crawford for the chaos. He was pretty sure Crawford had set the fire that occurred ten days ago. Now Crawford had somehow gained entry into the office and interfered with the computer system. He also thought Crawford had sent the email about the O'Neill supply chain issue.

Lang was so occupied with the IT staff that he didn't have time to look for Gracie until late in the morning, only to find that she still hadn't shown up. When she didn't arrive, he sent Peggy Lincoln to her apartment to check on her. Peggy returned saying that she had called and knocked, but no one had answered. No one in the building had seen Gracie since the previous week.

By Monday afternoon, the financial assistants had reported irregularities in the accounts, but without the CFO and her deputy, they hadn't taken any action. They were waiting for instructions from the front office.

Lang was still blaming Crawford for the confusion. He wanted to find Gracie. She would know what to do.

He had a key to Gracie's apartment. He left the building to search for her.

Chapter 83

Simon Lang rang the doorbell several times, without success. Then he unlocked the door of Gracie's apartment and stepped inside.

He called a greeting, but there was no answer. Gracie normally turned on the security alarm when she left, but it hadn't been activated. He closed the door and ventured further, walking slowly through the apartment, checking the rooms one by one.

The living room held a sofa and two easy chairs. The television set was in one corner of the room. Another corner held a small desk. Everything looked as it usually did.

In the bedroom, the bed was made, the crimson duvet and black pillows arranged the way Gracie always left them. The towels hanging in the bathroom were red and black, with the red hand towels placed symmetrically over the larger black bath towels.

But there was no sign of Gracie.

He went down to the underground garage. Gracie's car, a Ford Fiesta, was parked in its regular location.

Lang returned to the apartment and began a more thorough check.

The kitchen was neat and tidy. The trash had been emptied. The refrigerator was stocked with juice and water, along with fresh fruit and vegetables. The freezer held meat. Gracie didn't do her own shopping. She had groceries delivered once a week.

The closets held Gracie's clothes, all neatly organized according to type and color. *Hell,* he thought, *she might as well be in the military.* The closets at West Point wouldn't be any better arranged.

The suitcases she occasionally used were stacked in a corner of the closet. He looked in the bureau. Lingerie, sweaters, stockings. Everything was where it always was.

Except for Gracie.

The remainder of the apartment was the same. The desk held a small computer, along with a few office supplies. Gracie did most of her personal business and banking on-line and paid her bills with direct debit.

He could report her missing, but the police wouldn't be greatly concerned. Gracie was an adult and there was no sign of foul play.

He looked through the kitchen cupboards for the bottle of Scotch Gracie kept on hand for him. She rarely touched alcohol, although occasionally she would drink a glass of wine.

He poured himself a drink and returned to the living room. As he looked around, he realized that although Gracie's apartment looked like Gracie, it was also impersonal. He could be in the suite of a high-end hotel, recently cleaned and prepped for the next guest.

Lang was an intelligent man when he wasn't preoccupied with his dislike of Crawford. He believed Gracie's non-appearance this morning was somehow connected to the disruption of LB Freight records, the open safe, and the note on his desk. The question in his mind was whether it was voluntary or not.

Lenny was the one who had brought Gracie to LB Freight, hiring her as a financial assistant. Lenny had always had an eye for good looking women. He might have chosen her for her looks, thinking he could lure her into bed, but Lenny wasn't up to Gracie's standards. She had never treated Lenny as anything other than a younger brother.

Gracie was the complete professional, handling everything LB Freight sent her way. Lang hadn't intended for her to become involved in the illegal side of the business, but you couldn't hide anything from Gracie. She had come to him one day, saying that she had payment from the Bosqueros for conveying the drugs, and how did he want her to enter it in the books.

Lang, pondering the many liabilities of any answer he might provide, hadn't spoken right away. But Gracie, as usual, had a suggestion.

"I'll enter this as miscellaneous proceeds," she said. "But we have a number of ongoing dealings with the Bosqueros. If you agree, I'll work with them to set up a systematic approach with coded labels. That way both parties will have matching records, in case the matter ever comes up for audit."

Lang didn't know if the Bosqueros ever allowed an auditor to examine their books. He doubted it. However, the FBI had always had suspicions about LB Freight's activities. Keeping the in-house books clean was a worthwhile goal.

Then Gracie had turned and left him sitting behind his desk, his mouth hanging open.

"Can we trust her?" he had asked Lenny.

"As soon as she puts her signature on anything, she will be in it as deeply as we are," Lenny had said.

As Gracie became more enmeshed in LB Freight's affairs, Lang had collected and filed the evidence against her. He kept it in his private safe at the office. He was the only one who knew the combination.

This morning his safe had been empty. It wasn't the loss of records that worried him – he had copies of everything in the safe at his residence – it was the identity of the thief. Who was it? Gracie or Crawford?

In addition to the evidence against Gracie, Lang had wanted a stronger hold over his incidental partner in crime. And that was why he had begun the affair with her. Initially, it had been a way to determine her weak points, find out what made her tick, and look for other potential threats.

Gracie was an attractive, charming woman. An affair with her had been pleasurable, and sex with Gracie was a great deal more satisfying than with his wife, Venetia. Lang had become accustomed to having Gracie around.

And now that he thought about it, he hadn't found any weaknesses. Gracie was the least vulnerable person he had ever met. Not only that, he still knew very little about her. She had never revealed anything about her past, her family, or her friends.

He wanted to look for Gracie, but he had nowhere to start.

"What the hell," he muttered. He would have someone come over to sweep the apartment, searching for anything out of the ordinary. He had no idea what it might be.

He would also take her computer. The techs would be able to discover anything that was on it.

Lang was studying the abstract wall art over the sofa with its swirling shapes when the door opened. He must have forgotten to lock it. Then he sensed movement behind him.

He had a brief moment to realize that he did know one thing about Gracie. She liked bright colors.

It was his last thought.

Chapter 84

"We can't find the woman," Espinoza said. "Her car's in the garage. We're in the apartment. There's a man here."

"Alive?"

"Unconscious. We hit him pretty hard to knock him out. Want us to stick around and question him?"

If Ochoto knew Gracie, and he was pretty sure he did, she wouldn't have told anyone what she was going to do.

"Did the man see you?"

"Can't say for sure," Espinoza said. "I was behind him, but he may have seen Delgado come through the front door.

"Get rid of him," Ochoto said. "Search the apartment. Then come back to base."

"*Sí, jefe,*" Espinoza said. "We'll be back tonight."

Chapter 85

"I've got news for you," Jefferson said to Crawford on the phone.

"I've got some for you too," Crawford replied.

The meeting between the fake Ochoto and Simon Lang was scheduled for three o'clock that afternoon. Jefferson could sit in the trailer with Chloe and listen to the conversation as it was picked up by the miniature listening device that Darius would be wearing. The Squad had also installed hidden cameras.

"Simon Lang's body was found this morning."

"What?" Crawford felt the shock reverberate through his body. Then he felt nothing. His mind had gone blank.

It was as if he had taken a step into nothingness, an endless void.

"I take it you didn't kill him," Jefferson said.

There was no answer.

"Did you kill him?" Jefferson demanded again.

"No. What the hell? Where?"

"If you mean where the body was found, it was in the apartment rented by Graciela Martín."

"Huh," Crawford tried to digest the information, but nothing about the announcement made sense. How could Lang be dead?

"Is that all you've got to say?" Jefferson asked. "I

thought you would want to know. He was shot once in the head, execution style. Cleaning lady found the body."

When Crawford didn't respond, Jefferson added, "Look, I'm in a hurry. I've got a lot to do this morning. What news do you have for me?"

"OBE," Crawford managed to say. "Doesn't matter now."

He continued holding the phone even after it went dead. He couldn't think, couldn't even react. He had been seeking vengeance against Simon Lang for almost twenty years. Now, all at once, Lang was beyond his grasp.

Crawford sank into the leather armchair, the one with the pattern of cracks that looked like the Death Valley salt flats, and stared into space.

He had once wished to see Simon Lang dead more than anything else in life. Now Crawford realized that it wasn't just the man's death. He had wanted to be the one who made Lang suffer before he died.

He would have to ask Diego if the reports indicated whether Lang had suffered. But in the end, it didn't matter. Dead was dead.

Now what? Crawford asked himself. He didn't have an answer.

Chapter 86

"There's something you should know," Castellanos told Alice. "Maybe we could talk in person."

"Whatever it is, just tell me," she said. Her voice was husky and she sounded out of sorts. She was probably bored, cooped up in a safe house somewhere.

"Do you have a cold?" he asked.

"Cockroaches," Alice wheezed. "I'm allergic to them. Had to move out of my previous location. What have you got?"

Castellanos took a breath. There wasn't any way to sugarcoat his message and he didn't try.

"The police found your father's body this morning. He was shot."

When Alice failed to reply, he didn't push her. "Call me back when you're ready," he said. "I've got more information."

Then he ended the call. Alice Lang was a strong woman. He would hear from her soon.

Castellanos wasn't upset at the death of Lang. He thought Lang was a bastard. When Lenny was alive, Simon Lang had devoted himself to mentoring his son, ignoring Alice. But after she shot Special Agent Art Wilson, Lang had realized she could be an advantage to him.

Lang had established Alice as his hit woman. Alice had gotten rid of Lang's enemies much more efficiently than Lenny had. Alice had also done a few jobs for the

Bosqueros.

Castellanos liked Alice. They were friends. But that didn't mean he wouldn't use her.

It was two hours later when Alice returned his call. "Tell me what you know," she demanded. "All of it."

"How much information do you have?" he asked. He knew she would have checked with her contacts.

"The body was in Gracie's apartment," Alice said. "He was shot in the head." Her voice deepened somewhat on the last words, but it didn't waver. "Gracie has disappeared. But I don't think she's responsible. She hasn't been seen since Friday. And she didn't own a gun."

"It was a mistake," Castellanos told her.

"What part of that recital of facts was a mistake?"

"The shooting," he said. "It was a mistake. But you're right. Gracie didn't do it. It was Ochoto's men. Gracie was having an affair with Ochoto. When she broke off the relationship, he sent them after her."

"Son of a bitch," Alice muttered.

Castellanos didn't know if she was referring to Ochoto or Lang or himself.

"The gunmen didn't know who he was," Castellanos added. "Lang just happened to be in her apartment."

"Gracie was also having an affair with my dad," Alice told him. "That's why he was there. And stop laughing. Nothing about this is funny."

"I'm sorry about your dad," Castellanos told her.

"Thanks. But that doesn't end things, you know."

"I figured you'd feel that way."

Castellanos ended the call with Alice and gave a small nod to the mesquite trees growing in a *bosque* outside his window. The Bosqueros, like their namesake mesquite trees, had roots that were deep and strong. They could adapt to any type of soil and could remain dormant for years, waiting for the right conditions to sprout or regenerate.

The Bosqueros were equally strong and adaptable. Castellanos would make certain they stayed that way.

One way to do that was to get rid of the dead wood in the organization. Jerónimo Torres had sent Fay Courtney – Castellanos' sister – to Colombia to recruit for the Bosqueros. And that was where Fay Courtney had died. After Gina Hernandez told him that Fay's body had shown up, he had checked with the Colombian authorities. Unfortunately, the report was true. Fay's body was now on its way home.

Castellanos blamed Torres for his sister's death. Torres had been in prison for the last year, but he wouldn't be coming up for trial. He had been killed by a fellow inmate. Just this morning, in fact. Castellanos had already deposited the money for the hit in the man's bank account.

By killing Torres, Castellanos had been able to rid the Bosqueros of a man who had outlived his usefulness.

Torres had also been a long-standing rival with conflicting ideas. Internal dissention would have weakened the syndicate. Now it would not be a problem.

Castellanos was also concerned about the viability and vision of Ochoto. The Bosqueros should be moving more quickly to keep up with the competition, not basking in past successes, content to drift like children, lolling in inner tubes, as they followed the current down a lazy river. Castellanos wanted the organization to pick up speed, to shoot across the waterway like a powerboat, making waves that left their mark on the shore.

Then there was the matter of the tracker Castellanos had found in his car. He believed Ochoto had placed it there. The man didn't trust his own deputy.

Castellanos hadn't confronted Ochoto about the tracker. He had used a GPS jammer to block the signal when he didn't want to be tracked. Castellanos had also installed jammers around his house. Now, no one could overhear his phone calls or use other devices to spy on him.

Ochoto lacked the qualities that a leader of the Bosqueros should have. That was why Castellanos had told Alice that Delgado and Espinoza, acting on Ochoto's instructions, had killed her father.

He had also told her where to find them.

Chapter 87

"How much money is missing?" Sid asked.

Darius and David had been tracing the money that had been moved out of LB Freight's accounts. Diego had been trying to locate Graciela Martín.

"All of it," Crawford told him. "LB Freight is bankrupt."

"Not legally," David noted. "The company hasn't officially declared bankruptcy."

"Who is 'the company' anyway?" Sid asked. "Alice and Robbie?"

"There are a couple more owners," Crawford said. "I'm one of them."

They all turned to stare at him. Most of the members of the Squad were startled. Sid was the only exception. He looked resigned.

"Simon Lang was one of three brothers who inherited the company," Crawford said, "so the business was split three ways. Simon took over the management, but he didn't buy out his older brothers. They're dead, but their offspring inherited their shares."

"And you're one of them," Sid said. "I should have known."

"Yeah. My sister and I together own one third of the company. Another relative, Bessie Dawkins, gets a second third. Robbie and Alice control the remaining third."

"Then we have to round up the relatives," Sid said.

"We won't find Alice easily, but maybe Robbie can vote for her."

"No need," Crawford said. "I have voting rights for Bessie, my sister, and myself. Together we constitute two-thirds of the shares."

Crawford had emerged from his post-Simon-Lang inertia long enough to call his sister, Claire, and ask her what she wanted him to do with her portion of the company.

"It's not worth much anymore," he had told her.

"Treat my share as you do your own, Chase," Claire had said. She always used his birth name. She had told him she couldn't be expected to keep up with his numerous aliases. "I'll check to see what Bessie wants you to do with hers."

Bessie Dawkins, the daughter of Aaron Lang, had been expelled from the Roma community after she married a non-gypsy. She lived on Red Horse Island in Texas along with Claire, Claire's fiancé, and the O'Hancy family. In fact, it was Claire's search for Bessie that had first taken her to Red Horse Island.

Claire had called back to say that Bessie would concur with whatever Crawford determined. Then she had reminded him that she wanted him to come to Texas for her wedding.

"I want you to walk me down the aisle," she said. "You're my only male relative."

Crawford had considered reminding her that Robbie Lang, the parrot master, was a male member of the family. He might be available.

But in the end, Crawford hadn't actually refused to attend the wedding. He just didn't want to be the one to give his sister away to a mongrel *gadjo* like Paulo Simoneaux, a man who irritated the hell out of him.

"Excuse me, Crawford," David said, trying to get Crawford's attention. "Does that mean you can take over the company?"

"Yeah."

"You don't sound too excited. Wasn't that what you wanted?"

"Yes. No. Not exactly," Crawford tried to explain. "I want the Squad to take over."

"Will you replace Lang as head of the company?" Dave asked.

"No. I don't want Lang's job. I was hoping Sid would take it."

"Me?" Sid asked. "You're out of your mind. I'm not a CEO. I'm a machinist with unionist sympathies."

"You're the best man I know," Crawford argued. The others nodded.

"I can see it in you," Dave concurred.

"My brother, the big chief," Carter added. "You always were bossy."

"And I think Dave should be the chief financial officer," Crawford said.

"But I never worked for LB Freight," Dave protested.

"Doesn't matter. Everybody else on the Squad gets a job if they want it."

"But the company is still out of money," Dave, ever the realist, told the group.

"The Squad has money," Sid reminded them. "Couldn't we buy into the company?"

"Yeah," Diego spoke up. "We wanted to make it employee-owned. The Squad owning it wouldn't be that different."

Dave thought about it for a few moments. "Chapter 11 would be a last resort," he said almost to himself. "But we could merge the Squad and LB Freight without a bankruptcy. That way no other company could move in and buy off the assets. And all of us would become partial owners."

"There may be creditors," Crawford reminded him.

"Not a problem," Dave replied. "Like Sid said, the Squad has money."

Crawford and Sid were standing beside the refurbished bar at Virgil's Roadhouse. Crawford had been able to get the key from Gina. Everything that was set up for the meeting that Simon Lang would never attend would soon be dismantled.

Virgil had installed a new rustic wood bar top with a matching rail that not even the Bosqueros would be able to destroy. The bar stools had been replaced, and the pool table had a new piece of red felt cloth, but the juke box was back in its usual corner, and the piano had been returned to its small alcove next to the bar.

Crawford had made it a point to check out the graffiti. The restrooms had been painted a dark adobe red, covering all of the décor that previous patrons had added. Probably a good thing, Crawford thought. Most of the additions had been downright crude.

But the graffiti in the hallway was just as it had been before the renovation. Crawford hadn't felt compelled to redo anything.

Since the bar wasn't officially open yet, Diego and Harrison had brought cold six packs of beer from a convenience store down the road. The group was celebrating the death of Lang, discussing which jobs they wanted at LB Freight, and trying to convince themselves they wouldn't miss being members of the Squad.

"We can have monthly meetings," Carter reminded them. "Drink a few beers, talk about old times."

"Yeah, but it won't be the same," Diego said.

"You and Ximena going to get pregnant now?" Darius asked.

"Looking forward to it," Diego said. "Then she can buy clothes for the baby and leave me alone."

"You won't be alone," Barney said. "You'll have the baby to keep you up all night."

"The Squad kept me up before," Diego said. "Baby won't be much different."

"Just a lot of diapers," Connor said. He'd had some experience with children, having helped his sister raise three of them after her husband was killed in an automobile accident.

Connor and Darius were talking about chemotherapy. Darius, who was foregoing alcohol during his chemotherapy, was sticking to soft drinks.

Connor had been exposed to the toxic chemicals, but so far he hadn't been diagnosed with cancer. He was also abstaining from alcohol, but for a different reason. He was taking his nephew to soccer practice later.

Sid and Crawford stood to the side, watching the others.

"What do you plan to do with Lang's sports betting operation?" Sid asked. "Not to mention the swanky high-end escort service?"

"Castellanos contacted me about them," Crawford said. "He wanted to know if we planned to continue in those areas. He offered to buy both on behalf of the Bosqueros."

"What did you tell him?" Sid asked as he finished his beer and crushed the can, his fist destroying the aluminum container as he once had wanted to destroy Simon Lang.

"That they were Simon Lang's personal business undertakings, and not strictly a part of LB Freight. I told him to talk to Alice."

"Good answer," Sid said with a grin. "That will keep him busy. But what are you going to do?"

"Hell if I know," Crawford replied.

"What about Chloe?" Sid asked.

"She's finishing up the investigation with Jefferson. But he won't let her go until he finds out what happened to the money in that account in the Dominican Republic."

"Then she'll be here for a while," Sid remarked.

"Yeah."

At least he hoped she would be.

Chapter 88

Ochoto looked up from his computer screen to find Alice Lang standing in front of him holding a gun.

"How did you get in here?" he said in surprise, his hands hovering over the keyboard.

"Same way your men got into Gracie's apartment," she said. "I broke in the back door."

"This is about your father, isn't it?" he asked.

"Yes," Alice told him. "Only this time it's your turn."

She shot him just as he was reaching for his gun. He didn't have time to press the panic button that Castellanos had told her was located along the right edge of the desk. But it wouldn't have mattered. She had already cut the connection. Alice checked to make sure Ochoto was dead. She took a photo as proof in case she needed it. You never knew when someone might decide to move a body just when you required it as evidence that you had completed the job.

Alice had never had any qualms about killing people. Even if she had had to shoot her mother to prevent an arranged marriage, she wouldn't have been troubled by guilt. Alice sometimes wondered if she had missed the particular DNA or gene related to the human abhorrence of taking another life. She didn't feel any repugnance. Nor did she feel any elation or twisted thrill. It was no more significant in the overall hierarchy of things than changing a flat tire or buying a new computer. It was just a part of life, a means to an end.

But with the slaying of Ochoto, just as with the killing of FBI Agent Wilson who had betrayed Lenny, she did feel something. She felt justified. Both men had deserved to die.

She left Ochoto's small retreat in the Sierra Ancha Mountains of Arizona, and headed back to her safe house in Phoenix, the one without cockroaches. On the way, she stopped to make a phone call.

"Job is done," she told Castellanos. She knew he wanted to take over the Bosqueros syndicate. He was going to be the new Ochoto.

"What are you going to do now?" he asked.

"Head for Mexico."

"Come to work for me," he offered. "Excellent salary and benefits. Health insurance and Worker's Comp."

"I prefer being my own boss," she said flatly.

"Then we'll continue the same arrangement we've always had," he concluded.

"No, Castellanos. It won't be quite the same," she reminded him. "But I'm willing to take occasional assignments. Give me a call if something comes up."

"Sure thing, Alice. I'll miss our drinks."

Alice would too, but she didn't tell him.

Chapter 89

"I want a straight story from you, Crawford, and I want it now." Chloe's blue eyes were simmering, sending out sparks. He thought she might ignite at any moment, erupting like a volcanic cone, spewing pyroclastic material over everything in the vicinity.

"Why didn't you tell me you were related to Simon Lang?" she demanded.

"It didn't seem important."

"Not important that he was your uncle?"

"Great-uncle." That clarification didn't seem to mollify her. She was still fuming. "You don't talk about your family, either," he noted.

"That's not the same," she started to say. "We're not investigating my family, not that . . ." Then her voice trailed off.

Crawford decided to change the subject. "Gus found my father's papers," he told her.

When she looked confused, he added, "My father was gathering evidence against Simon Lang."

"Something else you didn't tell me."

"I didn't know until lately about his activities. Gus had O'Neill's and Darius's papers, as well. Not that they'll do us any good now."

Gus hadn't lasted long in rehab and was back on the street, carrying the pillow Patty had given him. But he had stayed sober and clear-headed long enough to contact Crawford about the miscellaneous assortment of documents and floppy disks he had stored under a pile of blankets in Frida's shed.

The papers prepared by Michael Colby, Darius Taylor, and Ernest O'Neill, and zealously preserved by George "Gus" Chaplin, documented repeated instances of chemical exposure of LB Freight employees, including the names, dates, types of chemicals used, and how the fluids had been recycled. The records might at one time have served as evidence in lawsuits against LB Freight, but it was unlikely that would happen now.

David Huang was moving quickly to complete the Squad's buyout of what remained of the company. In a few days, LB Freight would no longer exist. The Squad, wanting to sever all ties with the business entity once known as LB Freight, was deciding on a new name for the organization.

But even without lawsuits, the Squad was already taking care of those LB Freight employees and families who had suffered under Simon Lang's regime. The newly restructured corporation would continue that effort.

Crawford and the Squad members had found other information in Gus's hoard. Wesley Bernard had left a signed statement saying that he had watched from behind the warehouse as Lenny Lang hit Ernest O'Neill on the head with a tire iron. Then Lenny had set up the fake accident by placing O'Neill's body in an LB Freight truck and sending it over an incline.

Gus had witnessed Bernard's signature and had kept the statement.

The death of Ernest O'Neill hadn't been a heart attack that resulted in an accident, as reported by Lenny Lang. It had been murder.

"Why didn't Bernard or Gus say something?" Sid had asked.

"Bernard was scared of the Langs," Darius told them. "He must have left that signed statement about what happened. Then he retired and moved to Mexico. As for Gus, it was about that time that he began to drink."

"Didn't do Bernard any good to run to Mexico, did it?" Sid said. "Alice still found him."

"What would be useful would be if you were a little more forthcoming," Chloe said crisply. "I want honesty from you, Crawford. Tidbits of information from time to time aren't enough."

Crawford brought his thoughts back to the virago who was storming around his apartment.

There were a lot of things he hadn't mentioned, but he had good reason. He had altered the court order and modified the software. If he told her, she might never recover from apoplexy.

Then there was breaking and entering, arson, and theft. He didn't think she would approve.

Crawford searched for a suitable topic of discussion. He had spoken to Jefferson, going over the possible scenarios for Lang's death. He could tell her about that.

"Jefferson and I think the Bosqueros killed Lang," he said.

"Yeah, I know," Chloe replied. She was pacing the floor, kicking at anything that got in her way. Fortunately, Crawford didn't have many possessions. And she probably wouldn't injure herself on the makeshift furniture in the small apartment. He decided to let her continue mutilating the shabby trappings. There wasn't much he could do to stop her, anyway.

"Jefferson said the bodies of two of Ochoto's men turned up," Crawford continued. Jaime Delgado and Elmer Espinoza were both enforcers. They had signs pinned to their bodies saying they killed Lang. I think Alice shot them in retaliation."

"Yeah, I heard," Chloe muttered.

He wasn't sure why she had insisted on a discussion when she already knew everything, but now that he had started, he was determined to continue.

"Ochoto must have learned about the affair between Lang and Gracie," Crawford surmised. "Then he sent his men to kill Lang. Gracie may be hiding out with Ochoto."

"No," Chloe said bluntly. "You're wrong. I think Gracie took the money and left both of them."

Crawford began to relax. If she was talking about Gracie and Ochoto, she might forget about all the things he hadn't told her.

"Then why did Ochoto kill Lang?" he asked.

"I think it was a case of wrong place, wrong time," Chloe said. She stopped pacing to argue her point. "If Gracie took the money and ran, Ochoto could have discovered what she'd done. He wouldn't have let Gracie go. He would have sent his men to look for her. She was probably the target. I know from Peggy that Lang was searching for Gracie. Peggy went to the apartment earlier and couldn't find her. Then later Lang went there to look for Gracie. He must have been there when Ochoto's men showed up. The only thing that was planned was Gracie's disappearance with the money."

"You think Ochoto killed Gracie?"

"I think he wants her dead. Gracie is the only person we know of outside the Bosqueros who has first-hand information about him," Chloe replied. "She's a threat to his survival."

"So it was Gracie who took down Simon Lang," Crawford concluded. "All she needed was a little help from the Bosqueros."

All the efforts he had made, the activities of the Squad, and Jefferson's investigation were for naught. The thing that had succeeded in ridding the world of Simon Lang was the byproduct of one woman's pecuniary activities.

Apollyon, Gus had called Lang. Apollyon was the destroyer, and Lang had certainly been a destroyer. But it was Gracie who had led Lang to his doom. She was the angel of the abyss.

Then there was Gus, who had started the recent series of events. Gus had sent the message to Lang saying he knew what had happened to O'Neill. Gus, like Gracie, was another inadvertent player in Lang's death. He couldn't have foreseen the results of his email.

Frida and Yanko had returned to town after their

adventures in Dollywood. Their lives – and Gus's – were continuing, generally unchanged. Crawford was the only one who had lost his purpose.

"Talk to me, Crawford," Chloe demanded. "What are we going to do now?" She handed him a bottle of cold water, having evidently gone into the kitchen while he was lost in thought. She could have been talking to him during that time, as well, but he had missed whatever she might have said. He didn't know how to respond to her, and uttered the first thing that came into his mind.

"Now that Lang is gone, it isn't how I thought it would be."

"What did you think would happen when he was out of the picture?" Chloe asked. She flopped down on the sofa, which squeaked in protest. Then she stretched out and stared at the ceiling.

"I never really considered it." Crawford certainly hadn't thought he would be depressed. He still felt the shadow of Lang hanging over him.

"I know," she said. "That happens when you get wrapped up in a case. If it turns out differently than what you anticipated, even if you didn't realize that you had a particular goal in mind, you aren't satisfied."

"Yeah," he concurred. "But more than that, I'm not the same person anymore. It's like part of me is gone. I don't know who or what I am."

"You were caught up in the goal," she counseled.

Crawford thought it was strange that she was the one lying on the couch and he was sitting in the chair.

"You were trapped in revenge, on autopilot," she continued. "Now you're grieving for what you lost."

"But I got what I wanted."

"Did you?"

He didn't have an answer. He didn't know.

"The next phase of your life can start now," she added. "You can take the lessons you learned and move on."

Crawford wondered what he had learned. Not much.

"You also have the Squad," Chloe reminded him. "You have a lot of friends."

"Yeah," he mumbled. The Squad was moving on all right, but they were doing it without him.

"I've got a meeting with Jefferson," Chloe said. "We're closing the case and turning in our report."

She got up from the sofa and headed for the door.

"Does that mean you're leaving?" he asked.

If she and Jefferson closed the case, Chloe would go on to another assignment. He was losing her. It was another shock, almost as great as the one he had received when he learned that Lang was dead.

Another example of not planning ahead. He had to find a way to keep her until he figured out what he was doing.

"Yes, Crawford, I'm going to a meeting." She picked up the keys of the Audi, which the Highway Patrol had released and Eugene had repaired for her.

"No. I mean are you leaving Nevada?" he asked.

"I have a job in Buffalo," she reminded him.

Crawford got up out of the fractal chair with its patchwork of cracks and furrows – *infinite complexity,* he reminded himself, *just like his life* – and crossed the room to stand beside her. "Maybe we could stay in touch," he said. "I could come see you after I get things straightened out here."

That sounded simple enough to Crawford. Maybe his life wasn't so complicated after all.

"I'll think about it," she said.

Then she was gone.

Not so simple after all.

Chapter 90

"I shouldn't have arranged for you to work with Craw-ford. We can't trust him." Jefferson stared out the window in his office. "But you did volunteer."

Jefferson evidently believed in combining apologies with criticism. And in repeating himself. He had already said the same thing twice.

Chloe had had enough of moody, morose, down-in-the-mouth men. Crawford was troubled about the death of Simon Lang and the end of his quest for venge-ance. Jefferson was struggling to come to terms with the events happening around him. She was the only person who appeared to be in control.

Well, that wasn't quite true. The women with whom she had been associating recently were also in control. It was just the men who hadn't figured it out.

Chloe had heard from Trixie and Jolene, who told her that Gina was going to be the new treasurer of the Bosqueros syndicate. Gina didn't even have to masquer-ade behind Otto. She would be the first woman to hold an office in the syndicate.

Jolene also said there was some mystery associated with Ochoto. There were rumors that he was dead, and that someone else had taken over, but no one seemed to know for sure, and orders were still coming down from the main office.

Trixie and Jolene were buying a house, and they had adopted a dog that liked to ride on Trixie's bike. They weren't letting past events hold them back.

Alice Lang appeared to be in charge, as well. There were two new murders attributed to her, and the FBI still hadn't been able to track her down. There were reported sightings of her from across the country.

"She's creating false trails," Crawford had told Chloe. "Providing too much information. In order to confuse the authorities, she has trusted personnel in major cities using her ATM cards, but she's paying in cash. The FBI won't be able to trace her cell phone calls because she's using prepaid phones. Wherever she's living, she will have adopted a modest, low-profile lifestyle. And she will be paying a lot in bribes. It's the age-old tactic of misdirection."

"Is that what you would do?" Chloe had asked him.

"Yeah."

Jefferson had also blamed Chloe for the lack of success in finding Alice. He had asked repeatedly if she was sure it was Alice who had been in Huntridge Circle Park. Chloe had reminded him that they found the bag Alice had been carrying. Also, one of the security cameras on the pharmacy had picked up Alice as she walked around the side of the store.

"Why didn't you take her when she stopped to change her hair style?" Jefferson had asked Chloe.

"Perhaps I should have, but you told me not to approach her."

Jefferson grumbled a bit. Then he asked, "How can we be sure it was Alice?"

"Both Crawford and I saw her," Chloe had replied. "It was Alice."

"Crawford can't be trusted," Jefferson muttered.

"What have you learned about the bank account in the Dominican Republic?" Chloe asked. She was trying to move the meeting along. Otherwise, it might last until spring.

"The money's gone," Jefferson said.

"Yes, I'm aware of that," Chloe replied. "What did the techs learn about it?"

"The money disappeared at the same time the LB Freight money did," Jefferson conceded. "The computer guys say the funds were withdrawn by the person who set up the account."

"Then it had to be Gracie Martín, right?" Chloe demanded. "She not only set up the fund for Lang. She drained it."

"Yeah. I guess."

Chloe refrained from rolling her eyes. She didn't want to start an argument. She wanted to leave her temporary assignment with style and grace. She was a professional, after all.

Jefferson sat down again and picked up his pen, tapping it against the desk. "You and Crawford are friends, aren't you?" he asked, seemingly apropos of nothing.

"Yes," Chloe answered.

"Then there are a couple of things I should tell you." He cleared his throat, a sign that he was embarrassed.

Chloe waited, outwardly patient, for him to continue.

"Crawford's a criminal," Jefferson admitted.

Chloe manfully – or perhaps it was womanfully – didn't ask why he had set her up with a partner who was a criminal. Jefferson had promised that Crawford would help her with the technical aspects of her undercover role, including tapping into the LB Freight computer system. And he had.

Crawford, admittedly, had done more than that, but Chloe didn't bring it up.

"What makes you think he's a criminal?" she asked resignedly.

"He broke into the McCullough Sheriff's Office evidence locker," Jefferson said. "He and another man took material that would have convicted a car thief."

"Do you have proof that it was Crawford?"

"The men disabled the cameras at the evidence trailer, but a camera on a neighboring building had some clear shots. One of the men looked like Crawford."

"Looked like?"

"Yeah. I think it was Crawford," Jefferson said.

"I see." Chloe kept her voice even. "What kind of evidence was taken?"

"A pair of shoes and a cap left behind by a man driving a stolen car."

"Shoes and a cap?" Chloe asked.

"The car got stuck in a flooded stream," Jefferson explained. "The unknown perp must have taken off his shoes to push it out of the water. When the sheriff's deputy showed up, the perp ran, leaving behind the shoes and a cap. Now they're gone. The same night the evidence disappeared, the car was destroyed in a fire. The sheriff doesn't have a case anymore."

"Why would Crawford steal evidence?" Chloe asked. But she already had an idea. It must have something to do with the Squad.

"He's always pulling some cock-assed stunt," Jefferson grumbled. "The other night, he started a fire at LB Freight. Clear-cut arson."

"I'm going to ask you again how you know it was Crawford," Chloe said quietly.

"DNA," Jefferson replied.

"You are aware that he owns most of LB Freight, aren't you?" Chloe noted. "His DNA could legitimately be anywhere in the building."

"Yeah, but Simon Lang was in control at the time of the fire. Crawford shouldn't have been there. Somebody also gave the guards false orders. That's the sort of perverted shenanigan Crawford would play."

"Whoever started the fire might have wanted to get people out of the way," Chloe suggested.

"Yeah. Crawford hasn't killed anyone that I know of," Jefferson admitted. He stared at the calendar on his wall. It was a month behind. "Crawford also stole a shipment of drugs from Willy's Truck Stop."

"Huh," Chloe replied. Crawford used that particular form of speech whenever he didn't want to respond. She found it worked quite nicely.

"Well, the investigation of Simon Lang is finished," Jefferson continued as he rose and extended his hand. He must have decided it was time to end the conversation and go home to his dinner. "I'll send Regina a note for your performance file. I'm sorry I got you involved with a criminal. I knew that Crawford had a few rough edges, but I misjudged the extent."

"Are you going to prosecute him?" Chloe asked as she shook hands with Jefferson.

"No. It's over. Crawford and I have a long history, some good and some bad. I'm ready to move on. Alice is still out there. So are the Bosqueros."

Besides, Chloe thought, *Jefferson knows he would never be able to pin any of those crimes on Crawford.*

"Just one last thing before I go," Chloe said as she picked up her purse. "Why did you have me followed?"

Jefferson appeared startled. He harrumphed and cleared his throat before he spoke, his eyes avoiding hers.

"I never had you followed. And we couldn't trace the license plate. You must have given me the wrong number. Perhaps you just imagined that someone was following you."

Chloe decided not to bring up the tracker that had been found in the Audi, and the fact that the car that was following her had been rented by the FBI. Jefferson was lying. "Good luck," she said to Jefferson, and walked out the door.

Chapter 91

"You haven't been straight with me," Chloe said.

Yogi Berra was right, she thought. *It was déjà vu all over again.* She kept accusing Crawford of not being honest with her, and he kept assuring her that he was. But this time, she had specific information from Jefferson.

"When did I lie to you?" Crawford asked.

"Lying includes not telling the whole truth," she informed him. "Why did you take the shoes and cap from the evidence locker?"

At first, Crawford looked as if he might deny all knowledge of the event. Then he changed his mind. "If I give you an answer, will you tell me how you know about the locker?"

"Jefferson knows it was you. You missed the security camera on the building next door."

"Son of a bitch," Crawford muttered. "Was anyone else spotted?"

"Spotted but not identified," Chloe told him.

"Mutual trust?" he asked. It was what he had said to her when they first met.

"It doesn't appear to be mutual," she snapped. "But if you're asking if I will testify against you, the answer is no. Not that you deserve that kind of consideration."

"Carter Allenby was driving the car. Black men don't fare well in the judicial system."

"What was he doing with a stolen car?" she demanded.

"He didn't steal it, Sweet Cheeks. I borrowed it, and Carter was returning it for me."

"Borrow to you means taking the vehicle without informing the owner?"

"We gassed it up before Carter left to take it back."

"I understand the car was destroyed in a fire the same night the evidence was taken from the locker," she said.

"The owner received money to purchase a new one," he replied.

"And that makes it right? Why in the hell did you steal a car in the first place? You're a wealthy man. You could buy any car you wanted."

Crawford stared at her for a long time. "I am what I am," he finally said. "I informed you in the beginning that I lived below the radar, that I couldn't tell you who I was or what I was doing or why. You agreed that everything would be off the record."

"That was before we were involved in a relationship," she reminded him.

"You know who I am and why I was trying to convict Simon Lang," he acknowledged. "Isn't that enough?"

"No," she said. "It's not enough. You took the drugs from Willy's Truck Stop. You started the fire at LB Freight."

"Jefferson knows all that?" He actually looked concerned.

"Don't worry. Jefferson's not going to prosecute. As for me, I'm tired of trying to get information out of you. I'm going home. To Buffalo. And don't bother coming to see me. I won't be there anyway."

With that, she flounced out the door, letting it slam behind her.

As Chloe drove back to Patty's house, she had a lot on her mind.

She had wanted to be Reynard, the clever fox, the one who triumphed at the end of the story. Instead, she was writing reports about what others had done. She hadn't been the fox. Gracie had.

Chloe, with her drawer full of coordinated lingerie, her highlighted hair, and her determination to make things right, hadn't managed to resolve anything.

What she had done was end up in traffic school. But she had paid the fines. The points Reinhart had given her would be deducted, and she would go back to New York with a clean driving record.

Diego had found through on-line research that Reinhart was Jefferson's cousin. Perhaps Jefferson had asked Reinhart to keep tabs on her.

Surely that was against the rules, but that hadn't stopped Jefferson and Reinhart.

Thinking about rules brought her mind back to Crawford and the Squad. They hadn't worried about rules. And if they hadn't exactly succeeded in their efforts to take down Simon Lang, they hadn't lost either.

Simon Lang was dead, and the Squad was remedying much of the damage he had caused. That was a reasonable outcome.

Chloe reluctantly admitted that she had enjoyed associating with the small group of determined vigilantes. The rules had seemed less important when she was with them.

And it wasn't only the Squad who ignored the rules. There was also Patty, who presented herself to the world with a unique blend of confidence and originality. When it came to style, Patty made her own decisions.

Patty had been the one who instilled in Chloe's mind the idea of principles.

"You weren't born to be a rule follower, Chloe," Patty had told her. "You don't have to be controlled by rules. Use your principles – and I know you have them – as a guide."

Crawford had given her his opinion, as well. "You try to behave and follow the rules," he had said, "but there's something in you that wants fewer restrictions. You like the wind in your face. You look for unexpected challenges, and when you find them, you go after them."

Much as she hated to admit it, Crawford had been right. She did like the wind in her face.

As Chloe drove through Las Vegas, the city of unlimited possibilities, she sensed the glimmerings of an idea, as faint and undefined as a mirage on a desert highway. It had to do with life and freedom, with rules and principles, but before she could grasp it, the vision evaporated, leaving her feeling that she had missed something important.

Chloe tried to recall the idea that had been germinating in her mind. But it had gone the way of all mirages, leaving only a shadowy impression, and Chloe's thoughts soon returned to more immediate matters.

As soon as she got back to Buffalo, she was going to take a leave of absence. "You can know the rules and not know the game," Regina had said before Chloe left Buffalo. Now Chloe wasn't sure about either the rules or the game. She needed to understand, to get it straight.

In addition, the newspaper article she had read a few days ago continued to obsess her. Chloe had questions about her parents' deaths. She wanted to go to Kansas and investigate.

She had received an envelope enclosing the voucher for $4,000 that she had left in the Lazy Lake Casino. Finding the voucher in her mailbox had restored some of her belief in rightness.

She didn't know who sent it, but she was pretty sure it wasn't One-Eye. He had disappeared. Crawford thought Uncle Joey and the Bosqueros motorcycle gang had something to do with that.

With the proceeds from the voucher, plus her savings and a small legacy from her grandmother, she would stay solvent until she decided what to do next.

Whatever it was would not involve Crawford. He had been right when he said the two of them didn't have a relationship. A relationship with him would be impossible. First of all, he would never admit they had one.

Second, the man didn't understand the concept of honest communication, and probably never would.

She was going back to Buffalo. She would drive the Audi home, towing her Fatboy behind.

She was buying the car from Fergus, who had four more years of his sentence to complete. She had convinced him he would be better off getting rid of the Audi and buying a new car when he got out. It was just like a man to think the car could sit unused on the lot for that period of time and still be in good working condition when he was finally able to collect it.

Any future relationships Chloe had would be limited to love affairs with her sports car and her bike. The great thing about machines was that if you took care of them, they took care of you. That was more than you could say about men.

Besides, she didn't want another man, she thought as she blinked back tears. Disentangling herself from this one would provide enough pain to last a lifetime.

Chapter 92

One Month Later

"Where've you been the last few weeks?" Sid asked as he met Crawford at the front door of the Gonzalez and Associates building.

"You the new greeter?" Crawford asked belligerently. "Like at Walmart?"

"You're the big boss," Sid replied. "I figured it was worth a few minutes of my time to show you around."

"I didn't come here to see the fucking building," Crawford growled.

"Yes, you did," Sid replied with a grin. "Besides, the employees want to meet you."

"What did you tell them about me?" Crawford accused.

"That you single-handedly saved the company," Sid replied modestly. "That you're Superman and Captain America rolled into one. That you can take out villains with one hand behind your back."

Crawford didn't bother to reply. As they walked through the corridors, he noticed that Sid had incorporated his own version of down-hominess into the company. Sid greeted the employees by name, asked if they had everything they needed, and reminded them of the employees' meeting the next day.

"What's the meeting about?" Crawford asked. Simon Lang had never held employee meetings.

"They're thinking about a cafeteria. We also need to set up a clinic and hire medical staff."

"Huh," Crawford replied. He was uncomfortable. The employees might like Sid, but they were looking at him as if he had come from another planet. Several edged away nervously as he and Sid passed.

"They're afraid of me," Crawford grumbled.

"That's because you're scowling," Sid told him. "Smile. Act polite."

"Don't know how," Crawford replied. "This is as nice as I get."

"Let's go to my office, then. You won't have to meet anyone there."

Sid had turned Simon Lang's elegant, austere office into a conference room of sorts, having added a large round table and a dozen chairs near the window over- looking Las Vegas. "If they get bored in a meeting, they can always look out the window," Sid told him.

Peggy Lincoln brought in two bottles of cold water from the new refrigerator in the small executive kitchen.

"Hi, Mr. Crawford," she said. "Welcome to Gonzalez and Associates."

Peggy had a smile for Crawford, but she winked at Sid, and he beamed back at her.

"Chatting up the employees, are you?" Crawford asked snidely.

"I like her," Sid replied. "You've heard of office ro- mances, haven't you?"

"But you're her boss."

"Now you sound like Chloe," Sid told him. "I'm only going to remain as CEO until we get the company on its feet. Then I won't be her boss. Sit down." He motioned Crawford to one of the easy chairs in front of Simon Lang's elaborate desk.

"Simon didn't have these chairs," Crawford commented.

"We found them in a closet in the basement," Sid told him as he kicked off his shoes and ran his sock-covered feet across the thick carpet. "Old Isaiah Lang used to have them up here in his office. They're comfortable. Where've you been?" he repeated. "What have you been doing? You don't look good."

"Out of town," Crawford replied. Sid was his best friend – maybe his only friend – but he didn't want to explain that he had been hanging out at his cabin, so depressed that he hadn't bothered to go into town to buy food.

Azariah had heated up cans of chili, beef stew, and corned beef hash for him. But Crawford had been too caught up in his misery to eat much, and he had never liked that stuff, anyway. Even Orville and Wilbur had given up on him, detouring around the cabin instead of dropping by for a handout.

"Have you heard from Chloe?" Sid asked.

"No."

"So that's it. You're just going to let her go? Why aren't you going after her?"

"Just because you're CEO and you renamed the company doesn't mean you can run people's lives,"

Crawford complained.

"The Squad voted to rename the company after Luis," Sid protested. "If Darius goes, we'll add his name. Then we'll be Gonzalez, Taylor, and Associates."

Luis Gonzalez had died shortly after Simon Lang had been killed. The Squad had arranged the funeral and assured his widow that she and the children would be taken care of.

"Darius' cancer has spread," Sid told Crawford. "He's in the hospital."

"Yeah. Diego and I went to see him last night," Crawford muttered.

"It's not too bad," Darius had assured them. "I made it to Hawaii. And Lang is gone. I just want to get that helicopter ride in before it's too late."

Diego had arranged for a helicopter to fly Darius and his wife over the Grand Canyon today. They were probably in the air right now.

Sid brought Crawford up to date on the merger and the missing funds. "No one has been able to track Graciela Martín," he said. "She seems to have disappeared into thin air."

"She may be dead," Crawford noted.

"Dave and his tech buddies traced some of the money," Sid told him. "They managed to retrieve almost the entire employee retirement fund. Evidently Gracie didn't get around to moving it quickly enough. They think Gracie is alive. They can tell by how the funds are being shifted from one institution to another. But, other than the retirement fund, they can't keep up with what she's doing."

"We should have co-opted Graciela," Crawford said. "Then we could have sat back and propped up our feet while she did all the work." He finished his water and looked for a place to put the empty plastic bottle.

"Just throw it in that gold-plated monstrosity of a trash can," Sid instructed. "You wouldn't believe where I found it. In the executive washroom, of all places. You get three points if you hit the basket while sitting in the chair."

"What if I miss?" Crawford asked.

"Then you get to pick up the bottle and try again. What are you going to do about Chloe?"

"Do you think I challenge the norms and disdain convention?" Crawford asked. He set the empty bottle down on the small end table.

"Chloe said that to you, didn't she?" Sid laughed.

"Sort of."

"You want her back, don't you?"

"Yeah."

"Think of it as a journey," Sid counseled. "Like in Pilgrim's Progress. A way to get from your world to hers. You've left the City of Destruction and are on your way to the Celestial City. But you're going to have to make a few changes."

"What kind of changes?" Crawford asked. He was tired of being sunk in misery. At first he had wanted to go to Buffalo, find her, and carry her off on his motorcycle. But that wouldn't last long with Chloe. She would probably shoot out his tires.

If he had to make adjustments in his approach to Chloe, he was willing to consider it. He didn't know where to start.

"Like recognizing the existing social order," Sid said. "It's as easy as saying good morning and not frowning at people."

"You think that's what she wants?"

"What did she tell you she wanted?" Sid asked patiently.

"How do you know she told me?"

"Because I know Chloe," Sid reminded him. "She would have said exactly what she felt."

"Honesty," Crawford admitted. "She wanted honesty. For me to tell her things."

"Yeah, I can see that," Sid said, trying to hide a smile. "What are you going to do about it?" He tossed his empty bottle toward the executive wastebasket.

"Nothing but net," Sid gloated as the bottle dropped directly into the container. He picked up the bottle Crawford had placed on the end table and sank it into the basket as well. "Three more points," Sid crowed.

When Sid glanced at his friend, there was no response. Crawford hadn't answered the question about what he was going to do. He hadn't paid any attention to Sid's basketball prowess as he stared out the window, lost in his thoughts.

Crawford might moon around for days before he found the path to the Celestial City. He would be a pilgrim lost in the wilderness, and during that time he would be a pain in the ass to his friends.

What Crawford needed was a kick in the butt. But Sid decided shock therapy might be just as effective.

Sid leaped on to Simon Lang's desk, and in his stocking feet, slid along the surface of the stainless steel and Russian birch monstrosity, looking like Tom Cruise in Risky Business, gliding across the floor in his skivvies.

Except that Sid was fully clothed, and was headed directly toward the floor-to-ceiling plate glass window that overlooked Las Vegas.

Just as he reached the end of the desk, Sid abruptly pivoted to a stop, turned, and faced an open-mouthed Crawford.

"Time for you to make up your mind," he said in a deep voice. "I'm going to dance on my desk until you do."

Sid liked to dance, and the Charleston was one of his favorites. Besides, he knew it would irritate Crawford.

"Around the world," Sid said, kicking, turning, and changing feet, twirling his foot in the air as he spun around. "Scissor kick," he hummed, "or maybe that was the Savoy kick, I can't remember. Spank the baby," he shouted as he shuffled across the desk. "Shim sham," he sang.

Drop steps, crossovers, swoops. He was into this. He tried a hitch-hike move, thinking it might inspire Crawford to hit the road.

"What are you doing?" Crawford growled.

"Getting your attention," Sid panted as he came to a stop. "Are you going to let her get away?"

It was what Azariah had said to Crawford. It was why he had come back to Las Vegas.

"No," Crawford announced as he stood up, walked to the door, and left, letting the door slam behind him.

"*And he's outta here,*" Sid announced in his Funky Kong voice.

Really, Sid thought as he climbed down from the desk and picked up his shoes. *A CEO's job is like a vaudeville performance, complete with contortionists, jugglers, comedians, acrobats, ventriloquists, and plate spinners. Being a production machinist had made more sense.*

"What's going on?" Peggy said a few seconds later when Sid poked his head out the door.

"Did Crawford smile and say good morning before he left?" Sid asked.

"No. He just mumbled something about it not being a bootless errand. Do you know what that means?"

"No," Sid sighed. "But I believe he's going to shuffle off to Buffalo. How about lunch?"

"Sounds good," Peggy told him.

The Lang Family

Isaiah and Sylvia Lang (deceased) – Great-grandparents of Chase and Claire Colby

Jacob Lang – son of Isaiah and Sylvia

Gloria Meyer Lang – wife of Jacob Lang; daughter of Alex Meyer and Julia Varady (deceased)

> **Belle Lang Colby** (deceased) – daughter of Jacob and Gloria, granddaughter of Julia Varady Meyer

> **Michael Colby** (deceased) – husband of Belle

>> **Chase Colby** – son of Belle and Michael

>> **Claire Colby** – daughter of Belle and Michael

Aaron Lang – son of Isaiah and Sylvia

Livia Meyer Lang (deceased) – wife of Aaron; daughter of Alex Meyer and Julia Varady (deceased)

> **Bessie Lang Dawkins** – daughter of Aaron and Livia, granddaughter of Julia Varady Meyer

> **Wally Dawkins** – husband of Bessie

>> **Rodney Dawkins** – son of Bessie and Wally

Simon Lang – son of Isaiah and Sylvia

Venetia Hoffman Lang – wife of Simon

> **Lenny Lang** – son of Simon and Venetia

> **Robbie Lang** – son of Simon and Venetia

> **Alice Lang** – daughter of Simon and Venetia

Isaiah Lang's second wife was Lizzie McCauley. She had two sons at the time of her marriage to Isaiah Lang. Jameson and Robert McCauley are their descendants.

Members of the Squad

1. Joe Crawford (Chase Colby, Donlevsky, James Whistler)
2. Sid Allenby worked for LB Freight as a production machinist. He was fired when he tried to bring in union organizers. Sid is the de facto second in command of the Squad.
3. Carter Allenby, Sid's brother, was a truck driver for LB Freight. After Sid was fired, Carter was let go on trumped up charges.
4. Diego Gutierrez lives in Vegas. He has a cousin on the police force in Phoenix. Diego's father, Aurelio Alejandro, worked for LB Freight until he died of cancer. Diego is married to Ximena who used to clean Crawford's condo.
5. David Huang does the financial work for the Squad. He didn't work for LB Freight, but his father was fired for cause when he opposed the takeover.
6. Darius Taylor helps David with the money. He has cancer resulting from exposure to toxic chemicals, but is still able to get around. The Squad sent him to Hawaii with his wife for a vacation.
7. Luis Gonzalez is hospitalized with cancer. He is a victim of chemical exposure.
8. Connor Jackson was accidently exposed to the chemicals. There is no information yet on whether he has cancer.
9. Barney Watson lives in Boulder City. His brother, Clarence, died of cancer.
10. Harrison Knight worked in the Las Vegas plant until fired by Simon Lang. He was another would-be union organizer.

Bosqueros Motorcycle Gang

President: Uncle Joey Lancaster

Vice-President – Otto Hernandez (Gato)

Treasurer – Gina Hernandez

Sergeant at Arms – Alfred Woodson

Road Captain – Sergio Lucero (Spider-Man)

Big Mike Terry, the former president, is in prison.

Bosqueros Syndicate

President: Bartolomeo Joaquin Reyes (Ochoto)

Vice President: Enrique Castellanos

Vice President: Jerónimo Torres (in prison)

Roma Terminology

Chovihano – gypsy shaman or ghost

Rom baro – a big man politically and physically

Divia-mus – crazy man

Baxt – luck, good or bad

Dadengero – bastard

Bre – brother, boy

Gadjo – non Roma man

Pikie – gypsy expelled from tribe